I slipped
formless
of the o̶v̶e̶r̶m̶i̶n̶d̶...

▶ ▶ ▶ ▶ ▶ ▶ ▶ ▶ ▶ ▶ ▶ ▶ ▶ ▶ ▶

and began shaping it into the likeness of one of my favorite places, a mountain meadow beside a swiftly running stream.

Then I sent forth a summons. "Cowards! Meet me here if you dare, in the seeming of your natural form. Meet me in a contest of wills, to determine fairly and honorably who is the stronger!" This message I sent forth to the Mantics who had attacked me. Their names I did not know, nor their castella, but the "flavor" of their essences I knew.

They came, but not in their natural forms. They burst into my little universe as a variety of monsters: a dragon, breathing fire; a shambling giant, reaching for me with hands that could have twisted me into two halves; a coldly beautiful witch-queen, wielding a wand; and a hybrid monster of hideousness, fanged and clawed, pelted and red-eyed, that walked upright like a human being.

The dragon-fire washed about me...

BRIGHT and
SHINING TIGER

Also by Claudia J. Edwards

Taming the Forest King
A Horsewoman in Godsland

Published by
POPULAR LIBRARY

BRIGHT and SHINING TIGER

CLAUDIA J. EDWARDS

POPULAR LIBRARY

An Imprint of Warner Books, Inc.

A Warner Communications Company

POPULAR LIBRARY EDITION

Popular Library®, the fanciful P design, and Questar® are
registered trademarks of Warner Books, Inc.

Cover illustration by Kinuko Craft

Popular Library books are published by
Warner Books, Inc.
666 Fifth Avenue
New York, N.Y. 10103

W A Warner Communications Company

Printed in the United States of America

First Printing: January, 1988

10 9 8 7 6 5 4 3 2 1

For Tex Hill
Who is absolutely merciless
to stylistic errors and awkward constructions.
Thanks.

CHAPTER
1

SOMETHING Big and invisible had been stalking me for hours. The chest-high grass parted before it as the ocean parts for the bow of a ship. There was an occasional liquid gleam as of sunlight on polished flanks, but the stalker itself was as invisible as night. Now it was moving in.

Caution was called for, clearly, but not fear. When the rollers in my horses' noses had informed me that something dangerous approached, I began to gather the latent energy of the overmind into my grasp, shaping it into a weapon. As yet, I only held the surging energy within myself, curious. In two years of rootless wandering, I, Runa, exile and wielder of power, had met many supernatural threats and fought some. Nothing like this, however, had crossed my path before. It radiated menace as the sun radiates warmth.

The wake in the grass was arrowing straight for me now. My horses danced, on the point of hysteria. "Stop right there," I said quietly, casting a little barrier of energy between me and the charging supernatural—not enough to hurt it, but enough to jolt it.

There was a yowl of startled rage and pain. The grass thrashed. The thing charged again; I cast another magical barrier. The invisible creature screamed and struck at the energy that balked its advance. A little more power sent it reeling back; I strengthened the barrier enough to kill it should it attack again. Killing things needlessly is stupid, but this particular supernatural seemed mindless and blood-thirsty. The world could well do without it.

It didn't charge again, however. There was a grunting

1

cough. A swathe of bending grass lashed back and forth before the barrier. Abruptly, the creature became visible. It was a great silver feline, as tall as a horse and much longer. Its silver fur was marked with pewter stripes, like the mythical tiger in legends of the western continent. Footlong fangs curved from its upper jaw, and the tail lashed like a baffled housecat's.

The beast sat down, curling its tail neatly around huge paws. It blinked once, lidding the white-hot fire of its eyes, and spoke. "You don't fear me, woman-creature."

It was startling to hear sapient speech from what was manifestly an animal, even though a supernatural one. "Indeed yes," I said. "I do fear you. Enough that I'll kill you in self-defense, if need be."

The feline yawned. Its lower jaw almost unhinged itself, gaping wide enough to provide clearance for those enormous fangs. "You do not fear me, woman. There is no scent of fear about you." The creature began to lick its chest and foreleg. Presently it looked up, purring, "You are my food and I shall eat you."

"Will you?" I said, drawing a little more energy from my store and holding it before me, ready to blast the feline if it should lunge at me.

"Not today." The tiger stretched, hindquarters high in the air, flexing enormous claws. "In good time. You are my prey. You are the Silvercat Mantic and I am the Silvercat. At the end of your life, you will come to me of your own free will, unafraid, to be devoured."

"Be sure not to eat anyone else while you're waiting for me to sacrifice myself to you," I suggested. I was only passing through these plains; the creature's territory couldn't be more than a few days' ride. "When I'm ready to accept your invitation, I'll come back."

"You will not leave. Your fate is here in this land. I shall not be far." It was gone, extinguished like a blownout candle. The grass parted itself in a line leading away from me.

My horses were half-mad with fear; it took awhile to soothe them and resume my eastward journey. This had been my direction for many months now, across the mountain barrier that fenced my homeland against the sea. For the last few days, the countryside had been rich and verdant. My two horses, old

Whiskers who had come over the mountains with me and the young mare Biscuit, acquired from the plains nomads on this side of the ranges, were fattening on lush grass.

There seemed to be no people in this fair land—perhaps the supernatural feline explained that. If magical predators were common this might be a risky place to settle, in spite of rich soils and plentiful water. People without my magical skills would be hard-put to defend themselves against a killer so large and strong that its invisibility seemed unnecessary.

Was that a cabin up ahead, between the creek and a little copse of nut trees? It was. I smoothed my short mouse-brown hair and straightened worn shirt and trousers. Perhaps the folk of this little farmstead would offer a meal to a weary wanderer.

My heart beat faster. Loneliness had been my constant companion. Solitary and rootless even in my homeland, I at least had acquaintances and visited scenes familiar to me since childhood. Now, drifting aimlessly as a wind-driven cloud across the face of the world, going nowhere but away from the Kingdom, I was truly alone in an alien land.

Whiskers stopped a little distance from the cabin. It looked vacant, weeds growing around the porch. The stock pens were empty and no chickens scratched about the yard. There should have been chickens; it was that sort of place. "Hallo, the house!" I shouted.

Wind rustled through the grass. At the porch, I swung down from my saddle, dropping the reins. When there was no answer to my repeated call, I pushed the door open. A night in a cabin's shelter would be a welcome change from hard ground under distant stars.

There was a brownish skeleton lying on the floor. My appalled gaze flashed over the musty interior. Another skeleton lay by a table; a smaller one huddled in a chair by the fireplace, a quilt over its lap. An open door offered a glimpse into the other room; on a bed sprawled another tangle of bones. I gulped.

These poor souls had died suddenly and together, leaving no one to bury them. The skeletons were several years old, clean but not yet bleached. The remains lay undisturbed; the finger bones of the one by the door balanced precariously on the handle of an axe. Each bone lay next to its proper neighbor, with no scars of teeth or claw. Shuddering, I backed out and closed the door. "Rest, strangers," I muttered. "All's well." Then immediately felt foolish. Talking to dead bones!

Nothing had disturbed my horses; bones were of no interest to them, nor speculations about the origins of this tragedy. The pack horse's lead rope in one hand, I leaped hastily into my saddle.

A hard-packed road followed the creek; the horses turned readily onto it. No more than a couple of miles farther, there was another homestead. This one had burned, and wasn't worth pausing to inspect.

Near a little rise I saw a third farm. These had once been comfortable homesteads, large enough to support a family, and not isolated beyond assistance—except in the final emergency.

It was getting late. I reined my horses into this farmyard and bent down from my saddle to peer through empty windows. There were no visible skeletons inside, so I rode on toward the barn. Whiskers stepped on something that crunched like dried sticks . . . he had put his forefoot through a human rib cage. These bones, outside and exposed to weather, were bleached and brittle. Hastily, I backed him out of the pile of bones.

Nameless fears chilled my backbone. Heels clapped into his sides with panicky force, Whiskers galloped out of the valley onto the clean, windswept hill. Drawing rein, I looked around. Evening was closing in, but I could still see the meandering, wooded creek bottom, the farmstead below, and one or two others just as silent and lifeless. A cricket began to sing. The urgency of locating a safe campsite could no longer be ignored.

Not far away, the creek flowed into a river. Miles away, half hidden in the twilight, bluffs reared above the river bank. Squatting on the heights, square, solid, uncompromised by frivolous decoration, was a massive fortress.

No flags flew above the ramparts, no smoke from cooking fires rose into the darkening sky. It must have been enormous, but even from a distance it gave an impression, not of death, but of emptiness. Was this land entirely deserted?

There! Was that a fire? A gleam of light and a twist of

smoke were barely visible against the twilight sky. This land wasn't completely deserted, then. I longed for human company as never before.

Whiskers slid down the slope, iron-shod hooves clattering among the rocks. The fire was across the creek, a mile or so to the east. My horses splashed through the shallow water and headed for the flickering spark.

There was no movement in the camp. My horses pricked their ears, but neighed no greetings to others of their kind. The wind rushed unheeding by, kicking up a shower of sparks from the untended fire.

"Hallo, the camp," I shouted.

There was no answer to my hail. Could this be a trap, or was the camper displaying prudent caution? Nervously, I gathered a fistful of energy, reminding myself that there was no danger to a wielder of power like me, whom the ignorant and prejudiced would call a witch.

Abruptly Whiskers tossed his head up, pricking his ears and snorting. His sharper perceptions were to be trusted; he sensed something interesting but not frightening. In response to a nudge of my heels, he moved forward readily.

Equipment was strewn untidily about the camp, blankets and food trodden into the dirt. The gaunt body of a man lay to one side, throat messily cut. This was not what had caught Whisker's attention, however; his ears pointed at a clump of brush. Within was a small hunched shadow.

"Come on out," I called. "I won't hurt you."

The response was quick. Whoever was hidden there must have been frightened and possibly hurt. I had expected some hesitation, but the brush rattled and a little figure crept out. A boy in middle adolescence climbed shakily to his feet. He was sixteen or so, small and slight, fair-haired, with staring pale blue eyes.

"Hello," I said gently. "Are you hurt?"

He gaped at me. "A mantic," he breathed, awestricken. "A mantic, with two horses!"

He called me "mantic," as had the supernatural beast. The word meant nothing to me. The dialect of this place was strange to my ear, though many of the words were familiar. Had I been transported here directly from the Kingdon, the language would have been unintelligible. My travels through the lands between had allowed me adapt to the changing vernacular.

"I'm not a mantic, whatever that is. I'm just passing through. What happened here?"

"Bandits, Lady Mantic. My father and I were going to the market at Cherry Creek village to sell our calf and buy seeds. They killed him and took the calf."

"I'm sorry, lad," I said. "Are you hurt? I'm a healer." Moving slowly so as not to frighten him, I dismounted. He stared at me wide-eyed, trembling.

"No, Lady Mantic, I ran and hid." He eased forward, drinking in my appearance with his eyes. This boy was small, less than five feet tall. I towered over him, though in my own homeland, I was not considered tall.

"All right, then, we'd better take care of your father's body. What's your name?"

"Bion, Lady Mantic." He bobbed an awkward bow.

A blanket, shaken free of dirt, covered the bloody corpse. "We'll take him home to your mother in the morning," I told the boy. "For now, we'll have some soup and I'll make you a tea that will help you rest."

"Yes, Lady Mantic," he said obediently. "What if the bandits come back?"

"Don't worry about those bandits," I said grimly. "I hope they do come back."

His face cleared. "Of course! You're a mantic! You wouldn't be afraid of a few ragged outlaws."

"Not a mantic, Bion, just a traveler. Why don't you clean up the campsite while I make soup?"

Given a task to occupy him, the boy brightened a little. As he scurried about, I unloaded my horses and picketed them. A pot of water with dried meat flakes and vegetables was soon simmering over the rebuilt fire. Dough had been rising in my pack all day. Two loaves were pinched off and set to bake in the coals. Passiflora, a mild tranquilizer, steeped in another pan.

Strange how trustfully Bion had taken up with me. After his terrible experiences that day, he should have been either frightened or hostile, yet he seemed content to follow my instructions. He was undoubtedly hungry; his fingernails had the curled look of a lifetime without enough to eat.

Our meal finished, he drank the tea readily and wrapped himself in a blanket. I walked around camp, setting powerful magic wards. Signs of protection would keep away supernaturals like the feline; a barrier of energy would warn me of human marauders.

It had been a long day and my own blankets beckoned. I stretched out in my bedroll, wondering about the incongruities of this land, fair to the eye, but filled with dangers. It had once been populous and cultivated; now the dead weren't even buried and bandits murdered and robbed as they pleased. If Bion was typical, the people of the richest land I had ever seen lived on the thin border of starvation. The conditions in this place were an offense to civilization. What had gone wrong?

Two long poles from the woods along the creek made a convenient litter between my two horses—much to Whiskers's indignation. He was a pureblood of the old mountain breed and inclined to value his own consequence. Bion and I loaded the stiffened corpse on the litter. The boy, still unnaturally meek, led the mare as we transported our sad burden.

It was a long, melancholy walk to his home. As we went, I questioned Bion about his country. He readily explained the skeletons. "It was plague," he told me. "Almost everyone died. In the old days, when there were mantics and margraves in the castella, the tillers were protected. They worked the soil under the direction of the mantics and there was plenty for all."

As he told this story, his voice dropped into a singsong chant. He had heard it many times. "The tiller folk grew resentful of the nobles for taking too large a share of their crops, enriching themselves while the farmers lived simply. There was a great uprising and the mantics and margraves who weren't killed, fled."

"What exactly did the mantics and margraves do for the tiller folk?" I asked.

"The mantics held the magic. They knew the healing ways. The margraves were the warriors and monster-slayers.

Both rode upon horses." He cast an awed glance at Biscuit, walking placidly beside him.

"When they were gone, the evil creatures of the night were loosed upon us. We were the prey of creatures that eat human flesh and drink their souls. We died of a hundred diseases that none of us know how to treat. Evil men drifted into the land and were unchecked by margraves."

He continued sadly, "The tilling people suffered and dwindled. They regretted their uprising against the nobles, but it was too late. The folk lived in great misery. Ten years ago there was a terrible epidemic. So many died, that there aren't enough hands to work the fields. Our only hope is that the Burdened Ones may return." He glanced at me sidelong.

I soothed the disgruntled Whiskers. "Instead of longing for your nobles to come back, you'd do better to choose leaders from among yourselves," I told the boy tartly. "If you wait around to be rescued, you all may die. It sounds to me like you were well rid of the mantics and margraves. You don't need them."

"But," Bion protested, "we do need them. We don't have the magic or the healing skills of the mantics. None of us knows how to fight. It just isn't right for tiller folk to try to do things beyond their station."

"Would you rather die?"

"Yes, Lady Mantic, we would rather die. It was stepping out of our proper place in life that caused this sorry mess!"

I sighed. Adolescents always see things in such uncompromising terms. Either everything is the way it ought to be or it isn't and there is no middle ground.

"Who lives up there?" I said, pointing to the huge fortress. We were passing beneath it.

"No one, Lady Mantic. When the nobles lived among us, that was the castellum of this march. It was the mantic's residence and the margrave's fortress. All the folk lived there and went out to the fields by day. At night the gates were shut and the mantic's magic protected us against supernaturals. She treated our injuries and diseases. We served her gladly."

"How long ago was this?"

"Longer than my great grandfather could remember, but his grandfather was the mantic's last head plowman."

"That must be—h'mm—at least a hundred and fifty years. You should just move in and take it over. I'm sure the original owners wouldn't object."

The boy stopped in his tracks and stared at me. "Go into the castellum? Oh, no, Lady Mantic! It's haunted! The ghosts of the last mantic and margrave guard it. It's death to even walk through the gates. Many have tried, for there was a great treasure of tools, weapons, and fine furnishings there. But the mantic and her family were tortured to death by rebels, and their maddened spirits remain. They take terrible revenge upon all who enter." He sighed wistfully. "It's a great shame upon us that our good mantic and her folk were so foully murdered. We deserve all the sorrow we've suffered since that day."

"Nonsense," I said briskly. "Unfortunate as those deaths may have been, you aren't responsible for crimes committed a century and a half ago. Besides, I've seen almost every kind of supernatural there is, and I've never run across a real ghost. The dead don't linger at the site of their deaths."

The boy was pale with fear. He glanced away. "Forgive me, Lady Mantic. I forgot that naturally you wouldn't fear the ghosts of your own kind. Your powers would protect you from them."

We walked on in silence. It was reasonably certain there were no ghosts up at the castellum, but there must be something on guard. Curiosity began to tickle.

The formidable walls had been well built. Six generations of abandonment hadn't dislodged a single monumental stone. The wooden gate had rotted, hanging in fragments from bronze-green hinges; entrance would present no difficulty. I suppressed an urge to investigate. Our melancholy burden must be delivered first.

CHAPTER
2

THE Walls of the fortress loomed high above me as my horses climbed the paved road that zigzagged up the bluff. The walls were built of huge blocks of the native cream-colored stone; the cheerful color kept their sheer immensity from overwhelming my spirits. The castellum beckoned me with an imperative that I couldn't deny. I drew my horses to a halt before the gate.

Awed, I leaned back in my saddle and looked up and up to the lintel of the gate. There, carved in high relief, was the only decoration I had seen on the exterior of the structure. Crouched there, peering down at me, was the great feline supernatural I had encountered. The carving was three times life size, the stripes indicated by hatchings on the polished stone. The expression was alert but not threatening, as if to say, "Enemy beware, friend be welcome."

I hesitated on the threshold. This was a portentous moment. Until I rode through this gate, I could still turn back and ride east, drifting as I had for the past two years. Passing under the watchful feline would be a commitment to this place and its mysteries, for a time at least. I turned and looked out over the river valley below, scanning the rich alluvial soil, the willow-lined river, the green plains beyond. To my desert-bred eye, it was an alien land. The very air was thick and heavy with moisture, scented with greenery, sluggishly stirred by a warm breeze.

I turned back to the castellum and gazed through the portal. The opening had once been closed by a massive wooden gate, but only splinters clung to the huge bronze hinges now.

Beyond the gate was a courtyard, its paving stones heaved and cracked by the trees and bushes that had taken root there and grown to maturity since its abandonment. Once a company of cavalry could have entered there and dismounted. Farther back, I could glimpse the creamy facade of the interior building through the trees. I saw no ghosts, but it was bright midmorning, not the stormy midnight associated in the old stories with manifestations of spirits.

I turned again to look down the road, and Whiskers shifted impatiently under me as if to say, "Well, make up your mind. Are we going on or back?" I patted his neck absently. I had caught a glimpse of silvery reflections on pewter-striped flanks; we were not unaccompanied. The feline supernatural waited a few yards from the foot of the road.

"All right, then," I said aloud. A touch of my heel sent Whiskers through the gate, Biscuit following obediently.

My horses picked their way through the buckled paving stones and the trees until we came to the foot of a broad flight of shallow steps. There was a wide porch, the balustrades drifted in the corners with the accumulated leaves of many autumns. Once, I thought, important visitors would have been met here by the lord and lady of this keep, and servitors would have been waiting to take the horses away to some well-appointed stable. I was met only by the twittering of birds and the scurry of small animals, which peered at me unafraid and commented shrilly to each other upon the intrusion. How many of their little generations had it been since their ancestors had been the target of small boys with stones?

I dismounted and tied both horses to the balustrade, where they couldn't entangle themselves in their ropes. Climbing the steps, I paused before the mossy old door. I gathered enough energy from the overmind to form a weapon that could be counted upon to stun a charging bull; true, I didn't believe in ghosts, but it didn't hurt to be prepared.

The gates, exposed to the elements, had rotted away. The door, sheltered by the outer wall and the overhanging second story, had fared better. It was still more or less whole, shrunken from around the bolts that secured it to the elaborate hinges and blackened with age, perhaps. When I laid my free hand upon the greenish ring that served as a handle and pulled, it swung outward. It grated and the hinges groaned, but it opened wide enough for me to walk through before it stuck.

All my life I have paused upon thresholds and surveyed what lay ahead of me, and this was no time to deviate from an excellent practice. Before me, dim and cool, was an entrance hall. A grand staircase rose from the back, with lesser flights upon either hand. Doors flanked each staircase and the corners of the room, some opened, some closed. The bannisters of the staircases were carved of the same creamy stone, and beneath the coating of dust, they were polished and graceful. Several wooden settles, dark with age, were placed about, with small tables—for refreshments for guests, I supposed—near them.

There was no sign of violence or intrusion. The stone itself showed no mark of the passing of time, but the woods were aged and shrunken.

I walked into the room, my boots clattering upon the stone floor, setting echoes reverberating into the silence. Perhaps the noise served as an alarm to the guardians of the castellum, for as I reached the center of the floor, six grim and grisly apparitions manifested themselves, drifting toward me in utter silence.

Each was the representation of a dead person, one who had died in horrible torment. They reached for me with broken fingers, and I dodged their touch hastily. These were not ghosts. They were formed of the stuff of the overmind by some powerful will—powerful beyond imagining, if they had persisted for a century and a half after their creator's death. If they touched me, I knew, I would be drawn into the overmind, where there was no doubt a re-creation of the death scenes of the unfortunates who had been the models for the apparitions. I slipped past them; they were slowly reorienting upon me. I shaped the energy I had gathered into another form and released it. Energy was not wanted here; the ability to draw away the power that held the formless gray material of the overmind into the color and shape of specters was needed.

I dodged again, eluding the apparitions and pausing by the

door. Reaching into the overmind, I tapped the binding energies. They were strong—so strong that I knew I would have to find somewhere to drain them away or I would be blasted. Glancing out the door, I noted the overgrown courtyard. That would do. Chanting a focusing and directing spell, I diverted the surging energies to the task of clearing the undergrowth and forcing the paving stones back into their places.

My horses shifted uneasily as bushes and small trees heaved themselves out of the ground, roots and all, broke themselves into convenient firewood size, and stacked themselves against the wall. Blocks of stone grated and squirmed their way into position. The drifted leaves leaped suddenly into the air, flashed with little spurts of greenish fire, and were gone, leaving a sweet smoky smell. A few of the larger and more attractive trees shuddered and stripped away their tangled lower branches, and the paving stones that their growth had pushed aside crawled into neat rings about each trunk.

Still the energies I had tapped fought to be free of my control and to burn me away as the leaves had been burnt. I directed the power at some of the larger tree trunks I had removed from the courtyard. If I focused the energies just so, it should be possible—I had never worked with such a tremendous amount of energy before. The first tree trunk burst into a cloud of splinters that sparked green and spat as they were consumed. I groaned with effort as I shifted the chant. The next log shivered and fell into slabs. A surge of heat cooked the sap out of the wood that only seconds before had been living. Other logs followed suit.

When I had a pile of massive boards, I turned my attention to the splinters of the old gate that hung from the hinges. This was dry, old, powdery wood that flared up in a flash of heat and light as it was consumed. Corrosion-frozen nuts backed themselves off green-crusted bolts. Slabs of wood that I could not have begun to move with my natural strength heaved themselves up, jockeying for position, rubbing away uneven edges so that they fitted so closely a knifeblade couldn't have slipped between them. Crosspieces clamped themselves against the standing slabs and bolts impelled themselves like arrows to pierce both gate leaves and crosspieces. Nuts leaped from the ground and whirred into place. The hinges clanked into their proper positions as the huge leaves rose to meet them, and were secured by their own bolts.

I was beginning to waver with exhaustion. If the binding energy was not spent soon, I would lose control of it and be consumed. Yet there was still more. I looked up. Sure enough, there was a cloud in the sky. I raised my hand, refocusing the power yet again, and releasing it with a yell. A lightning bolt speared from my hand into the sky, forking and splitting, leaving a smell of ozone. The abused cloud gave up its moisture; rain poured down. The energy was gone, and I glanced over my shoulder as I sank down to lie sprawled upon the doorstep in the rain. The apparitions were gone too, leaving only a few floating flecks of gray where they had dissipated back into the overmind.

I lay for a long time in the sluicing rain, resting from my labors and gathering my own strength as the water cooled my overheated flesh. The downpour completed the cleaning of the entry court, and I wondered bemusedly what the tiller folk would think when they saw the tidy courtyard and the renewed gates of the castellum. I had had to have somewhere to bleed away the energy that bound the apparitions. How incredibly powerful the sorcerer or sorceress who formed those must have been! At my strongest, I couldn't have invested a thousandth as much in one of my creations, and mine usually faded away in a day or two. I would try to discover how it was done.

As the rain slackened, I regained enough strength to drag myself to my feet and to fetch food from the pack upon Biscuit's back. Refreshed, I went to explore the castellum.

I climbed the grand staircase. It was strange, I thought, that Bion and his family had betrayed no resentment or fear when I had told them that I was coming here. They had seemed cheerfully accepting of the notion. They evidently took it for granted that I would go to the castellum—after all, it was where I belonged, wasn't it?

At the head of the stairs was an ornately carved door, with the feline as its central motif. Here the creature sat complacently on its haunches, looking out at me with cool superiority. Dark halls led away to both sides. Above the door was a legend, carved in a tantalizingly familiar script—almost, but not quite, enough like the alphabet of the Kingdom that I could read it.

I pressed on the latch handle; it grated and the hinges squealed as I pushed the door open. Delighted, I wandered among the rooms of what, by their size and central location, had once been the suite of the mantic and margrave of the march. They were placed around another courtyard, where the remains of a fine herb garden still lingered. The rooms themselves—offices, bedrooms, sitting rooms, well-drained bathing rooms—seemed not to have been disturbed since some long-gone maid had last straightened them. The margrave's rooms were full of armor and arms; the mantic's gave directly into a fascinating library. Most of the rooms had been protected by shutters closed across the outside of the windows, and when I opened these, the rooms were light and airy, placed so as to catch a cool breeze. I felt at ease and at home, as though the very proportions and colors of the rooms welcomed me.

The mantic and margrave of this castellum had not lived luxuriously. There was little that could be called treasure. They had worn embroidered homespun robes, if the fragile remnants of fabrics I found were any indication, and had eaten upon hand-thrown earthenware, attractively patterned in red and black upon a light tan slip, but by no means as valuable as the delicate snowy porcelain favored by the rich of my homeland.

I chose the mantic's quarters to be my own. Both the feline supernatural and the tiller folk had called me mantic, though if the position required the kind of skill and power that had been employed in building the apparitions, I was a sorry pretender! But the rooms were next to the library, and I was certain that I could decipher the script. The bedroom adjoined the bedroom of the margrave's suite; there was a door between them secured only by a simple latch, from which I inferred that the mantic and the margrave had customarily been husband and wife.

I found the stables. There were a dozen or so boxes for

horses, and many tie-stalls where from the narrow little
shoes and the withered remnants of leather bridles, asses had
been kept. The stables were on one side of a courtyard with
a well in the middle; on the other sides were cow byres,
dairy rooms, and other facilities for livestock which my limited agricultural knowledge couldn't identify. The hay and
grain for the animals, and straw for bedding them, had long
since perished, but this courtyard too was overgrown and
there was enough grass there for my two horses for the
night, so I turned them loose and propped the gate shut.

When I had carried my gear up to my rooms, I went exploring in the rest of the castellum. The place was an incredible maze, built without order or plan, and I wandered in it
for the rest of the day without seeing every room. I frequently got lost, but all the rooms in which people had lived
or worked gave on to one of the multitude of courtyards, and
an occasional glimpse of the sun reoriented me.

The kitchens were a complex of bakeries, sculleries, but-
teries, and pantries that must have fed hundreds and required
a staff of dozens. The well in the kitchen courtyard was right
across the castellum from the stables, I was pleased to note.
The dining hall was huge, once open down both flanks to
garden courtyards, now securely shuttered. There was a stair
that led down from the master suite above to a door in the
rear of the dais where the head table was placed and surrounded with carved chairs; the main part of the hall was
filled with ranks of long narrow tables and benches. Each
table had a chair at the end of it facing the dais, and from
the carvings on the backs of these chairs, it seemed that the
chiefs of the various occupational groups sat there—here the
herders, there the plowmen, beyond them the shoemakers
and blacksmiths and weavers and so on.

The rest of the castellum contained living quarters and
workshops, and if there was one apartment the same size and
shape and decor as any other, I didn't find it. All the rooms
faced onto courtyards, all were orderly and clean. Many had
usable furniture in them. I was overwhelmed at the thought
of the many hundreds of people who must have lived here in
the castellum's heyday. But even before it was abandoned,

the population must have been declining. Many of the apartments were shut and unfurnished.

It seemed to me that the castellum, though similar in its defensive function to the ancient ruined structures that we of the Kingdom called "castles," was actually more like a town than a fort. But what economic principles governed the exchange of goods and services within the castellum, I couldn't discover. There were no chambers that could be identified as shops, nor strong rooms for the keeping of currency.

The castellum differed from the castles I had seen in another respect: those ancient structures remaining from the First Civilization invariably included several levels of grim dungeons, which in modern days provided a good living for guides and lecturers who escorted gaping sightseers through their cells and torture chambers. There were no dungeons in the castellum, apparently not even a cellar. I was a little disappointed; after all, ancient abandoned stone fortresses really ought to have dungeons.

There had been no great difference in the lifestyles of the mantic and the margrave, and the tiller folk who served them. They wore much the same clothes, and their possessions had differed but little. Possibly the head table had received the choicest cuts of meat and the freshest fruits and vegetables, but the food was all prepared in the same kitchens and was kept in the same storerooms. The quarters of the tiller folk had been smaller than the master suite, but contained the same type of rooms except for the library and armory.

Looking about, I couldn't believe the story Bion had told me of rebellion and destruction. If such things had happened, they certainly hadn't happened here. There was no trace of violence. The whole vast place gave the impression of having been left carefully closed up for a vacation, perhaps, and never reinhabited. When they left, its folk had gone peacefully, with the intention of returning. But that was almost as unbelievable as the story of rebellion. Hundreds of folk, going off to the seaside or the mountains, and then never returning? Without leaving a single caretaker?

But if that were so, then why the specters out of the overmind, left to entrap and destroy intruders? Why had they been made so gruesome? To protect the place, doubtless, but it had been no casual undertaking to place them here. Something truly cataclysmic had inspired their making. Perhaps the explanation would be found among the journals in the mantic's office or the books in her library.

I kindled a small fire in one end of one of the enormous stoves to boil my soup and to dry my damp clothing and another in one of the ovens to bake my bread; there was wood in the woodsheds—well dried, after a century and a half. The folk of the castellum had used oil lamps made of the red-and-black ware; I had found hundreds of them, many still with wicks, but I had no oil for them and had to use a torch to light my way up to bed. The mantic's bed was sound, even if the bedclothes were too dusty and fragile to use, and I spread my blankets upon it, enjoying the springiness after many nights of sleeping upon the hard ground.

My first concern the next morning was to find pasture for the horses. There was no other gate out of the castellum than the one by which I had entered, which meant that the nearest grass was down on the river bottom. I pulled open the new gates, noting with approval that they swung freely on their hinges, which needed oil badly but bore the many hundred-weights of the gates easily. Then I went to get the horses. I took the picket pins and ropes out of the pack and scrambled up on Whiskers bareback so I wouldn't have to carry the saddle up the bluff.

I rode to the gate and glanced down the road. There I halted, amazed. A procession was at the foot of the bluff, preparing to climb. There were people—a couple of dozen, enough in this empty land to qualify as a crowd. There were carts and wagons drawn by asses and oxen, all heavily loaded. There was a herd of sheep and three or four milch cows. Dogs frisked and barked.

They saw me sitting bareback on Whiskers, framed by the gate, and they pointed and chattered to each other. "Our tiller folk are prompt to arrive," said a voice beside me, and Biscuit shied, nearly yanking me off Whiskers. I looked, and there sat the feline supernatural, for all the world like a cat at the hearth.

I stared at it, amazed. "What are you doing here?" I asked faintly.

The feline looked at me and blinked slowly. "It is my place to be beside the mantic of the castellum when the little folk come to make their obeisances. How else are they to know that I have chosen you?"

"If you attack them, I'll have to kill you," I warned.

The cat gave me a look of cool inscrutability. "I do not attack the folk of my own castellum," it said haughtily. "It is my place to protect them. I am the familiar of this castellum, and you are my mantic."

"I beg your pardon," I said. "But you do intend to eat me?"

"Of course. You are my proper food. I eat no other. Once in a generation I feed upon the mantic and the margrave of my castellum, and choose a new mantic to replace the old one." It ran its long gray tongue curling over its lips. "I have not eaten for a very long time now."

"No," I said. "I can imagine that you haven't. May I ask when you intend to eat me?"

"When you and the margrave come to me of your own free will. You will know when the time has come."

"There is no margrave," I pointed out.

"I will choose one."

Baffled, I looked at the creature. It was magnificent in the slanting morning sunlight, its silver flanks touched with gold. "But what if the mantic and the margrave don't want to be eaten?" I asked.

"You will, when the time has come. It is proper." The feline yawned impressively, dismissing the subject.

I looked down the road. The tiller folk were climbing up, the asses straining in their harnesses, oxen swinging their heavy heads under their yokes. There was Bion, driving the livestock, grinning up at me proudly. This was not an indignant lynch mob; people bound on that sort of violent errand don't bring their sheep and household goods. They must be planning to move in. If that were so, they must know that I had disposed of the apparitions that had kept them out for so

many generations. Perhaps they meant to demand that I
serve as their mantic. I gulped, beginning to feel trapped.

"Come," said the cat. "We will greet our folk and accept
their allegiance from before the door as is proper." It flowed
through the gate. The creature certainly had definite ideas of
propriety. I shook my head, but I followed it and turned my
horses back into the stable yard.

I placed myself beside the feline on the stately porch before the aged doors. The tiller folk, arriving at the gate,
peered timidly through and then filed in, gazing about at the
cleaned courtyard. There was no surprise on their faces,
only acceptance and a growing excitement. When they had
all entered, and the sheep were herded off to one side, the
wagons and carts parked, and the cattle secured, the people
began to gather in family groups before the porch, peeking
at each other, each waiting for someone else. The feline
yawned, its foot-long fangs gleaming in the morning sun; an
awed whisper ran through the folk.

At last Bion's mother stepped forward. She had at least
met me; I had helped to bury her husband, two days ago.
"Lady Mantic," she began, and stopped and cleared her
throat nervously. "Lady Mantic, we beg that you will accept
the goods and services of myself and my family and grant us
in return your protection and support." She gestured, and
Bion's gray-haired grandmother and his two little sisters
moved forward to kneel with her and Bion on the lowest
step.

"I am not the mantic—" I started to say, when the great
silver feline interrupted me with a snarl that started somewhere far below the registers of sound that I could hear and
rattled its way through my bones into audibility.

"You are the mantic," it hissed, its ears laid flat against its
head. Its eyes blazed like little silver suns. "I have chosen
you. Your only escape from the office lies down my throat."

Involuntarily, I recoiled. I had almost begun to think of
the creature as friendly. "Accept the service of these folk.
Touch each one upon the forehead and say their names," the
feline continued. I hesitated. It moved forward, gliding like
a stalking cat.

I could—perhaps—have destroyed it. But as close as it

was to me, I would not have escaped unscathed. It takes time to gather enough energy to form so potent a weapon. Besides, the creature was obviously an integral part of the culture of these people, choosing their leaders, protecting them from supernatural predators. I didn't want to destroy it while I was uncertain that great harm wouldn't result from the action. On the other hand, I had no wish to burden myself with the responsibility for the tiller folk. However, wish or no wish, I was going to have to make a quick decision; the creature was sinking into a crouch, its tail lashing.

"Please, Lady Mantic," said Bion's mother. "My name is Tildis."

I stepped forward and touched her forehead. "Tildis," I said. The feline stretched and sauntered forward, sniffing at the woman as if to remember her scent. She submitted unafraid.

Bion came forward next, and then the rest of the tiller folk were crowding around, each kneeling and offering his or her goods and services. I touched each forehead and repeated each name, and even the littlest child, too young to speak for itself, was presented. The feline sniffed each.

They seemed to know what to do when the ceremony was over. They picked up their goods and unpacked the wagons and carts, entering the castellum with the air of those who had a right there, exclaiming. Tildis asked me shyly where the kitchens were, and I went with her to show her. Bion bustled after us. "Shall I take your horses down to the pastures, Lady Mantic?" he asked.

"Would you, please?" I answered. I was obviously going to be busy the rest of the day. None of the tiller folk knew their way around the castellum; quarters would have to be allocated, jobs apportioned, arrangements made for feeding and sanitation and the storage of the food supplies on the carts. I wasn't going to be able to make a start today on deciphering the script in which the books were written.

CHAPTER
3

I Tilted the journal to try to get the light onto the scrawled writing; it got no clearer. The last mantic had had atrocious handwriting. I was able to puzzle out a few words in the printed books in the library, but the mantic's journals still defeated me. I was intensely curious about the entries of the last few years before the castellum had been abandoned.

Perhaps that word there was "children." Then the one just before it would be either "red" or "ret." That didn't make any sense. I sighed and laid the journal aside as there came a scratching on the office door.

The door opened and Tildis came in. "Lady Mantic," she said, "there are three people in the entrance hall who wish to seek your protection."

"Did they bring any food with them?" I asked. Provisions were becoming a major worry. Nearly every day two or three tiller folk came seeking to join us at the castellum. In the three weeks since I had entered, the number of indwellers had swelled to nearly fifty. The custom was for them to turn over all their possessions to the mantic, in return for which they expected to be fed, sheltered, and cared for. But many of those who came were nearly destitute.

"A little," Tildis answered. I had made her housekeeper of the castellum, a job for which she was well suited. "They brought another team of oxen and a cart. The woman claims to be a weaver."

"A weaver? That's good. We're going to need a weaver."

"Yes, Lady Mantic. Shall I give them quarters near the weavers' hall?"

"Ask them first. Maybe they'd rather have an apartment near the rest of the folk." The castellum had been arranged so that each category of craftspeople lived around the court into which their workshop opened, but there were so few people here now that they had all chosen to live in the plowmen's quarters, which was conveniently near to the kitchens and dining hall.

"Yes, Lady Mantic. We have food for three more days if no one else comes in with supplies."

"Can't we send out hunting parties?"

Tildis looked at me, shocked. "Hunting is the responsibility of the margrave, Lady Mantic. None of us would know anything about it."

"I know," I said patiently, "but there isn't any margrave. I'll ride out and see what I can do. Have Bion harness up a donkey cart and follow me with some of the men in case I get anything."

"But, Lady Mantic, you can't hunt. You don't even carry weapons."

"There are different kinds of weapons, Tildis," I said. "I can't let everyone go hungry, either." I was beginning to feel enclosed by the stone walls; I needed to get out. I didn't explain this to Tildis. The tiller folk regarded the castellum as a shelter and ventured out of it only upon orders. I myself had been no farther than the fields that were being put into production down on the river bottom. It was late for planting but many of the crops should make it to maturity, and they were absolutely necessary if the tiller folk were not to starve during the winter.

As I rode along the river valley looking for a convenient way up the bluffs to the prairie, I thought about the little people who were insisting upon making themselves my responsibility. They were indeed "little" people, so small and delicate that sometimes I felt like a hulking giant among them. A few of the men might approach my inches, but none could begin to match my weight, and I was thin for my height. The women were like children beside me, and the children—there were very few—were impossibly ethereal. The folk seemed intent upon forcing me to accept the responsibility for their safety and well-being, gladly turning over their farming tools and supplies to me and keeping only the most personal of possessions.

I was wary of the trap they set. Once before I had been lured into accepting the responsibility for another person, and with the best of intentions I had come within a hair of destroying both of us. Had I not been arrested, convicted of witchcraft, and sent to prison, I would have. I missed him still, the slave I had bought to save his life and had come to care for more than I had ever cared for anyone.

I felt that if I let these people saddle me with the responsibility for their lives, something even worse would inevitably happen. A good friend—a kind man—had told me that there was a place for me somewhere. But this was not it. A solitary, rootless wanderer, I was not the proper person to take charge of these folk.

I didn't even feel at home in this moist green land. Of all the places I had seen in my roving life, I loved and understood the deserts best, the sun-filled space and the stillness and the secretness and even the furnace-hot air of summer. Next, I loved the grand wild mountains. The low green plains were alien to me, the very air uncomfortable to breathe in its syrupy thickness.

Even if the tiller folk were dying, what was that to me? I couldn't save them, I told myself. Only they could save themselves. What if the silver feline supernatural had chosen me? If it tried to keep me when I wanted to leave, I would kill it. I had destroyed more fearsome supernaturals. The limits of my magical strength and resolution had never yet been tested.

There was a good path up a lower place in the bluffs, and I headed Whiskers into it. Up on the prairie it was windy and open; although there were many trees, they tended to nestle in the draws and along the creeks and rivers. The soil was thickly sodded and yielded reluctantly to agriculture, nor was it periodically refreshed by silt from the flooding waterways as the bottomlands were. The tiller folk grazed their livestock up here occasionally, but in the main it was untamed land, given over to the huge slaty wild cattle, and the wolves and little tawny panthers that preyed upon them.

It was a herd of the cattle that I sought. The tiller folk

feared them, not without reason. The bulls particularly were big and aggressive and adorned with sharp-tipped upstanding horns that they used freely in defense of the cows and calves. They weighed fifteen hundred pounds or more on the hoof, and two or three carcasses would provide the materials for a lot of soups and stews and even meat to salt away against the winter.

How exactly I was to reduce the beasts from the state of being "on the hoof" to "carcasses" I had not yet considered. It was true that the energy I could gather and shape could be formed into a formidable weapon, but I was loath to use it for this purpose for several reasons. It was dangerous to handle, and slow to gather. It exhausted me to do so. And finally, all my life I had had to hide my skills as a wielder of power and I was vastly reluctant to exhibit them before the tiller folk.

I had seen several herds of the gray cattle as I entered into the prairie, but I had made no attempt to kill any. I limited my hunting to the trapping and snaring of small game: rabbits and quail and the speckled grouse. If I had killed anything larger, most of it would have gone to waste.

Whiskers was fresh and well fed and we soon succeeded in locating a herd of cattle. They were not greatly disturbed by our presence. The bulls looked up from their grazing to shake their great horns at us with a sharp cracking sound. The cows with young calves drifted in their grazing to the far side of the herd.

I circled far to the right of the herd, until they were between me and the river. I thought perhaps it would be possible to drive a few of them over the bluffs. The bulls, lowing uneasily, followed me and the cows began to herd their calves to the interior of the herd. I unfastened my jacket from behind the saddle. Putting my heels suddenly into Whiskers's ribs, I whooped and waved the jacket over my head as we went charging down upon the herd.

The cattle didn't react as I hoped. Instead of stampeding toward the river, they bunched. The bulls, heads lowered and forehooves scraping at the earth, bellowed threateningly. As Whiskers and I went pelting down upon the herd, one scarred old patriarch charged, tail stiffly erect. His horns were directed as straight as lances at us, and behind him the younger subordinate bulls tossed their heads and made shorter charges.

Whiskers, who had been none too convinced in the first place of the wisdom of charging down upon these monsters who weighed half again as much as he did, plunged to a stop and shied wildly; the old bull charged past us. For a moment it seemed as though the whole earth shook with the force and turmoil of the charge. The younger bulls were nearly upon us. Whiskers lunged into a gallop and before I could stop him we were in full flight back to the west. The cattle were slower and clumsier; they chased us for only a quarter mile or so before they stopped and returned to the herd, snorting and congratulating each other upon having routed the intruder.

I checked Whiskers and pondered. Obviously a lone rider couldn't herd the cattle. I considered firing the grass; surely the beasts would run before a grass fire. But I shuddered to think of the destruction, the small creatures that would die uselessly, the ugly black scar upon the green land. I thought about returning to the castellum and raiding the margrave's armory for a bow or lance, but I never carried weapons and would be unlikely to hit one of the young cows. Nor could I see Whiskers and me charging down upon the herd and lancing one. Whiskers was going to be very reluctant to go near them again after his fright. No, there was no help for it; I was going to have to use magic.

Gazing back over the restless herd, I pondered. I was evidently far enough away not to arouse the aggressive instincts of the great bulls, but too near for them to be entirely easy. I would have to separate the two-year-old cows I wanted from their protective bulls. How could the power I could draw and shape be put to this particular use? I peered nervously around. No one was in sight. I gathered a quantity of energy and held it, seething sullenly, between my outstretched hands, muttering a controlling spell. More and more I added to it until it was as much as I could conveniently handle. Then I sighted on a plump heifer. The chant became one of the focusing and directing; as it reached its climax, I hurled the hissing globe of energy from me with all my force and will.

The crackling ball traveled toward its intended victim, who stared dully at it. If she had run, she could have outdistanced it and stayed ahead until it dissipated, for it moved no faster than a trotting horse. She could have dodged, too, if she had tried, but she just stood, chewing and unafraid, until it struck her. Convulsing as the energy surged through her nerve channels, she dropped in her tracks and died, stiffened legs paddling at the air.

The other members of the herd stared for a moment, then returned to the grass, apparently not connecting the quivering hulk with the late member of their herd. I began to gather another energy weapon. It was harder this time; I had taken nearly all the readily available energy in the area for the first one, and I was tiring with the immense effort of will it took to control and shape the destructive stuff. I struggled for a long time with the obdurate energy, while Whiskers shifted uneasily under me. He was used to my sorcery, but he didn't like it.

At last I was ready. A second heifer too dropped without a struggle. I swayed wearily in my saddle as I began again to collect power. This time I had to reach to the farthest limits of my range to collect enough energy to make my weapon, and I found that I was gasping through my open mouth as I fought to control a globe of energy that seemed inertly intent upon turning on its creator. By the time I had readied my last bolt, the herd had grazed a quarter of a mile farther to the north, leaving the still carcasses with complete unconcern. I nudged Whiskers with my heels and he sidled unwillingly closer. I couldn't see the herd well enough to choose my target so carefully this time, so I hurled the weapon at a young bull, the nearest to me. This unfortunate creature didn't die as easily as the heifers had done, but struggled half-paralyzed to regain its feet, churning up the sod in a circle about itself before mercifully expiring at last.

The old bull finally seemed to sense that something was amiss, for he lowed uneasily and moved off to the north, the depleted herd falling in behind him obediently.

I sagged in my saddle, holding a double handful of mane

to keep myself on. I felt weak and listless enough to slide to the ground and just lie there, but there were things to be done. Whiskers was glad enough to set off in the direction of the river under my feeble urging. I found Bion and his party with the donkey cart just coming up out of the river valley. Thankful that they hadn't seen me, I led them back to the kill site and left them to butcher the carcasses and bring the meat while I turned Whiskers once again toward home. I managed to stay aboard until we reached the castellum, though Whiskers was left to his own resources to find the way.

I only realized that we were within the forecourt when I found that Whiskers had been standing still for some time, one of the tiller folk patiently holding his bridle and waiting for me to dismount. The distance from his back to the paving stones seemed vast, and I slid awkwardly down his shoulder and stood for a long time clinging to the saddle. At last I gathered my strength to totter up the steps to my room, where I sagged bonelessly onto the bed and slept the rest of the day and all night without even removing my boots.

I was tired and weak for several days thereafter. The meat was welcome, but clearly I couldn't supply the needs of the castellum by such methods. I went into the armory and looked at the weapons there, but the bows, the obvious hunting weapons, were too stout for me to draw. The swords were clumsy things, meant to be swung two-handed. I could see no way to use them for killing cattle without being gored. The objects I had thought were lances turned out to be short heavy throwing spears, not at all useful from horseback. There was nothing that I could use effectively as a hunting weapon.

It was becoming obvious that the castellum needed a margrave, but I had no idea how to go about recruiting one—and the implication of the adjoining bedrooms disturbed me deeply. I wondered if the mantic and the margrave were necessarily wed to each other, or if it was only a custom. I certainly had no wish to marry in this land, especially when I had every intention of keeping the way clear for my eventual departure.

I needed more desperately than ever to be able to read the

local script. I was making only slow progress even with the printed materials, since the tiller folk made constant demands on my time and energy for decisions, medical treatment, the resolution of quarrels, and the allocation of what few goods we had. The task of discovering anything was made doubly difficult by the lack of any index or table of contents in the books. I had to read quite a lot from each volume to determine its content, and since I was still spelling out each word one letter at a time, that was a lengthy process.

I was still lonely. There seemed to be a vast social gap between the tiller folk and the mantic. There was no conversation or easy companionship. Any attempt I made to join in was met by tongue-tied and apologetic embarrassment. Of course, I was used to solitude, but I had always had the consolation in my loneliness of consulting no one's convenience but my own. Here I was run to distraction by the demands made upon me. Perhaps an aristocrat born might find the consequence a fair exchange for the burdens, but I was by nature an outsider. I began to regret more and more deeply that I hadn't ridden on when I had left Tildis's homestead.

I soon found out that the social gap between the tiller folk and their adopted mantic was narrow compared to that between the outsider and the high-bred folk of the true aristocratic bloodlines. I was supervising the cleaning and setting to order of the harness shop near the stables when Bion came running to inform me that the margrave of the nearest inhabited castellum, the Bearsnake, was in the entrance hall and demanded my immediate presence.

I was inclined to take this imperious message amiss. Who, after all, did the fellow think he was, giving me orders in my own castellum? Then I grinned at my bristling reaction. *My* castellum? Not if I could help it!

I soothed my feelings by keeping him dawdling while I washed and changed clothes, though there was little to choose between my two outfits; one was a rose shirt and gray trousers and the other was a pale green shirt and tan trousers, but all were faded and worn.

The margrave was a balding thin man built to my own

scale, and he was not favorably impressed by my attire. A sneer curled his lip as he looked me over. "Good morning," I greeted him politely.

"You are the female who claims the Silvercat?" he asked coldly.

"Eh?"

"This castellum. The Silvercat. You claim to be mantic here?"

"The tiller folk of the area have called me by that title."

"You have no shadow of a right here. Or do you claim descent from an extinct family?"

"I'm a traveler from the far west. I'm not related to any family in these plains."

"How dare you claim to be a mantic? How dare you make free use of this castellum?"

I controlled my anger and answered evenly, "These folk needed the protection of the castellum. Apparently their ancestors lived here."

"What concern is it of yours? If these people had deserved the help and protection of a mantic, one would have been provided by the familiar of the castellum."

"I've made it my concern. If that displeases you, send a true mantic and margrave here to protect the folk and I'll go about my business."

The man sneered again. "Such a statement could be expected from a mongrel usurper. You have no inkling of the burden or responsibility of the office of mantic. You think nothing of destroying the guardians that were set over this castellum to protect it for the return of the true rulers, nor of letting these helpless tiller folk come to depend upon you and then callously abandoning them, do you?"

I flushed. A small green spark popped from the tips of my fingers. When I lose my temper, I find it hard to control the power that surges through me; it manifests itself in green sparks. The phenomenon has exposed me for what I am more than once. "Make up your mind," I snapped. "A mongrel usurper could hardly be expected to feel any scruples, and it seems to me that anyone who accepts that sort of responsibility is truly a mantic whatever bloodlines she may carry."

He leaned back on his heels and crossed his arms. "Now you claim to be a true mantic. Yet if you were, you would have foreseen my visit."

I felt at a loss. How should I have foreseen his visit? He must have seen the puzzlement in my face, for he laughed scornfully. "I see you did not. Nor seemingly do you even know what a true mantic is." He smiled maliciously. "The meaning of the word *mantic* itself is *prophetess*. The administrative functions of the mantic all come from foreseeing the future. I see that you are causing your plowmen to plant the bottomland. Have you looked into the future to foretell the next flood? Do you know when the first frost will be? Have you divined the intentions of the savage hordes so that your margrave may prepare the defense of your castellum? Have you laid in your medicines against the next epidemic?"

I took a deep breath. I didn't believe that it was possible to foretell the future. Coming events were too fluid, changing as factors shifted. There were those in the Kingdom who claimed that ability, and credulous souls who paid them for their predictions. They were one and all charlatans, worse even than the multitude of priests and cult leaders that infested the cities, some of whom were at least sincere in their beliefs. "I am not a prophetess," I said coolly.

"No, nor are you a mantic," the margrave said. "You are to leave this castellum at once. Shut it up, put everything back the way it was, and go."

"If I were to do that, what would become of the people here, about whom you were so concerned?"

"They may apply for entrance at another castellum. If they are refused—and they will be, no better than scum, supporting a false mantic—they may do as they like."

"I must decline to obey your commands, Sir Margrave," I said. "I should think that your own mantic could have foretold that your visit here would be in vain."

"She did. She also foretold that you and your folk would come to an extremely unpleasant end as a result of your obstinacy."

A few more green sparks crackled. "Did she advise you to attempt to bring us to that end?" I asked, challenging him. I gathered a few scraps of energy, enough to sting if I cast it at him. In the dim light of the entrance hall, I began to glow, ever so slightly, with the energy I held.

He looked at the glow with fascination. "It will be unnecessary for me to bother myself," he said loftily. "A castellum can no more survive with a false mantic than a bird can without its wings. Nor can it survive for long without a margrave."

"Thank you for visiting, Sir Margrave," I said. "Do give your mantic my regards."

"Leave this castellum."

"Good day." I walked to the door and stood beside it.

The margrave made no move to leave. "I have heard that you have two horses. Is that true?"

"It is."

"It isn't proper for such as you to own a horse. They should be confiscated from you. But I'm willing to purchase one of them."

"They aren't for sale."

"I'll give you ten donkeys loaded with trade goods."

My eyebrow rose. That was a princely offer for an aged gelding or a mare of undistinguished breeding. But I needed both the horses and ten donkeys were no use to me. "Neither of my horses is for sale," I repeated.

"Very well," the margrave said impatiently. "I'll give you twelve donkeys and see to it that three are loaded with Bearsnake woolens."

"No. My horses are not for sale at any price."

The margrave made an impatient gesture. "You're a commoner. What do you want with horses? It's highly improper for you to ride one. The Bearsnake Mantic has no horse. I demand that you sell me one of your horses!"

"I need both horses and I care little for your ideas of propriety."

"You will care when the Silvercat appears to chase you out of this castellum." The Bearsnake Margrave was beginning to redden with anger and frustration.

"The creature seems to be too intent upon threatening to eat me to do much chasing."

"Do you claim to have seen the Silvercat? You're lying. It would never appear to a usurper."

"Nevertheless, it has appeared to me," I said. "Now, Sir Margrave, you must excuse me. I have things to do." I pushed the door open and stood waiting for him to leave.

He swept past me, pausing to sneer, "You needn't think that any man of breeding will consent to marry you. Even if you were the true Silvercat Mantic, none would want that badly to become the Silvercat Margrave."

"You relieve my mind wonderfully," I said coldly.

He stamped down the stairs to the coarse-headed horse Bion was holding for him. The animal was little better than a dull-eyed nag, teeth projecting nearly horizontally with age. The Bearsnake Margrave wouldn't be mounted for much longer, himself. I thought that I had better take measures for the security of my horses. They were evidently more valuable here for their social distinction than for mere transportation.

"Tildis," I said thoughtfully, "do any of your stories tell how to go about finding a margrave?"

"No, Lady Mantic. The Burdened Folk arranged such things among themselves. We tiller folk had nothing to do with it."

I sighed. "Then we'll have to get along without one. One of your men is going to have to learn to hunt. Send them to me and we'll see who can draw one of those bows."

"It isn't proper for one of us to handle weapons, Lady Mantic."

"Propriety is going to be the death of you all! Is it proper to starve to death?"

"It's more proper than for those who aren't suited to it to try to hunt, Lady Mantic," she said with the stolid obstinacy that I was coming to recognize. They were vastly conservative, these folk, and if something didn't suit their notions of propriety, they weren't going to do it, even if they or their children died because of their stubbornness.

"Very well," I acquiesced. "I don't suppose that any of you could have pulled one of the bows anyway. I'll ride to town tomorrow and see what can be done about hiring hunters."

* * *

Not much could be done about hiring hunters, I speedily discovered. The town was a dull and alien excrescence upon the landscape, grown up in the last century. There was a half-empty livestock market and a few shops, but not even a place to buy a bit of lunch. Most of the inhabitants were tiller folk, and not the better class of those. There were a few traders come to purchase linens and woolens. These were all packing up frantically and preparing to leave—the town was astir with the news that the savage hordes were moving in this direction early this year, driven by drought on their home ranges.

I was treated with deference to my face—being horseback was enough to ensure that—and sneered at when no one thought I was looking. I didn't mind that, but I objected to the stares I attracted. I had always been, from direst necessity, unobtrusive, my comings and goings unnoted, my presence unmemorable. Among these folk even my quiet ways and subdued movements and modes of dress were not enough for invisibility.

Nor did I get any response other than amazed stares when I inquired about people willing to hire out as hunters. All the needs of the people were met within their castella, and the few luxuries they acquired were bartered for their fabrics and surplus food. Gold money was scarce, nor was there much that could be purchased with it. I rode back to the castellum in a thoughtful frame of mind.

CHAPTER
4

THE Savage hordes were drawing nearer every day. I struggled with the multitude of practical problems presented by the reanimation of the dormant hulk of the castellum and worried about what we were going to do when the savages arrived. The tiller folk confidently left the problems to me.

Tildis, rummaging in one of the storerooms, came across a useful find: a chest made of aromatic wood which contained some of the ancient gowns we had found in the suites, both colorful linen summer gowns and soft, subtly dyed woolen ones for winter. These, however, were usable, as sound as the day they had come from the looms. They were clearly meant for the mantic and margrave, as they were sized for one of my inches.

They were beautifully embroidered and laid away wrapped in sheets between layers of a pungent herb, which no doubt accounted for their remarkable preservation. Some were men's robes, but there were two dozen gowns meant for a lady to wear, and I accepted them gratefully and wore them to supper in the evenings and on days when I didn't ride out. I felt completely regal dressed in the flowing, gauzy summer gowns, though I had to laugh at what a comical figure I would no doubt make to one used to whatever the contemporary fashion was. I enjoyed wearing the beautiful things.

There were many other useful and beautiful things in that storeroom. It was the closest thing to a treasure we found. And the contents were lot more useful to us than a cold pile

35

of gold and jewels would have been. Besides clothing, there
were finely crafted small utensils and tools, bronze fitments
embossed with the Silvercat symbol, and a collection of sur-
gical implements and other medical tools tenderly wrapped
in oiled linen and stowed in polished wooden cases. The
mantics had evidently been more physicians than mere herb
doctors.

The thought gave me pause. I had never really been a
healer, but had supported myself for many years as a wild-
crafter, gathering herbs and medicinal plants in the wilderness. I knew the uses of the herbs I collected. I didn't
hesitate to give out teas and poultices for mild ailments, but
I felt no competence to wield these scalpels, obstetrical for-
ceps, and strange implements whose function I couldn't
even imagine.

I was feeling not only trapped, but also overwhelmed,
when suddenly everything changed. I was in the mantic's
office struggling yet again with the printed books of the library. I thought I had found an herbal, a book of the botani-
cal remedies and preventives used by the mantics of
Silvercat, and was groping through a fog of strange terms,
when Bion came bursting in the door. The lad treated me
with just a little less deference than the rest of the tiller folk.
He, after all had been the first to recognize a mantic in the
dusty, faded stranger and felt that he had earned a few special privileges.

"Lady Mantic, there are bandits coming up from the
river," he blurted.

I shoved my chair hastily back and leaped to my feet.
"The same ones that killed your father?" I demanded.

He shook his head. "No, there were only four of them.
There are many of these and their leader rides a horse."

"Run and shut the gates," I said, and hastened up the
staircase that led to the ramparts. The wall around the castellum was four feet wide on top and battlemented on the
outside; from that vantage point I would be able to get a
good look at the approaching strangers.

They looked like no one I had seen in all this land. They
were bearded and long-haired, ragged and wild as wolves,
barbarically dressed in furs and wide saddle-leather belts

over coarse tunics and gaiters. There were at least a dozen of them, just starting up the zigzag road that led to the Silvercat gate.

I pelted down the stairs to the front courtyard, where the tiller folk were milling nervously about, like a flock of chickens that senses the hawk's nearness. Halfway down, I nearly came a cropper, tripping over the flowing skirts of the gown I was wearing. I cursed the chance that had led me to put it on instead of my accustomed shirt and trousers that morning. It seemed as if the castellum was going to have to be defended, and of all the inhabitants, I was the only one who would fight even to save a life. I caught myself on the bannister and hurried on down. "Tildis!" I called when I sighted the headwoman, "are these the savages everyone's been warning us about?"

She looked at me in wonderment. "No, Lady Mantic, the savages are immensely tall and thin. They wear no clothes nor use any other tools or weapons than stone knives and fire-hardened stabbing spears. I've never seen people like these."

There came a thunderous pounding on the gate. "Ho, there, within!" roared a stentorian voice. "Ho, the Silvercat! To the mantic I wish to speak!" The voice was melodically accented, with an odd vowel shift that I couldn't place.

I paused and gathered up a good charge of energy while the pounding intensified. The barbarian must be using something to hit the wood; no fist could produce such an uproar. When I was ready, I moved closer to the gate. "I speak for Silvercat," I shouted though the wood. "What's your business?"

The pounding immediately stopped. I expected threats and demands. Instead the voice said, more moderately, "I can't yell it through the gate, Lady Mantic. May I come in?"

Certainly, I thought. *I'll just open those gates and we'll all line up nicely here for you to cut our throats.* Out loud, I said, "You may not enter armed and with an armed band at your heels, stranger."

There was a bellow of a laugh. "Fair enough," the voice replied. "My men I'll send to the foot of the trail with my battle sword. May I keep my dirk?"

I was considerably startled by this ready acquiescence. I dashed up the stairs to the battlements again, arriving out of breath in time to watch the footmen wind their way back down to the river valley. Only the horseman remained before the gate. I suspiciously considered hidden weapons and sudden attacks; there were certainly enough hiding places about his disorderly garments. But he was facing a wielder of power, one who was forewarned and ready. I could blast him to rags before he could do much damage, if I were careful to keep out of his reach and to be alert for thrown knives and such.

I hastened down the stairs—this time I gathered up my trailing hem in one hand—and bade the tiller folk open the gate for the stranger and bar it again immediately after him. I took a position on the porch and nodded to Bion. The gates swung smoothly open and the barbarian rode through.

My first amazed impression was that both he and his horse were incredibly huge, but I blinked and realized that they were not so much huge as wide. The stallion was probably no more than fifteen hands tall, but he was enormously broad across the chest and haunches. His legs were as sturdy as tree trunks and his hooves flared out to platter-sized dimensions. From the knees down, he sported a luxuriant growth of hair that bounced as he pranced across the courtyard, and as he came near, I noted with amazement that his rusty black coat was curly. His luxuriant mane and tail fell in waves. I almost could have sworn that the eyes that peered through the bushy forelock glared with a red light.

I wrenched my astonished gaze from the horse to the man, and found him to be a fit rider for so uncouth a steed. He was as hugely broad across the shoulders as the horse, and fully as hairy. He was grizzle-bearded and long-haired, and two thin braids wrapped with grimy scarlet ribbons hung on each side of his face. His forearms were nearly covered with a wiry pelt of dark hair. A fur baldric hung across his chest, its hooks empty of sword and scabbard, but his dirk was tucked into the foot-wide belt that crossed his belly. I would have called it a short sword, as it was at least a foot and a half long. There was a dainty skean in the huge brooch that fastened the fur cloak around his neck. He had left his battle sword, perhaps, but he certainly hadn't disarmed himself.

"Greetings, Lady Mantic; respectful greetings, as they say here," he bellowed, as if I stood fifty yards away and he had to shout against the wind. The castellum shrank about him, as if he and his voice filled it to overflowing. I took an involuntary half-step back as the stallion pawed sparks from the paving stones.

"Greetings, stranger," I replied cautiously. "What business brings you to the Silvercat?"

"Taharka, I am." The windows rattled in their panes. "Son of a chieftain of three manors and twelve ships. Outlier, I am, and my followers with me. Unwedded, I am, even in my own land far to the north. Of years, thirty-eight I have. Killed my man, I have, and slain my bear, and wear warrior's and hunter's braids by right. Mighty fighter, I am. None in these plains can stand against the least of my followers, nor the mightiest of my followers against me. Rememberer, too, I am, bard and chronicler both."

I eyed him dubiously. Did he expect a similar boasting recital from me? Among barbarians from whom he was undoubtedly sprung, bargaining sessions often opened with just such bragging. But for what were we bargaining? He was sitting upon his restless horse, waiting. "All very commendable, I'm sure," I said. "What do you wish here, Sir Taharka?"

"Estates have I none, being outlier," he said, with the air of one explaining the obvious. "Warriors have you none, Lady Mantic, and yourself an outlier if I hear aright. The margraves talk of attacking your castellum, taking your horses, and driving you forth. Furthermore, no more than three days away, the cannibal savages are. A great warrior I am, and followed by twelve men fierce and wild. We've need of each other."

"I see. You wish to hire on here as warriors?" I regarded the barbarian without enthusiasm. It would be like loosing a lightning bolt to light candles, to let him and his men, undoubtedly as uncivilized as himself, within the castellum. All very well to have help against the savages, nor did I doubt his story about the margraves of the nearby castella.

But once the danger was past, how was I to get rid of the defense?

"No, no," he roared impatiently, shaking his scarlet-wrapped braids. The stallion reared a little, and he slapped it on the neck, raising a cloud of dust. "Better, Lady Mantic. Marry you and become your margrave, I will."

"Absolutely not," I snapped. Marry this barbarian oaf? Give him not only my castellum but myself? My skin crawled at the mere idea. A shower of green sparks crackled at my fingertips.

Tildis was pulling at my sleeve. "Lady Mantic, Lady Mantic!" she said urgently. "We must have a margrave! What about the hunting? What about the savages? Please, Lady Mantic!"

"No." There was a sudden flicker of movement at the corner of my eye, and the Silvercat appeared, sitting on the step, tail twitching. The stallion shield. Taharka fingered his dirk.

"Lady Mantic, you don't fancy me for husband, I see," bellowed the barbarian. "Stranger here, you are, is it not so?"

"Yes," I said, agreeing to both.

"Ever seen the cannibals?"

"No."

"Bring your horse. I'll show you. Then ask you again, I will. Or ask me, probably you will. Come."

"No, thank you."

"Do you fear me, Lady Mantic? For your safety, word is given. And if I wished to harm you, take your castellum, I could, for all its walls and your magic. Come."

I hesitated. I had no reason to fear the man, of course, being a wielder of power, but I had always avoided situations where I might have to use my skills to defend myself. There is a very fine line between legitimate use of the power in self-defense and the arrogant overuse of it. To seek situations where the power could be used was the first step into evil witchery, and I had always guarded against it. He had given his word not to attempt to harm me, and while I placed no reliance at all upon that, he needed me if he really wanted to become a margrave.

If he did, he had no idea at all of the responsibility he was undertaking. He probably thought that being a margrave was all fine clothes and food and parties every night.

On the other hand, it was an opportunity to scout out the savages. I had been worrying about them for days now. "Very well," I said coolly. "I take you at your word, Sir Taharka, but I warn you that I'm by no means defenseless, in case you're tempted to dispose of me and take over here. Bion, will you please fetch Whiskers?"

He smiled, strong white teeth gleaming wolfishly between the grizzled mustache and untrimmed beard. "Dispose of her whom I intend to be my loving wife? Foolish, that would be. Defenseless, you are not, I can see, nor coward either."

"Will you dismount and have something to drink while my horse is being fetched?" I asked, remembering the duties of hospitality.

He swung down from his stirrupless riding pad with an agility reminiscent of the Silvercat's grace. On foot, he was only two or three inches taller than I, but much bulkier. He strode up the steps with complete self-confidence. The Silvercat rose as he approached and went to meet him, moving like a flow of quicksilver. The barbarian's eyes bulged and he stopped. The Silvercat sniffed at his face, and Taharka moved not so much as an eyelash. The great feline smelled him up and down, prowling around him.

"You are my meat," announced the supernatural. It vanished. Good heavens, did that mean that the Silvercat accepted this ogre for the Silvercat Margrave?

"Unusual pets, you have," Taharka said, coming the rest of the way up the stairs. Near at hand, he had a sweaty, musky odor. Not a stink, exactly, but a definite smell.

"That's the Silvercat. It's no pet, but the tutelary spirit of this castellum." I didn't explain the significance of the creature's words.

Tildis was waiting in the entrance hall with a flagon of the thin beer the tiller folk drank. "Lady," she whispered while Taharka was draining the quart-and-a-half container with one draft, "please take him. We need him."

I gave her a quelling look. "Give him more beer while I change clothes. Sir Taharka, excuse me for a moment."

He emerged from his second tankard of beer and bowed with a certain quaint ceremony.

I was back dressed in shirt, trousers, and boots in ten minutes. "While we're gone, have some beer and food taken down to Taharka's men," I told Tildis. "Sir Taharka, how far are these savages?"

"Back by nightfall, we'll be," he said, burping noisily and holding out the tankard to Tildis. "Proper lifewater, I'll teach you to make, housekeeper. Though your beer is very good." He slapped her on the bottom as she passed and she simpered with pleasure. I clamped my lips shut and vowed that if he tried that with me he'd be hunting for his teeth.

There was a stallion's ringing challenge from the courtyard, and a crash of platelike hooves. I hurried out to find the squat black stallion glaring at Whiskers, ears flat and a mean sneer on his face. Whiskers was regarding him with mildly astonished interest (from a safe distance).

"Butterfly! Quiet yourself!" roared Taharka beside me, nearly deafening me. The horse snorted and swung to his master, ears up.

"Butterfly?" I blurted incredulously. "You call that Butterfly?"

The barbarian grinned. "Cute little foal, he was. Besides . . ." he brushed aside the matted forelock. On the black forehead was an irregular white blotch that might look something like a butterfly if you tilted your head and squinted.

Taharka gathered up the straps he used for reins and a handful of mane and vaulted onto the horse's back as easily as stepping over a log. I reminded myself not to underestimate his physical prowess. He might be built like a bull but he wasn't slow or clumsy.

I mounted up, with the stirrup, and turned Whiskers toward the gate, which Bion had opened. Butterfly laid his ears back, received a clout on the neck, and seemed to accept the necessity of traveling with a mere gelding with resignation.

I was not expecting Taharka's next move. Bellowing, he clapped his heels into the stallion's sides with an audible thump and charged out the gate at a gallop, sweeping

Whiskers along in his wake. Surely he didn't intend to ride headlong down that steep, winding path! But he did. And Whiskers, his blood up, followed. I gritted my teeth and *rode* as we plunged down the bluff. If that awkward great stallion could do it, Whiskers, mountain-bred, used all his life to precarious trails in rough country, could.

We dashed through the waiting group of Taharka's followers, scattering them as they shouted and laughed. One held up the battle sword he had left with them and he gathered it in without breaking stride. "Going to visit the cannibals!" he roared, and then they were behind us and our horses' hooves were on the road east that paralleled the river.

On flat ground, Whiskers pulled up level with the stallion easily. My valiant little horse wanted to make a race of it, in spite of his years. He loved to run, and the cold-blooded stallion was built for power, not speed or endurance. The barbarian hunched over his horse's withers, lashed by the long woolly mane, and urged him on, so I eased up a little on the bit, and Whiskers threw up his head, flagged his tail, and stretched out his stride. We could have left the stallion in our dust, but I checked Whiskers a little whenever he drew ahead, conserving his strength.

"Up there," shouted Taharka, pointing at one of the side roads up the bluffs. I touched Whiskers and he swerved obediently. I checked him to a walk as we climbed. Only a fool and a horse-killer runs a horse uphill for any but the most pressing of reasons. Whether Taharka would have run his stallion up the bluff, I didn't know, for I had let Whiskers pull a little ahead.

Once on the plains above, I checked Whiskers and let the barbarian come up beside us again. "Northeast," he shouted, and his horse sprang into a gallop again, Whiskers matching his speed. I noticed that the black was beginning to blow, red-lined nostrils flaring to scoop in the air, while Whiskers was hardly warmed up. The mountain horses weren't known for great speed, but there were no horses I had ever seen or heard of that could match their endurance, and I was confident that he could run this clumsy great brute into the ground. But I wasn't sure that Butterfly's rider knew it, or that Taharka had enough consideration for his mount not to ride him to death in a senseless effort to outdo us on our own ground.

Side by side we raced, over the trackless prairie, keeping an eagle eye forward for rabbit holes. The stallion was beginning to labor in his stride, and white foam was forming around his bit and flecking his chest. I began to consider requesting a slower pace for the sake of the barbarian's horse. No doubt he would count it a victory.

The earth dropped from under the racing hooves. We had topped a slight rise to find a gully cut through the prairie sod by a meandering stream. It was only a few feet deep, but at least twenty-five feet wide, and Taharka put his horse at it without hesitation. The immense haunches thrust mightily; the huge beast sailed into the air like a great ungainly bird. And then Whiskers and I were flying. There was nothing else for it; we were going too fast. If I had tried to stop, we would have skidded right into the gully and no doubt broken several legs and a couple of necks. But I had never jumped my horse before. I had no idea whether he even knew how. I could only loosen the reins and hope desperately.

My gallant Whiskers triumphed again. Far, far below there was a twinkle of water; the opposite brink flashed past; there was an earth-shaking thud as the black stallion landed, and then Whiskers alit on the sod in the stride of his full gallop.

"Whoa, Lady Mantic! Whoa, there, say I!" shouted Taharka, leaning back against the stallion's bit.

Whiskers fought the bit; his blood was up and he wanted to run, and I had to circle him a couple of times before he would consent to slow down. I brought him dancing and shaking his head back to where Taharka sat on his lathered stallion.

"Gallop he can, your pretty little pony, and jump like he had wings," said the barbarian admiringly. "Run all day, too, I think. He'd run my poor Butterfly to death."

It's hard to make an enemy of someone by admiring her horse. Gratified, I answered, "He's specially bred for stamina. I don't think he could begin to match Butterfly in strength, though."

He laughed, a full-throated bellow of joy. "It's strong he has to be, my Butterfly. It's no stripling he carries." He swung his horse up beside Whiskers and looked at me appraisingly. "A fine wife you'll make, my sweet, and what wild sons and daring daughters we'll breed! And what joy we'll have in the making of them!"

I could feel the hot blood rush into my face, and angry words of denial rose to my lips. "Meant no offense, I did," he said hastily. "Save your wrath for the savages. Come!"

We traveled on at an easy jog, and spoke no more, but I thought furiously. I had no wish to make this smelly barbarian my margrave, but I certainly did need one, and soon. And where else was I to look? The old nobility of the land wouldn't supply me with one, even if I offered to abdicate and allow him to install his own mantic. The tiller folk were clearly unsuited. If there were other, more civilized outlanders in the marches, I knew nothing of them. There seemed to be no one but Taharka. But marrying him was unthinkable! I wouldn't do it. The Silvercat demanded too much of me if it demanded that.

We jogged on for another hour, and then Taharka pointed. "There, signs of the savages are. Look."

There was a pillar of thick greasy smoke ahead. We topped another low rise and stopped the horses. Before us was a savage encampment. A thin wailing arose from it. There were hundreds of naked men and women, all incredibly tall and emaciated; their hands and feet were grotesquely long. Seven feet tall must have been the average, and few could have weighed as much as a hundred pounds. Some moved about with a loping motion and some lay sprawled somnolently on the ground, their bellies mounded until they looked like galls on a branch. Then I saw what they had been feasting on and I nearly vomited. That long thing that one was gnawing on was a skinned and roasted human forearm . . .

"Prisoners they've got down there, still alive," said Taharka suddenly, grimly. I followed his gaze and saw three little figures, naked and bloody, huddled together. The wailing rose from them. One of the savages wandered over to them and thrust a burning brand against a thigh. The wailing escalated to a scream of agony, and the savage laughed hideously.

I watched in despair. There was nothing we could do to help those unfortunates, but I was half minded to agree to Taharka's proposal of marriage, gallop back and fetch his warriors, and enact a bloody vengeance.

There was a sudden ringing sound as Taharka drew his huge battle sword from the scabbard hooked to his baldric. "Stay close to me, Lady Mantic, and mind the horses," he ordered. He swung the enormous thing over his head until it whistled and booted his horse down the slope, bellowing a thunderous warcry.

Whiskers, sensing another race, bounded after him while I sat astonished on his back. The barbarian was a maniac! He couldn't be thinking of charging the encampment! There were hundreds of savages. It was suicidal for two people . . . We plowed right through the thickest concentration of savages, and the huge sword sliced through arms and legs and even a torso as if hardly impeded. We reached the cowering prisoners and Taharka leaped off his mount without slowing him, still swinging the sword two handed, cutting through savages like a scythesman cutting grain. I urged Whiskers up to catch the black's dangling reins, hauling him back to his master's side. One of the savages rose out of the dust of the melee at my side and clutched at me; I spoke a word and he dropped away, shrieking with surprise at the charge that stung him. Another grabbed at the black's reins; the beast laid his ears back and bit, and I heard bones crack.

Taharka was laying valiantly about him with his awesome weapon, bawling like an enraged bear, but he was badly outnumbered. I dropped off Whiskers behind the shield he provided and ran to the prisoners. They were tiller folk, strangers, battered, naked, and bloody. They stared at me with blank terror as I urged them to the stallion's side and boosted them one at a time up on his back. For a mercy, he stood fairly still; Whiskers was almost unmanageable, sidling and rearing. He had never been in a battle before, nor had I, and neither of us liked it.

The tiller folk once mounted—it was a good thing the stallion had a long back—I looked about. The savages were swarming more thickly before Taharka, and he was being forced back step by step. He glanced quickly back at me.

Grabbing the stallion's mane with one hand, I closed my eyes and concentrated with all my might on drawing a shape from the overmind. I formed it into the most horribly frightening thing I could think of, an enormous writhing worm, blind, with a gaping ciliated mouth dripping venom, large enough to sweep in half a dozen savages at one gulp. I gave it an eerie, keening voice and a poisonously slimy skin. I made it rear up out of the ground in the space Taharka's sword had created in front of him, groping hungrily for the savages.

I opened my eyes as the startled savages screamed in horror and recoiled. Taharka gasped and raised his sword. "No," I shouted "Leave it and come on!"

He bellowed one last defiant warcry and turned away. Sheathing his sword, he grabbed the cheekpieces of Whiskers's bridle and held him still by main strength while I scrambled on. I gathered both sets of reins in one hand and extended the other to him. He took my arm above the elbow and I grasped his as he swung onto Whiskers's croup. "Carry both of us, can he?" he shouted into my ear.

"Long enough," I yelled back. "Hang on." I turned Whiskers back toward the river and clapped heels to his sides, and he broke into a wallowing gallop, encumbered as he was with a third of his own weight. Butterfly followed, hampered by the frantically clutching tiller folk on his back.

We burst through the savages who had closed in on our escape route by sheer momentum. I discovered that they could run as fast as a horse; they easily outdistanced our overburdened mounts. Then we topped the rise and were clear, and the last of them fell away. I couldn't see what became of my monster worm, but from the ululating shrieks that rose behind us, it must still have been frightening savages. It had no power to actually harm them, unfortunately, and they would soon discover that.

We galloped on until I was fairly certain that we were out of danger. Then I checked Whiskers. "Where is your castellum?" I asked the tiller folk who were clinging to various parts of Butterfly and his harness. They stared at me wide-eyed. "Where would you like to go?" I asked.

"Too deep in shock to know, they are," said Taharka. "It would be best to take them to Silvercat and treat their injuries."

"What about you?" I asked. "Are you hurt?"

"Nicked a little here and there, I am. Nothing to interfere with the wedding."

I became suddenly aware that he was sitting on Whiskers's croup, separated from me only by the cantle of my saddle. Indeed, I could feel the puff of his breath when he spoke. I also realized that I had spent the energy I had built up to protect myself if he meant to practice some treachery on me. "What is it?" he said, quietly for him. "Is it hurt you are? Why did you jump?"

"No," I said nervously. "I'm fine. Just scared to death. I'm not used to charging into the midst of hundreds of enemies."

He laughed delightedly. "Very well you did. You'll soon be as fierce a warrior-woman as Grith out of the old tales."

CHAPTER
5

I Nudged Whiskers with my heels and he started back to the castellum. I held him to a walk. The old fellow had had a hard day. I suddenly realized that I was trembling myself. Worse yet, Taharka, riding double with me, was so close he couldn't help but notice. He'd put it down to fear and reaction, I thought. In fact, it was anxiety. There was no doubt about the barbarian's courage, or his warlike skills. I had to give him reluctant credit for compassion, too, for he had charged into deadly danger to help three complete strangers. And he was needed at the castellum.

But how could I marry him? He was rough and noisy and violent and he smelled! I shuddered when I thought of the wedding, and of the wedding night to follow. He had made it clear that he would expect to be husband to me in every way, and the very thought of permitting him to touch my body brought on quaking nausea. There was no gentleness in him, and I was terrified of him. He frightened me far worse as a prospective husband than he would have as an enemy.

There was a problem. I had been an outlaw, hunted and on the run since before puberty. There had never been time or opportunity to get to know a man, to come to trust one. Then there had been Laddie, the slave I had bought to save his life. But my scruples had prevented me from forcing (or permitting) him to become my lover. I had been on the verge of succumbing to my baser self when at last my pursuers had caught up with me. I had gone to prison, saved from hanging by Laddie's eloquent plea in my behalf, for five years, then pardoned and immediately exiled. Since then I had drifted rootlessly, completely alone most of the time. In short, I was entirely inexperienced in the ways of love. Taharka would have no way of knowing that, nor likely would believe me—or care—even if I could bring myself to confess it.

I had no very clear idea of what the wedding night would be like if I married him, but I was absolutely certain that it would be terrifying and painful and humiliating.

On the other hand, I would probably survive it. Women had, from time immemorial. If I closed my eyes and gritted my teeth, I could endure it. After five years in that soul-destroying prison, I could endure anything if I really had to.

But why should I have to? It wasn't fair. I didn't need Taharka. I had a right to a life of my own, a life unbrutalized by exuberant barbarians. Had I survived so much for this? Surely I deserved something better.

I was seething with rebellion when we rode up to Taharka's men at the foot of the trail. He slid off Whiskers's rump and shouted, "Come up to the castellum. A home we've found!" There was an exultant cheer that echoed off the bluffs across the river and made Whiskers, tired as he was, shy a little. The band of warriors gathered around, talking and laughing far too loudly, hugging Taharka and each other, joking and exclaiming.

One of the barbarians seized my hand and kissed it. He was younger than Taharka. "Thank you, Lady Mantic!" he roared at me. "For a very long time have we searched for a home. Defend you bravely, we will." I pulled unavailingly on my hand.

"Bedata, let go of the Lady Mantic," bellowed Taharka good-humoredly. "She needs to take these tiller folk up to the castellum and treat their injuries. Come on, bring our things!"

I rode up to the castellum escorted by a yelling crowd of barbarians, all talking at once, while Taharka led Butterfly with his load of frightened, shivering victims.

Tildis met us at the door, and Bion to take Whiskers, with another of the men to take Butterfly. "Cool them out well," I instructed wearily. "They've worked hard today. Tildis, these tiller folk need treatment; put them in the surgery and

I'll come to them. See if you can get them to tell you where
they belong."

"Yes, Lady Mantic," she said happily. "The warriors'
quarters are ready for the new margrave's men. I've sent for
the observers of rites from the village to witness the wedding. The margrave's apartment is being turned out right
now." She darted away to conduct the shouting, laughing
barbarians to the quarters she had prepared for them. I stood
staring after her, choking on angry reproaches.

One of the other women came to inform me that the injured tiller folk were in the surgery off the entrance hall and
that hot water was being brought to wash their wounds and
brew tea, and for the next few minutes I was busy. None of
the victims, two men and a girl of fifteen or so, was much
hurt. They were cut and bruised and burned, but nothing that
wouldn't heal if cared for. They were frightened into inco-
herence, though. I gave them each a calmative cup of sage
tea and coaxed them into telling me that they were not indwellers in any castellum, but smallholders, father, brother,
and sister. The mother had been eaten.

Doron, the father, begged to be allowed entrance at Silvercat, and they all seemed relieved when I sighed and accepted. I had one of the kitchen women settle them in an
apartment; Tildis was still running about making the barbarians comfortable.

The whole castellum seemed full of barbarians. They
were few in number, but they laughed and shouted and
strode about exploring delightedly until the walls reechoed
with their presence and one never seemed to be out of hearing of them. It was a change. The tiller folk were quiet and
soft-voiced; I had long and assiduously studied silence and
unobtrusiveness, until I had become nearly invisible even to
myself. The uproar made me feel ready to jump out of my
skin, like a wild colt newly brought in from pasture.

I went in search of Taharka, who had mentioned that he
had been a little injured. (It was miracle, I thought, that
either one of us was still alive!) I found him in the margrave's armory, examining the weapons. I should have
looked there first. "Sir Taharka," I said.

He looked inquiringly at me and laid the javelin he held

back in its rack. Then he came toward me so suddenly that I shrank back into the margrave's office. Seeing me recoil, he stopped. "Yes, Lady Mantic?" he asked.

I flinched at the loudness of his voice. "You said that you were hurt. I came to see if you wished me to treat your wounds. I'm an herb doctor."

"Not much hurt, I am, but easing of the pains and a little stitching would be welcome."

"Then if you would come to the surgery downstairs?"

He gave that quaintly courteous bow again and followed me. "What means 'sir'?" he asked as we went down the stairs.

"Eh? Oh, 'sir'. It's a title of respect among the ox-nomads to the west. Anyone who fails to name a nomad 'sir' had better be ready for a fight. I picked up the habit when I was passing through their land."

"You're not of the ox-nomads yourself, then?"

"No. My homeland lies even farther to the west, on the shores of western ocean. Will you sit here and show me where you're hurt?"

"Take off my tunic, I must."

"Then please do."

Undressing was an extensive task, given the layers he wore. First the wide belt had to be unbuckled, and it was fastened with half a dozen little buckles, the thick leather so stiff that it was no easy job to tease the ends out of their keepers and the tongues out of their holes. Then the shaggy furs had to be unwound. Beneath the furs was a coarse woolen tunic, none too clean, which laced at the throat. When that was finally removed, he wore only gaiters up to his thighs and a sort of breechclout between his legs and lapped over a rope belt.

His "few little nicks" were cuts and gashes that would have put a civilized man to bed for a week. There was one under his shoulder blade that was at least eight inches long, and another on his left upper arm so deep I could see the white membrane that surrounds the bone at the bottom of it. There were half a dozen others. "Why didn't you tell me you were hurt this badly?" I scolded. "These should have been treated first."

He grinned. "Wanted to impress you with my courage, I did. A woman doesn't want a man that complains about every little sore. Bleeding badly, they were not."

I set to work, and for a time concentrated wholly upon washing and cleaning and stitching and salving and bandaging. Actually, the wounds bled very little, nor did Taharka flinch and complain, although the stitching process was a lot more painful than the original injuries. He bit his lip once or twice.

Finally I reached for a clean cloth to swab away the last smears of blood. "I don't suppose," I said acidly, "that if I made you a cup of poplar bark tea to help with the pain and fever, you'd drink it."

"You'd suppose wrong. Very good about following doctor's orders, I am."

"Oh," I said, disconcerted. I'd rather expected him to refuse the medicine indignantly. Then I fixed him with a steely eye. "If you're not going to get an infection in these, cleanliness is very important. I want you to take a bath with plenty of hot water and soap, only don't get your bandages wet. Then put on clean clothes and I'll have your tea ready for you in my office. It has to be simmered for half an hour; you should just about have time."

"Yes, Lady Mantic," he said meekly. "I'll bathe; beginning to smell a little anyway, I am. Only I have no clean clothes."

"I'll send Tildis to the warriors' quarters with something for you to wear."

"Bathe in the margrave's quarters, I will. They aren't so far away." He stood up and I realized how very powerful he was. As long as I had been stitching, he had been just another patient. Confined in the surgery with him, I saw him to be as muscular as a great draft horse, and as solid. His bulk was not fat. I backed away nervously before I could stop myself. He paused in the act of pulling his tunic over his head. "Frightened of me you need not be," he said.

"I'm not frightened of you," I said with dignity. "You couldn't hurt me if you wanted to. I just like to have a little space around me."

He gave me a shrewd look. "A powerful mantic you are,

Lady. I've never heard of a mantic who could summon up such monsters as that worm. But between husband and wife there should not be space or need for it."

"We aren't husband and wife."

"Getting used to the idea, you should be." He gathered up his furs and belt and opened the door.

I simmered the poplar decoction over an oil lamp, and when the door in the side of the office that led to the living quarters opened, I turned to give Taharka a cup of the strained liquid. Before me stood an imposing figure, somehow even more exotically barbaric in the flowing robes of a margrave. Clean, still damp and sleek, there was some order to his grizzled dark hair and beard. He had chosen a somberly magnificent robe of dark purple, surely the most elaborately embroidered of those we had found in the storeroom. Tildis or someone had found for him gold ribbons to match the embroidery on the yoke and sleeves of the robe, and he had rebraided and wrapped his warrior's lock and hunter's lock with those. As before, the spacious room shrank around him.

He stepped forward to take the cup from my hand and a drift of a clean herbal scent wafted toward me. "Different I look, don't I? Smell better, too, I do," he said with his booming laugh. "Fit to be a bridegroom!"

I felt as if I shriveled to insignificance in his presence. I was still dressed in dusty and disheveled shirt and trousers, decorated with a few splashes of blood and drops of medicine. It occurred to me that I probably smelled a bit, myself.

Taharka held out his hand to me. "I know you'll want to bathe and change for the wedding yourself, and I told Tildis have hot water fetched to your bathroom, but come and sit with me until the water comes. Talked a lot this day, I have, and said nothing at all have you."

I eluded his outstretched hand and he dropped it, but I followed him into the sitting room. He sank down upon the wide padded bench and leaned against a pile of cushions. "Less than pleased with me for a husband, you are," he said.

"Less than pleased with marrying anyone," I countered. I sat gingerly upon one of the chairs.

"But no choice have you, Lady Mantic."

I looked at him sharply. He was watching me from under his bushy brows. His tone was not threatening; he spoke as if pointing out a fact I had overlooked.

"Oh, I shall not force you," he said. "But a margrave you must have, true?"

My glance fell. "True," I admitted.

"The cannibals are coming and you need help to withstand them, true?"

"Yes," I mumbled.

"The noble folk of the other castella will not help you, true?"

"True."

"The tiller folk of this castellum, who trust you to see to their safety, want you to accept me, true?"

I nodded.

"The Silvercat has accepted me as margrave, true?"

I looked quickly up at him. "How did you know that?"

"Tildis told me. True, is it?"

"Yes, it's true."

"Then no choice have you but to take me to husband, true?"

"You have no idea what the responsibilities of a margrave are. If you did, you wouldn't want to be one."

"Son of a chieftain am I, and leader of warriors. I know about responsibilities. My men need a home. A time to stop wandering comes. A place where one is needed and wanted has to be found. A warrior pays in blood, a margrave pays in care." He paused, but I could find nothing to say. "Answer, Lady Mantic. No choice have you, true?"

"I—I guess not," I said unwillingly. I knew I would just have to make up my mind to endure his husbandly caresses and hope he wouldn't hurt me too badly. There would be no choice about that, either. Perhaps his wounds would bother him and he wouldn't feel well enough to enforce what he would no doubt consider his rights. But one quick glance at him, alert and vigorous, dispelled that hope.

There was a scratching upon the door. "Come!" roared Taharka, as if he had already taken possession of the castellum.

"Lord Margrave, the Observers of Rites are here to witness the wedding. They await you downstairs. Lady Mantic, your bath water is ready and I've laid out your best gown for you. The wedding feast is cooking."

"Well done, Tildis," boomed Taharka. "Don't be too long about your primping, Lady Mantic. An impatient bridegroom, I am."

I made for the door, to be stopped by an urgent shout. "Lady Mantic!" I whirled, to find Taharka bearing down upon me. "Leave us a moment, Tildis!" he barked. I sidled toward the door, my heart pounding. "Lady Mantic, I don't know the custom of your people, but among my folk, a husband has the right to know his wife's personal name. I don't want to offend against the customs of the witch folk, but like to know yours, I would."

I blinked at him. I hadn't realized that he didn't know my name. I seldom mentioned it out of the old habits of secretiveness, not because of any magical significance to anonymity. "Oh, of course," I said. "My name is Runa."

He gave me a courtly bow. "Runa," he repeated, giving the vowels that slightly different glide. I slipped out the door and hastened to my bathroom.

I felt better for having bathed. I soaked lavender and camomile in the buckets of hot water, and the fragrant steam soothed and calmed me. I was determined to go through with the wedding with as good a grace as I could. If it proved unendurable, well, I had two good horses and a world to explore. Once he was established here, I could see no reason why Taharka should care whether I stayed or left.

The gown Tildis had laid out for me was one I had never worn before, a light rose-colored gauze embroidered in patterns of ripe ears of grain. I had only boots, which seemed incongruous, or the woolly knitted slippers I wore indoors, so I went barefoot. I fluffed out my short hair, curly in this damp climate, and glanced at myself in the mirror. I was dressed festively enough to be a bride, anyway, even if the sober expression and anxious eyes suggested a funeral more than a wedding. At least my usually colorless cheeks were a little pink.

I paused at the private door behind the head table of the dining hall, from which an impressive amount of noise was

emanating. The entire populace of the castellum was gathered there — not so many, considering the size of the vast
room, but Taharka and his twelve barbarians went a long
way toward filling it up. The tiller folk were all dressed in
their best and brightest garb, and the barbarians had evidently all bathed. They were milling around the room,
shouting and laughing, and Tildis was guarding an impressive array of drinkables, some of which I had never seen
before.

The noise and chaotic movement were overwhelming, and
I shrank back into the shadows. Should I saddle up and ride
out at once? I would rather have fought the Silvercat than
walked into that room. It was already too late; a sharp-eyed
barbarian spied me and bellowed out the news that I had
arrived, and I was surrounded, buffeted, and herded forward
on the dais until I stood beside Taharka. He grabbed my
hand roughly, holding me in a grip that threatened the little
bones of my fingers.

"What ceremonies are current here?" he bellowed.
"Shall we be married by the rites of this place, or the rites of
my folk, or the rites of the Lady Mantic's homeland?"

"Or all three?" shouted one of the barbarians. "Be sure
that the ceremonies are binding on all parties, you should."

There was a storm of other suggestions, some of them
offensively lewd, as to how the rites could be made permanent. I would have stepped back but Taharka checked the
movement. "Quiet, you bastards," he bellowed, in so vast a
roar that dust drifted down from the arched ceiling. "This is
my wedding and I'll smash the next man who disturbs it!"
Then he turned to me. "What rites do you wish? Your wedding too, it is," he added, generously.

"I don't care," I said desperately. "Just get it over with!"
A spark popped at the fingertips of my free hand, and I
noted with distracted wonder that it was a sullen purple
rather than the usual angry green.

Taharka turned to one of the three strangers, the Observers of Rites who had come to witness the ceremony, who
stood in a prim row near the wall. "What rites do you call
binding here?" he said.

One of them sniffed. "A simple declaration of assent by

each party will be enough," he said. "If the Silvercat recognizes your claims."

"Declare our assent, we can do," Taharka said. "But as a ceremony, it seems unmemorable. In my land we are wed by bread and blood. Will you object to that, Lady Mantic?"

"No," I said. "Get on with it."

"From the kitchen bring an uncut loaf of bread and a sharp knife," Taharka shouted to Tildis. When the items were brought, he turned to the witnesses again. "I, Taharka, outlier, declare and affirm my willingness to wed with Runa, Lady Mantic of the Silvercat," he said clearly.

He and they turned to look at me. I cleared my throat nervously. There had been no hesitation in his affirmation. Mine would have to be as clear, if not as loud. "I, Runa, declare and affirm my willingness to wed with Taharka — " and something prompted me to add—"Lord Margrave of the Silvercat."

 Instantly there was a feline scream that set the hairs along my arms prickling, and the Silvercat appeared at the far end of the hall. Lashing its tail, it prowled the length of the room, ears flat, eyes blazing white-hot, as tillers and barbarians alike fell back before it. Up the step of the dais it flowed, and sniffed at my feet, and Taharka's, and our linked hands. Then it sat up. "Mantic and Margrave," it said, in tones that filled the hall, "you are my meat." Then it winked out and was gone, and the held breaths of the whole hall full of people sighed out.

Releasing my bloodless hand, Taharka turned to the table where the items he had requested had been put. Taking the bread, he broke it in half and put one piece down. Then he picked up the knife and made a little cut at the base of his left thumb. Holding the cut over the broken surface of the loaf, he let a few red drops of blood sprinkle the white surface. "Runa, wife," he said, "I offer you my oath, to love you and trust you and to be faithful to you alone all my days. By this bread I convey to you myself and all my goods. By this blood I accept from you all your enemies to be my enemies and your cares to be mine." He handed me the gory thing.

"Say, 'I accept your oath, Taharka,'" said a quiet voice in

my ear. It was one of the barbarians. I obediently repeated the words. "Now eat the part with the blood on it." I nearly gagged. "Eat it!" the voice insisted. I closed my eyes and choked the nauseous mess down.

When I opened them, Taharka was offering me the other half of the loaf and the knife. I nicked the base of my left thumb and dribbled blood on the bread. "Taharka, husband," I followed my coach, "I offer you my oath, to love you and trust you and be faithful to you alone all my days. By this bread I convey to you myself and all my goods. By this blood I accept from you all your enemies to be my enemies and all your cares to be mine." I gave him the bloody bread.

"I accept your oath, Runa," he said gladly, and he ate the unsavory bread with every evidence of enjoyment, making sure that he got every speck of blood. I shuddered. He was not so very different from the cannibals we had seen. I felt very close to unseemly tears and a shower of purple sparks crackled around me.

Then I was swept up in a body-crushing hug, a smacking kiss was planted roughly on my lips, and the whole hall erupted into celebration.

CHAPTER
6

ONCE The wedding ceremony was over, the barbarians descended upon the liquor with howls of delight, and the kitchen workers began to bring in mounds of food. Each of Taharka's barbarians insisted upon kissing me and telling me his name.

When all his men were done with me, Taharka swept me into the crook of his arm and dragged me about with him wherever he went, as if I had been a rag doll. First he circled the hall and spoke to all the tiller folk, and they looked at him with the shining eyes of adoration. I strained against his grip from time to time, trying to free myself, but he apparently didn't even notice. Then he took me up to the head table, threw himself into the creaking margrave's chair, and pulled me onto his lap.

Tildis, who was utterly enchanted with the new margrave, rushed up with plates and plates of food and a beaker of some clear fluid. "Not too much lifewater, Tildis," he roared for the whole room to hear. "Clear-headed for tonight I must be, or risk disappointing my wife!" Then he kissed me noisily and off-center, and reached across me for a chicken while the crowd rolled with laughter. I saw nothing funny in it whatsoever.

When I struggled to rise, he pulled me abruptly back so that I was half lying across him, my head resting on his massive biceps. Flourishing the chicken, he buried his face in the curve of my neck. "What's the matter?" he whispered in my ear. "Patient you must be. The people must have their show. Then alone we can be."

"Let me up, damn you," I hissed furiously. "How dare you maul me about like this?"

He raised his head and gave me a puzzled look. "Newly husband and wife, we are," he explained. "The people expect us to show a little affection." He kissed me full and lingeringly on the lips, chicken grease and all. I heard the chicken go crashing among the plates. With his hairy, greasy lips pressed against mine, his newly freed hand began to explore my knee and thigh. A gleeful roar went up from the assembled company, along with shouted advice. "Put your arms around my neck," he said against my lips.

"Let me up!" I tried to snarl.

"Put your arms around my neck, or reach higher, I will," he growled. He pulled up the hem of my gown and clamped a bruising grip above my knee. I gulped and put my arms around his neck, suppressing with an effort of will the purple sparks that would have stung him. He let go of my knee and enfolded me in an embrace, forcing my head back and bruising the inside of my lips against my teeth as he pulled me more tightly against him.

At last, just when I thought I would die of suffocation and humiliation, he relaxed his hold and raised his head, accepting the shouting, whistling plaudits of his men as a victor at some athletic game might accept the applause of the crowd.

Swinging me upright on his lap, he handed me the beaker of lifewater. "Make you feel better, it will," he said, and I took a sip of the poisonous stuff and shuddered, giving the beaker back to him. "Well it would be if you'd drink some," he said warningly.

Then the men began to shout at him, "Sing for us, Taharka! Sing a love song for your wife!" each adding his clamor to the general uproar, and even the tiller folk piping up curiously.

Taharka rose to his feet, lifting me easily into the mantic's chair as he did so. "It isn't seemly for a man to sing at his own wedding," he said, raising his hands to quell the disappointed grumbling. "But tonight I can refuse my wife nothing, and if she asks me, sing I will." He turned and looked at me expectantly, and every eye in the room was turned on me, as I sat rumpled and smoldering in a corner of my chair, rubbling my swelling, stinging lips.

Under the force of all those eager stares, I could not order him to choke rather than sing, as I would have liked to. I had agreed to marry him and if he was to be an effective margrave he must seem to have the support of his mantic. I raised my eyes to his and forced my bruised lips to smile. "Please sing for me, husband," I said clearly and as sweetly as I could.

There was a delighted roar from the onlookers. Taharka grinned and held out his hand to me, and I came forward and took it.

The barbarian took a deep breath and threw back his shoulders; he *sang*. Clear and pure and true as star music on a winter night, he sang a ballad of love and longing, and from the barrel chest issued a volume of music that would have put an orchestra to shame. But loud as it was, unaccompanied by so much as a tapping foot, he never faltered on a note or missed a beat.

He looked only at me as he sang, and neither I nor anyone there could doubt that the tender words were directed at me. I found I was standing wide-eyed, staring at him with my lips parted in amazement. Realizing it, I blushed, and he squeezed the hand he still held.

I couldn't look away. He held me pinioned with his gaze. When the song was finished, and it was a long one, he pulled me into his arms and held me close, and I could feel him panting with the effort he had expended. He smelled of musky masculine sweat again, and he was hot and damp, like a horse just in from a hard run.

Then the momentarily peaceful spell was broken, and he swung me around him and back to the chairs at the head table, where he was soon roaring over the obscene advice his followers were offering and trying to feed me eggs with his fingers, bellowing that they would improve my fertility. He sipped a little at the lifewater, but my hopes for that were dashed when I saw that he never drank deeply.

As the evening wore interminably on, I could feel the sullen purple energy building up within me, and I struggled desperately to keep it from leaking out in visible showers of sparks. I had never had to deal with this sort of energy before, this turgid bitter-feeling purple power that threatened to overwhelm me with a destructive panic. When I lost my temper, or succumbed to strong emotion, the manifestation had always been green energy, and though I had to concentrate to control it, I usually could. But this energy just went on building up, with a metallic taste in my mouth and a dull buzzing behind my eyes. I began to fear that I really would lose control of it and blast the hall and its rioting occupants to splinters and rags.

I ate nothing. I couldn't unclench my teeth, and if I had, I couldn't have swallowed. I longed unavailingly for peace and privacy to calm myself and think things over, but Taharka never moved farther than arm's reach from me.

Periodically, Taharka squeezed me or kissed me messily or fondled my knee, and I concentrated upon controlling the building power and, with what slivers of attention I could spare, on forcing myself not to recoil from his rude caresses. My head rang with the noise he created, and I had long since ceased to listen to his words when finally—midnight, it must have been—he rose to his feet, dragging my stiff body with him. Bellowing, "We'll retire now, my wife and I. Tired, we are, and need our rest," he winked broadly at the hooting men. I shuddered with loathing.

But worse was yet to come. Before I could dodge, he picked me up in his arms. "Don't rouse us early in the morning. Late we'll be sleeping tomorrow," he continued, and he carried me through the hall, into the entrance foyer, up the grand staircase, and through the Silvercat door. The laughing, whooping barbarians poured after us, followed by the tiller folk, and Taharka put me down and leaned his shoulders against the door to bar their entrance. They made no serious effort to follow; after a few thumps and more advice shouted through the panel, they clattered noisily down the stairs.

I half expected him to collapse in a swoon, the last effort having proven too much for one who had sustained wounds, ridden miles, laughed and shouted and sung, all on his wedding day. Once again I underestimated his fortitude—or possibly his lust. When he was sure they were gone, he picked me up again and thrust through the door into his bedchamber, where he dropped me roughly onto the bed and turned away to pull the margrave's robe over his head.

I scrambled to my feet and backed away from the bed, feeling hysteria rising with the energy inside me. "What are you doing?" he roared in amazement when he emerged from the robe, naked but for a breechclout. "Take off your gown and lie down. Such a night of pleasure as you've never thought of, you're going to have."

"Get away from me," I said as he advanced across the room, massive and hairy.

"Your husband I am," he bellowed, and lunged at me.

The energy that had been building up in me exploded into fury and fear. I raised my hands and spoke one word of focusing and one of sending. A coruscating globe of lavender-purple light sailed across the room, propelled by all my terror and anger at his rough treatment. It struck him full in the chest and exploded, flinging him back half the width of the chamber to crash shoulders first into the wall. The partition shook under the impact and brought down the shield that hung there, clattering and bouncing. Taharka slid down the wall, leaving a smear of blood on the paneling.

I thought for a moment I had killed him. In the moment I flung the energy weapon, I had certainly meant to. But when I bent over him, he was breathing raggedly, the wind knocked out of him. His eyes were wide and amazed.

"Your stitches have torn out," I informed him, and turned to leave.

"Wait . . ." he gasped, and levered himself up on an elbow. "Your husband am I. A right to you I have."

"You have no rights over me that I don't give you. Never forget it."

"Agreed to marry me, you did." Incredibly, he was staggering to his feet. The man was like a reptile; no matter how battered he was, he kept moving. "My wife you are. This is our wedding night. We must lie together. A marriage unconsummated is no marriage."

"You wanted to be the Silvercat Margrave, didn't you? Well, you are. Be content."

"No!" he bellowed as his lungs fully inflated. "A wife I

wanted. A home I wanted." Leaning one hand on the wall he took a shambling step toward me. "I want you! Tonight! Come to me, Runa. Be my wife."

I wrenched the door open and stumbled through it, slamming it behind me, fleeing into my own unlighted room. I crouched in the darkness, listening, and at last heard a groan and the creak of the bed. What if he was bleeding to death? The torn-open wounds should be tended. But what if he wasn't and I went back in there? He would think that I had come to—to.... Trembling, I knelt on the cold floor, wracked with shame and indecision.

What had I done? I had made up my mind to be his wife and to endure his touch. But I had panicked like a green girl, I who was thirty-two years old and probably the widest-traveled human being on the whole continent. I should have kept my bargain and held to the oath I had sworn. It would have been all over with by now, and the future of the Silver-cat Castellum made as secure as I could make it. What was I to do? I was in the wrong here. If only he hadn't shouted so, and charged at me. If only he had been content to be a little patient and gentle—it was all his fault. But I had known what kind of a man he was when I had accepted his offer.

Gulping, I realized that I had done something tonight I had promised myself never to do—I had lost control of myself. In anger and terror I had done a wrongful thing: used the power as the tool of my own passions without thought for the harm that might be caused to others. I had not behaved so dishonorably even with the fear of an agonized and shameful death upon me.

There was another moan from the adjoining room, and I rose shakily to my feet. There was nothing for it but to try to undo the harm I had caused. Taharka might well be bleeding to death in the next room, and if I refused to go to his aid for fear of facing the consequence of my own decision, I would have murdered him. As far as I knew, he had meant to carry out his part of the bargain. It was I who had broken faith.

I pushed the door cautiously open and peered into the room, where the oil light was still burning. Taharka was sprawled face down across the bed. It was the shallow cut under his shoulder blade that had broken open, for the bandage over it was stained. The cut on his shoulder seemed all right. I edged nearer.

He wasn't bleeding to death, at least, but the cut needed attention. As I started to take another step nearer the bed, he rose up suddenly, his hair and beard all wild, and I started back, quivering. "Hurt you I will not," he said bitterly.

"I came to see if you were all right," I said. "Your wound has opened up. I'll tend it for you if you'll let me."

He looked at me for a long while without answering. I thought he might refuse my aid, but at least he said, "Thank you, Lady Mantic."

I approached the bed slowly, wary of a sudden grab, but the spirit seemed to have gone out of him. I laid my hand on his forehead; it was cold and clammy.

"I'll make you another dose of poplar bark," I decided. "Lie down and let me look at that cut."

Obediently, he lay down again and I examined the damage. Sure enough, three of my neat stitches had torn right out. He was silent until I had given him his bitter draft and resewn the cut. Then, as I was gathering up my things to leave, he spoke—a whisper compared to his usual bellow.

"Lady Mantic, if you sleep in your own bed, the folk will know that the marriage was not consummated."

I looked blankly at him. "Why should they care?"

"The customs of these folk I know little of, but among my own people, a marriage unfulfilled is no marriage."

I still failed to understand. Surely he wasn't still trying to get me into his bed; he was pale and weak and in no condition to do anything about it even if I had crawled in beside him.

"The other nobles, the Burdened Ones, may accept you as Silvercat Mantic and me as Silvercat Margrave now. But married to each other the mantic and margrave must be. The custom that is. Spies the margraves have among our tiller folk; if there is any doubt about the truth of the marriage, by noon tomorrow they will know."

I realized with astonishment that he was right. The marriage of a mantic and margrave was not entirely—not even mainly—a contract between a man and a woman, but a political event of overwhelming importance. All must appear to be well between us. I slowly put the medical bag down. "I hadn't thought," I said.

"Nor had you thought, not knowing the customs of my folk, that no man who could not satisfy his wife could long retain leadership among such men as my followers. By our customs, a man unwed is only half a man, but a wedded man whose wife fears and hates him is less than the plow-ox in the field. Fight, sing, drink, and love better than any other of the troop, must a leader of outliers."

I looked at him, and saw him shamed and diminished by my violent rejection of him. "What can I do?" I mourned. "It's too late."

He raised himself on his elbow again with a grimace of pain. "Desire me as a man you do not," he said wryly. "But an appearance, we can show them. Sleep here, with me, tonight. Touch you I will not." He laughed a little. "Easy it will not be, for I do desire you as a woman. But rest here in this bed. Tomorrow try you must to show affection for me. From my touch you must not shrink away, nor show that I am abhorrent to you."

"I'll try to do as you say. I . . . I'm sorry . . ." but I could not explain to him for what I was sorry or why he frightened and upset me.

He eased himself back down upon his pillows. "Plain it is that our customs are not the same. If we can but convince the folk that all is well between us, time we may gain for the sorting out of misunderstandings." He sighed heavily. "Come, then, and lie beside me."

His arguments were persuasive, but I stood frozen. I could not force myself to trust him so close to me. Lying at his side, I would have no opportunity to gather my power if he should attack, and I would stand little chance in a physical struggle, even weakened as he was.

He lay there quietly for a time. "My word I have given," he said at last.

I blushed hotly. I also had given my word, and broken it immediately. Jerkily I lay down beside him. As I did so, my knuckle brushed the skin of his back. He was cold. I sat up and arranged a warm blanket over him. Lying down again, I pulled the corner of it up to cover myself.

He stirred uneasily and I stiffened. But apparently he was only seeking a comfortable position for his wounds, for he kept his back toward me.

In time, I realized that he meant to keep his word, and my thoughts turned to the shambles of a marriage I had contracted. Unlike most young girls, as an adolescent I had not spent much time in dreaming of love and marriage. My mother had been hanged when I was twelve, and I had been too busy staying out of the hands of the witch-hunters to indulge in many romantic fantasies. But never in my worst nightmares had I envisioned this bitter and desolate wedding night.

I didn't expect to sleep that night, but I dozed a little. Whenever my restless bed-mate stirred or moaned in his sleep I woke with a start. At last I opened my eyes to find a dim dawnlight filling the herb-garden court and leaking into the room. Taharka had turned to face me; he was lying on his side watching me. I reached out and laid my hand on his forehead to feel if he were feverish.

His forehead was cool, but he caught my hand in his own and held it. I stiffened. "Well this morning I am," he said, with a grin. "A good doctor I have. But no more of your fever-drink do I want. Bitter enough to tan your tongue, it is!"

I tried to smile a little at him. "My patients often tell me that they'll get well if it kills them, rather than take another dose. But it's the best fever medicine I have. May I look at your wounds?"

"Not yet, Lady Mantic. Soon our men will be bringing the morning cup—a tradition it is, to strengthen and refresh the newlyweds. When they come, I will kiss you and pretend to be very indignant to be interrupted—expect that, they will. Don't be frightened when I do! Attacked by your magic again I do not want to be."

"I'm sorry. I don't suppose you'll believe me, but I didn't do that deliberately. The power is not always under my complete control."

"Why should I not believe you? An oath to trust you, I swore."

I squirmed. The broken oath I had taken ate into my conscience. "As I haven't kept my oath, I don't see why you should be bound by yours."

"Too soon it is to say you have broken oath. I do not free you of it—in good time, will it be fulfilled. Nor will I break mine and free you by my fault." He spoke very quietly, but with such intensity that I could hear his teeth clash together.

I realized how very little I understood this man. The things that seemed obvious to me were outside his ken, and clearly there were things that were of paramount importance to him that I hardly considered at all. It was certainly true that, having known each other for less than twenty-four hours, we had created an entirely disproportionate amount of havoc in each other's lives. I recalled my blithe assumption of the day before that once he was secure in his tenure at the Silvercat, Taharka wouldn't care if I simply rode away. Now I was not so sure of that.

I sighed, and in my bewilderment, said to him, "If only we understood each other better!"

"Learning fast, I am. When you understand that I'm not to be feared, you'll learn too."

"I'm not afraid of you, nor do I abhor you."

"My wife you are, yet you shrink from my touch. If not from fear or abhorrence, then why?"

I sighed again. "I can't explain it to you, Taharka. When I agreed to marry you, I meant to—to try to be a good wife. I still mean to, if I can. If you'll be patient, I'll try to overcome . . . to overcome . . ." My voice choked and petered out, but Taharka seemed to understand what I was trying to say.

"With your promise, then patient I shall try to be. Only hard it is, when for so many, many years I have searched for my wife and my home, to find them and then be denied my rights."

My breath caught in a little moan. I had treated Taharka wrongly, by my standards as well as his. If only he hadn't lunged at me so suddenly!

There was a thunder roll of knocks upon the door. "The morning cup is here," Taharka said. He pulled the blanket up. "They must not see that you're clothed. Peculiar they would think it. *GO AWAY! WE'RE TIRED! READY TO AWAKEN WE ARE NOT!"* he added, in the bellow I had come to expect.

"Time to get up, it is!" came laughingly through the door. "Spend all day at your new game you cannot!"

"GO AWAY, YOU BASTARDS!" roared Taharka. He folded me into his arms, rolling over a little so that he shielded me from the door. He pressed his hairy mouth against my split and bruised lips, but not with so much force as to cause more damage. In fact, this kiss was more akin to those gentle, tentative kisses I had taken and given to Laddie, all those years ago, the only kisses with which I was familiar. I was just beginning, shyly, to respond a little, when the door burst open and about half the populace of the castellum came spilling into the room.

"A boy or a girl will it be?" one of the barbarians inquired with interest.

"Both—from the looks of them they've been at it all night," commented another. "Such mighty labors should be rewarded by twins, at least." This remark was treated by the assembly as a great joke.

Caught unprepared by this rough raillery, I did exactly the right thing, blushing furiously (how were they to know it was from shame and not embarrassment?) and turning my face to hide it against Taharka's hairy chest. He held me protectively closer and cursed them blisteringly for a pack of tactless fools; apparently they were a little surprised by the vehemence with which he reacted to their horseplay, for the coarse jokes died away and one of them came nearer the bed. I heard a clinking as he put a tray down upon the table near the bed, moving my medical kit aside to make room for it.

"No offense meant, Lady Mantic. Your morning cup this is, and our good wishes with it," he said, and the visitors filed out of the bedroom in a subdued patter.

When the door closed behind them, I emerged to find Taharka staring at me in some amazement. "Learning to understand you I am not," he said. "Before they came in, kissing me you were, and exactly like a new bride of sixteen you acted—perfect, it was. Yet last night you cast such a spell on me that I thought I was a dead man, rather than be a wife to me."

I squirmed out of his grasp. "I told you I couldn't explain it," I said. "What is this morning cup?"

He sighed. "Very good, this is," he said, handing me one of the mugs and taking the other for himself. "Continue this conversation tonight, we will."

It was good, too—thick and fruity and nourishing.

CHAPTER 7

THE First necessity of the next day was to prepare for the arrival of the cannibal savages. "Defend the crop-lands we must," pointed out Taharka as we walked about. The new margrave was inspecting his castellum, and the mantic, like a devoted bride, was escorting him. "Harm us they cannot, if we stay safely within the castellum, but next winter we may all starve. Hunting parties will I send out today, so that if we must stand a siege we'll at least eat well. All three horses will I take, so that we can find the herds of wild cattle more quickly."

"No," I said.

It was apparent that no one ever said no to Taharka. He blinked at me, astonished rather than angry. "All of my men can ride a horse," he said.

I shuddered, remembering the heavy curb bit and the great strap-like reins he used on his stallion, and the way he had pulled against the bit with all his strength. "No one rides my horses but me," I said calmly, but a few green sparks popped.

"Hunting, the business of the margrave is," Taharka said. "We need the horses."

"You shall not have mine." We had been walking along the battlements, looking at the defensive arrangements of the castellum. Now we stopped and faced each other.

"Shall we quarrel then, Lady Mantic? For if you prove a contentious wife, I shall have to chastise you."

A shower of green sparks escaped my control. "You couldn't," I retorted icily. "And you'd better not try."

He lowered his shaggy head, reminding me of a wild bull. "Perhaps I couldn't, Lady Mantic, yet if I must, I shall try. A man who fears his wife, no better than a gelding is."

I shrugged. "Fear me or not as suits you, Taharka, but you will respect me. If you ever offer me physical violence, I will defend myself—and I don't think it'll be I who comes away from that battle the loser." I knew that I must not seem to yield in this first confrontation. This was not a civilized man who stood before me, but a half-wild barbarian. I couldn't reason with him. I would have to show him that I was as strong as he. I let a little glowing globe of energy form itself on my palm, in case he had forgotten that he was dealing with a wielder of power.

He stood facing me, as grim and inflexible as granite. "Strength against strength, is it to be, Lady Mantic? Slay me with your magic you can, as I can slay you with my warrior's skills. Or dare you lay your witchery aside and deal with your husband as a wife should?"

Challenged, I tossed my head and let the energy flow back into the overmind. "You're the one who threatened chastisement. I don't know what the customs are where you come from, though I can imagine that men beat their wives whenever it suits them. But I will not permit you to do so to me."

"The customs of my folk are different than you seem to think. Beat you I shall not. But my wife you are and my judgment you must learn to respect."

I realized that we were on the verge of a conflict that neither of us really wanted but that neither of us could stop. I could not yield, but I didn't want to kill him, either. I took a deep breath, calming myself. "Taharka," I said, "we aren't enemies. Let's not destroy each other."

"No. Enemies we are not," he said. Was there a note of relief in his voice? Perhaps his thoughts had paralleled mine. "Husband and wife we are. Friends must we become."

I gave him a startled look. It was a novel idea to me, that husband and wife could be friends as well. Yet I found the idea attractive. There had been very few friends in my life, and I had always felt that lack far more keenly than the lack of husband or lover. "I should like to have you for a friend," I said impulsively, holding out my hand to him.

He took the hand with the courtly grace he displayed from time to time. "Then friends we shall be," he said.

He didn't mention the horses again until we had completed our tour. Then he asked me if he might borrow my horses for his hunting party. I sighed. "I'll let you use Biscuit," I said. "But not with a bit in her mouth. If one of your men wants to ride her in a halter, he can. I'll go with you on Whiskers and help you scout."

"Traditional it is not, for a mantic to go hunting," he said.

"If you're going to fret yourself over the nontraditional and improper things I do, you'll die young," I said with a smile.

He grinned back at me. "Many of the women of my folk fine hunters are and wear the hunter's lock to show that their bear they have killed."

"I have no desire to kill a bear," I said. "I'll be content to scout out the herds for you."

"More fearsome game than bears have you killed, it is not so?" he said shrewdly.

I eyed him with astonishment. I had in fact killed two giant supernatural carnivores, eaters of human flesh. But how on earth had he known that? "I have," I admitted cautiously, "from time to time been forced to kill certain creatures that might otherwise have killed me or someone for whom I was responsible. I don't seek such encounters."

Taharka gave me a sharp look, but didn't pursue the question. I went to change into riding clothes—Taharka was already dressed in his shaggy native costume—while the horses were saddled. I returned to find the hunting party ready to set out and a train of donkey carts preparing to follow. One of the barbarians, Satha, was riding Biscuit bareback, since we had no saddle for her, and with a halter. The mare was broken to ride, but not well trained. Her rider probably got along as well with the halter as he would have with a bridle and bit.

The cattle herds were on the move. The savages didn't restrict their diet to human flesh, and the game animals moved before them as they would have before a horde of locusts. We had no difficulty locating a large herd—not the same I had hunted before, but a larger one. The bulls were restless and moody, inclined to attack with little provocation. The barbarians, armed with heavy bows, crept right into the fringes of the herds and drove the long arrows into their quarry at close range, dodging the charges of the maddened bulls with lighthearted agility.

Taharka didn't hang back, but left his stallion with me and dared more than any of his men. Once, when a cow whose calf he had just shot charged him, I saw him sidestep nimbly, grab her by the spreading horns, and wrestle her to the earth, roaring more loudly than she bawled. When he had taken her down, her head twisted impossibly far, one of the men ran up and cut her stretched throat.

Another time, when one of his men tripped on the tangled sod and fell before a charging bull, he dashed between the animal and its target and distracted it, dodging until it gave up and trotted off, while the barbarian picked himself up.

I stayed on Whisker's back and well away from the danger. At last the herd moved off, and Taharka loomed out of the dust, blood-splashed and dirty. "Seven, we got," he said, as he vaulted back onto his stallion.

"I was frightened for you. I hope you haven't torn your stitches out again," I said severely.

He flexed his shoulders experimentally. "I don't think so," he said. "But more tired I am than I should be. Aged I am becoming. Back to the castellum we can go and you can look at my stitches. With Satha will we leave the mare, so that he can lead the tiller folk with the donkey carts to the carcasses."

I nodded. I had watched Satha with the mare, and he had not abused her, though he had ridden her hard. The three of us had managed to mill the herd before the slaughter had begun.

The two of us rode back alone; the barbarians were butchering the kills. Taharka insisted upon checking the area around the castellum with a view to defense. It would be his strategy, he told me, to turn the savages rather than to enter into pitched battle with them. "Against so many, small chance have we to halt them," he said. "Many men would we lose and likely the crops as well. But too expensive can we make it for them to come through the river valley, and easy to veer off to the north." He showed me how the brakes of the river made a natural barrier that his twelve men could hold against the hundreds of savages. I had seen the same brakes every day for weeks, but their military possibilities had eluded me completely.

"I should have thought of that," I said with some chagrin.

"Warriors to do your fighting, you had none," Taharka pointed out.

"I could have made some, the same way I made the worm yesterday," I said.

"But only illusion they would have been, isn't it so?"

"Yes," I admitted, "and if the savages had discovered that I would have been in real trouble. But I can add to your forces if you like. Illusory warriors can be mixed in among the real ones to make the force look larger."

"No. Out of the castellum I do not want you to be. No," he added, looking at my suddenly stormy expression, "doubt your courage I do not. But if you were there, I would worry about you, and think not of my proper concerns. To think of your tender limbs as food for some cannibal savage, and that before ever I have sampled their sweeter delights, would be enough to set me distracted."

I blushed. "Very well," I said reluctantly. It was easy to tell by the set of his jaw that he was willing to come to blows over this issue, and I had no great desire to take part in the battle anyway. "I'll stay in the castellum and sew up the warriors like a good little wife."

He gave me an approving grin—and was there a tinge of relief in it as well?

When we got back, I inspected his wounds. I was amazed at the healing that had taken place. The smaller wounds were crusted over, and I left them open to the air. In the two larger ones I could see that the skin had begun to knit. I exclaimed in amazement. "A skilled and caring doctor have I," he said. "I wish only that the wife cared as much for her husband as the healer for her patient."

I paused for a moment behind him, my hands resting on his shoulders. We were in the surgery, and he had again divested himself of belt, fur wrap, and tunic. I wanted to say something reassuring; the words had been light but there was

an undercurrent of sadness in the tone. But the right words
wouldn't come, and finally I turned away to begin tidying
my instruments. "Don't get the wounds wet when you
bathe," I said.

We had a fine supper of sliced breaded beef hearts and
liver fried with onions. Taharka laughed loudly and joked
with his men, who ate at the warriors' table while he and I
dined grandly at the head table, but tonight he didn't attempt
to handle me, nor did he force any of his rough kisses on
me. When the meal was over and everyone dispersed to their
apartments, he came with me through the private door and
up the back stairs to our quarters.

"Would you like a cup of lemon tea?" I asked nervously
when we reached the sitting room.

"I thank you, Lady Mantic, but no," he said. His bearing
was more formal than I had ever seen it, his expression remote. He poured himself a small draft of lifewater and sat
with me while I sipped my tea, but we spoke only of com-
monplaces, like two strangers making conversation. Soon he
bade me a courteous good night and went into the margrave's quarters.

I put down my cup, surprised to find that I had to unclench white-knuckled fingers to do it. I had dreaded this
evening, fearing a repetition of the previous night's turmoil.
I was immensely relieved to be spared it, yet there was a
tiny germ of regret to find that he no longer desired me. I
didn't want his clumsy caresses, nor the guilt that came from
rejecting him, but no one had ever actually wanted me before, and a little lost crumb of feminine vanity somewhere
under my mental carpet had plumped itself upon discovering
that it was possible for me—me!—to be desired.

Satha, scouting upon Biscuit the next day—Taharka had
asked if his scout might borrow her—reported that the savages were on the move and headed in our direction. "Heavy
fighting there is, toward the village and at the ford of the
river. If the savages are turned there, the river will they
follow and land right on our doorstep this afternoon or early
tomorrow morning."

Taharka cursed. "Why are the margraves not turning the

savages north? Then out of this area altogether would they be forced." He was sitting at the desk in the margrave's office, looking at a map. I sat a little to one side, at Taharka's invitation, to hear the scout's report. He had not said so, but I guessed that he wanted me to be in possession of all the facts in case anything happened to him in the upcoming battle.

"I know not," said Satha doubtfully. "Almost it seemed to me as if they were deliberately sending them this way. Easier it looked to me to leave the way north open, but there are ditch fortifications thrown up on the prairie."

Taharka glanced at me. He knew, as I did, that the margraves were indeed making us a present of the savages. "Up to us it will be to turn them north, then," he said. "Go with the mare to the highest place you can find that offers a good view east, and when the savages come, ride back and give warning."

"Stop by the kitchen and get some food to take with you," I suggested. "You're likely to miss lunch." Then I glanced quickly at Taharka to see whether he was going to take umbrage at my interference with his orders. He didn't seem bothered.

"Thank you, Lady Mantic," said Satha, with a shy smile.

"Tell them at the stables to saddle Butterfly for me," Taharka said. When Satha was gone, he turned to me. "Well thought of that was, Lady Mantic. A warrior can miss meals when he must, but any man fights better on a full stomach and when he knows that someone cares for his welfare."

"Where are you going?" I asked. Then I added, realizing that he had addressed me formally, "Lord Margrave."

"Nowhere just yet, but ready it is well to be. Fast can those savages move when they have to. Beside us one ran as we galloped out of their camp, and stride for stride he matched your pony."

"Whiskers was carrying double," I protested.

"True, but fast was he galloping, nonetheless."

"I'll go see to it that all the tiller folk are within the walls," I said. "Shall I send you up something to eat, too?"

"Grateful would I be, Lady Mantic." As I left he turned back to his map.

Satha had indeed underestimated the speed with which the savages could travel. It was not long after noon that he came pelting back to the castellum with the news that they were in sight, coming fast with the forces of the other margraves harassing their flanks and rear—in effect, driving them down upon us.

In the next few hours, I found that waiting in safety for the men to fight a battle was more harrowing than being out in the thickest of the fighting. I would rather dash into the savage encampment a dozen times than to relive that afternoon.

Nothing could be seen from the battlements. There was a little dust, an occasional bellowed warcry from our men or an ululating shriek from the savages. That was all we in the castellum could discover of the battle. I went at last to my office and began to try once more to puzzle out the handwritten script of the plains folk. I was fortunate in finding the journals of some previous mantic whose hand was more legible than that of the last, and was soon absorbed as words began slowly to form from what might as well have been bird tracks before.

I didn't forget the battle or the plight of our men; they were always in the back of my mind, but the time passed more quickly when I had something to occupy myself. In fact, I was in the surgery, checking over my bandages and salves one more time to be certain that I hadn't forgotten anything when Bion brought me word that the men were returning. I dashed up to the battlements, to see that they were carrying three of their number, but that the savages were nowhere in sight. Then I hurried down and told Bion to admit them but to bar the gate firmly immediately after them.

I was waiting at the gate when they came through. First my eyes sought out Taharka. He was walking easily with the rest, having sent his stallion back to the castellum when the fighting seemed imminent. At least he gave no indication of being injured, though I suspiciously remembered the "few little nicks" from two days before.

I turned my attention to the men who were being carried. The first was the youngster who had taken my hand and thanked me for giving them a home, that first day. He was dead, haggled about with the stone knives of the savages, staring and bloodless. I bowed my head for a moment and then turned to the living wounded whom I might yet help.

One was gashed from hip to knee, a bloody wound that might well draw as it healed and leave him limping if it were not carefully stitched. None of the major blood vessels were cut, and I judged that his life was not in danger if he were cared for properly. The other had been stabbed in the abdomen with a filthy fire-hardened spear, and though he seemed in less distress than his pale, sweating comrade, I was more concerned for him. I had no expertise in the treatment of such wounds but I knew that infection was a grave danger, and I gestured his bearers to take him into the surgery first. I gave the other a thistle-poppy draft for the pain, patted his arm, and told him that he was going to be all right and to be content to wait.

"Assistance do you need, my love? A little battlefield wound-wrapping I have done myself, in my time," said Taharka from the door of the surgery behind me.

I glanced around. "Do you have any more of your 'little nicks'?" I asked. "Torn out any stitches?"

"Well am I, my love."

I felt a brief flash of wonder at his intimate mode of address when he had been so formal before, but was instantly too busy with the man on the surgery table to follow the thought.

The spear had entered and then broken off; part of it was still in the wound. I dared not give the man a poppy draft until I was sure that the stomach or gut had not been penetrated. "I can't give him anything for the pain," I said to Taharka. "Can you hold him while I remove the spear?"

For an answer, Taharka moved to lay his hands upon the man's shoulders. I bent over him. "I'm going to have to hurt you," I told him, smoothing back the dusty, sweaty hair from his forehead. "I'll be as quick as I can, and when I'm done you can have a strong poppy drink. It will help me to be faster if you'll lie as still as you can. Taharka will help to hold you. All right?"

He nodded solemnly, and I washed the blood away from

the entry site with a strong, boiled decoction of barberry roots, which most healers used as a fever drink but which I had found to be sometimes effective against infection. Then I took one of the shining scalpels from the medical tool kits I had found, warned both Taharka and the patient that I was about to begin, and opened the wound with a quick, decisive stroke far enough to remove the wood and clean away the fragments. I worked as fast as I could, but the patient must have suffered agonies. Even so, he clenched his fists and gritted his teeth and neither moved nor cried out. Taharka kept a comforting hand upon his shoulder, but had no need to hold him.

They both seemed to have complete faith in my skill, and I tried to maintain a calm and confident demeanor. They were not to know that I had never wielded a scalpel before in my life.

I was relieved to find that the spear hadn't penetrated any internal organ. The layers of fat and the crisscrossed fibers of muscle had been thick enough to protect the vital parts. I sighed. "You can give him the poppy drink now," I told Taharka. "Nothing important's been hurt and he's going to be all right." I didn't mention the danger of infection. They must both have been aware of it. I used my barberry root liberally. Then I began on my stitching. By the time I had the muscles sewn together with gut and was beginning on the skin, leaving a boar's bristle that had been boiled with the barberry root in the wound to provide drainage, the poppy drink had taken effect.

"Could you have some of your men carry him to his bed and see that he's warmly covered?" I asked Taharka.

"Shall I have the other brought in?"

"Not yet. I don't know why, but there seems to be less infection if the surgery is cleaned between each patient." I began to scrub the surface of the table vigorously as they carried the drowsy patient away. I removed all of my instruments to be cleaned and brought out fresh ones, as well as a fresh jar of barberry root, and scrubbed my hands thoroughly again.

When I was ready, the man was brought and placed on the table. He was already drugged with poppy drink, and Taharka had only to steady him. His was a nasty gash, and I regretted a little having taken the other man first. The edges of the wound had begun to swell, and that would make it more difficult to close it as neatly as needed to be done. He too was at risk of infection, and I cleaned his wound as carefully as I could. It took me a very long time to stitch him. Each layer of severed muscle had to be joined with gut and then the skin sewed together. When at last I straightened wearily, my back ached fiercely.

There were two or three small injuries among the warriors to be cleaned, exclaimed over, and sewn up. But finally I turned to Taharka. "All right, you're next."

"Injured I am not, my love." He put an arm around my shoulders. "Working hard you have been. Come up to our quarters and rest a bit. Perhaps Tildis will send our supper to us on a tray."

I nodded. "You haven't told me how the battle went."

He grinned wryly. "We won," he said.

CHAPTER
8

Our Lives assumed a strange pattern. During the days, while we were at work about the castellum and within the public eye, Taharka treated me with a warm familiarity, addressing me either as "my love" or by my personal name. Occasionally he put an arm around me or kissed me vigorously. But in the evenings after supper, when we were alone together in our quarters, he behaved with a formal dignity that made it easy to believe that he was the son of a chieftain. I could hardly reconcile the two facets of his personality. But I was becoming more at ease with both of them.

My own conscience was less easy. I had not lived up to the reasonable expectations any man might have of his wife, and I knew it. I was able to console myself not at all with the thought that Taharka had shown no further amorous inclinations toward me, for I knew that it had been my violent reaction to his first advances that had smothered his natural desires. I could only conclude miserably that there was not much I could do about it except to try to be a good wife to him in other ways. And even so, there were times, when he was at his loudest and most boisterous, joking with his men, pinching the middle-aged tiller women on the rear, roaring over some offense that irked him (for he was easily annoyed and loud in his ire, but soon over it and good-humored again) that I would shudder and vow internally that if I died for my fastidious tastes, he'd never be admitted to my bed.

I spent much time with the two wounded men, although I appointed nurses from among the tiller women to care for them. But I monitored their progress attentively, and was relieved to find that both injuries were healing cleanly with no sign of infection.

There was no immediate need for more meat, and Taharka came to me one day when I was working in my office on my journal. "Bored my men are becoming, Lady Mantic," he said. "Can you think of some worthwhile work they might be put to?"

"What do warriors and hunters do in your land, when they aren't fighting and hunting?" I asked, laying aside my pen.

"Most make something," he said. "They are leather-workers or goldsmiths or work at some such craft. The winters are very long in our homeland and idle men soon begin to drink too much and quarrel. Encourage their hobbies, my father did, though the materials cost him a lot. Cheaper than funerals it was, he said."

That was no doubt true enough. The lad that had died in the fight to turn the savages north had been buried with complex rites. There had been an all-night wake with continuous eating and drinking and a great deal of oration. The next evening, as the first stars began to appear in the dusk, the body, dressed in all its finery, was carried to the barrow the barbarians had spent the day constructing. There it was laid with an elaborate offering of grave goods, each item broken—killed, Taharka told me, so that the spirits of each item could accompany the lad to the afterworld. Besides, he added wryly, it kept grave robbers away if they knew that nothing in the barrow was usable.

As the last light of the day of mourning faded, Taharka stepped forward and sang. So liquidly sweet was his voice, so freighted with sorrow, so expressive of the sadness of youth cut down in all its promise, that I wasn't the only one reduced to tears. The northerners bawled like babies. When he had his listeners reduced to a state of helpless grief, Taharka changed to a rollicking, bawdy song of the joys of the warriors' afterlife, lifted our spirits again, and sent the boy's soul forth encouraged, cheerful, bidden a proper farewell and ready for new adventures in a place where there was no death.

I marveled once again, as I had on the night of our wedding. Taharka had named himself bard, and indeed in his voice there was a potent magic to stir the hearts of his hearers. It was a different sort of magic than mine, but powerful. I shook the memory off and returned to the matter at hand.

"I don't quite see how they can do leatherwork and goldsmithing here, though," I said, "although there are tanning vats in the harness-makers' workshop." I paused as a thought struck me. "Er—just how strongly do your folk feel about their work being appropriate to the sexes?"

Taharka gave me an inquiring look. "Understand you I do not."

"Well, most peoples have jobs that they consider to be women's work, and no man will do them. Among the ox-nomads, for example, caring for the oxen is men's work and women are terrified of the beasts, though they are as docile as oxen elsewhere. The men, on the other hand, would starve rather than prepare food and go naked rather than sew. I was asking whether there are any jobs that your men would feel insulted if they were asked to do."

"Our men are content to leave the bearing of babies to the women," said Taharka dryly, "and likewise women leave the fathering of them to the men."

"I think the ox-nomads would agree with that, and even my own people. What about spinning and weaving? Among the tiller folk, it's women's work, but among my own folk, either sex may practice the craft."

Taharka considered. "Most sewing is done by women, but much of our clothing is made of skins and furs and the preparation of these is men's work. Yet neither is thought to be shameful for the other sex."

"Then ask your men if they would like to work in the weavers' workshop. Besides the needs of our own folk, fabric is the only product these people make to trade and sell, and we have only one skilled weaver. It takes four or five spinners to keep one weaver supplied with flaxen thread and woolen yarn, too, and our weaver has to stop often to spin."

Taharka nodded. "Well thought on, it seems to me. The work would be pleasant if we all worked together. Increase our resources, it would, too. Some will wish to learn to weave, doubtless. Interested in the patterns woven into the cloth here, Satha has been since we arrived. Suggest it to them, I will, and set the example by learning to spin myself." He hesitated. "Lady Mantic, take offense I hope you will not."

"Of course not, unless offense is meant."

He cleared his throat diffidently. "Very cool to me, you have been, in the presence of our warriors and tiller folk. Beginning to comment upon it, they are."

"I don't understand. I've been perfectly friendly."

"Yes. Friendly you have been. Loving you have not. After the battle, you did not come to me or seem pleased that I had survived."

"I could see that you'd survived. There were wounded men to care for."

"Yet you did not seem concerned. A wife should show a little relief that her husband was unhurt. Unnatural it seems to the warriors that your demeanor is so cold."

"What do you want me to do?" I said angrily. "Throw my arms around your neck and cry?"

He looked at me. Then his eyes fell. "Of course not," he said defeatedly. He turned as if to go.

"Wait," I said. I didn't like to see him so downcast, and I was thoroughly ashamed of my little flare of temper. He paused and half turned. I rose from my desk and went to him, putting my hand on his arm. "I'm sorry, Taharka. You're right and I'm wrong."

He turned to face me and I realized that I had come too close to him for comfort. I held my ground, but let my hand fall away from his arm. He said nothing, merely waiting for me to continue. "What is it that you think I should do?" I asked humbly.

"Lady Mantic, I mean no disrespect," he said, with a touch of irony in his tone. I flushed. I had become uncommonly touchy of late. "If a deception of a happy marriage we are to carry out, glad to be in my company you must seem. It is not unknown for happily married pairs to touch one another. Even, in extreme cases, call one another by pet names they might."

"Very well," I said. "Unfortunately, I have never had need

of pet names before. I don't have an extensive vocabulary of them. What would you like to be called?"

He looked at me with a touch of exasperation. The thought of picking out his own pet name was evidently uncomfortable to him. Then suddenly he chuckled. "Answer I will to any name given me in affection. If offered with a hug and a kiss, even 'Stupid' will I accept."

I had to smile at that. "But it would hardly serve the purpose of convincing the indwellers that all is well between us. I'll think about it and try to come up with something. Is there anything else?"

"Always it is I who offers a caress when parted for a while we have been. Nor do you respond to my touch."

"I thought that men disliked women who pawed them about all the time," I said.

"Speak for all men I cannot, but for myself, grateful I would be to be 'pawed about' even a little."

I was seized with a sudden mad impulse, the kind of thing that gets you halfway out of a tightrope or astride an unbroken horse before you quite realize what you're doing. "Like this?" I said, and stepped closer to the startled barbarian. Slipping my arms about his middle, I touched my cheek to his shoulder. I had intended to give him a quick hug, I suppose, and leap away, but his powerful arms closed reflexively behind me, not tightly, but forming a solid fence to confine me against his chest.

"Yes," he said, a little breathlessly. "Very much like that."

I was dizzy with my own daring. I meant to withdraw from his embrace, but for the first few seconds I was too astonished at myself to move. If he had handled me aggressively, as he certainly would have had a right to—after all, I had made the first advances—I would have pulled away indignantly. But he just stood there, solid as a cliff, and I just stood there, arms encircling his formidable circumference.

In the next few seconds, I realized that it was really not so unpleasant to stand there with my cheek on his shoulder—that in fact it was rather comforting. Then I began to wonder what I could possibly say to explain what I was doing, since I didn't know myself, and no lie I could think of sounded even remotely convincing. "Oh, dear, oh dear," I said use-lessly. "I don't . . . I mean, I can't . . . oh, dear."

Taharka let his arms fall and I stepped away quickly, avoiding his eye. "If you would do that occasionally where seen we can be," he said remotely, "stop the talking it would." He left quickly. I stood staring after him, wondering what he must think of me and why he had hurried away. Had my touch become as distasteful to him as his was to me? I found that I was a little piqued at that thought, and shook my head ruefully, laughing at my own foolish inconsistencies. Fair, as Taharka would say (but never had), I was not being.

I puzzled considerably over the matter of an appropriate pet name. I felt sure that Taharka wouldn't like anything lacking in dignity. The warriors would tease him about it if I called him "Cuddles" or something of that nature, and in any case I couldn't have brought myself to call him a name so utterly unsuited. "My dear," on the other hand, seemed con-descending. I thumbed through some of the storybooks in the mantic's library, but none of the characters seemed to use pet names for each other. I did find one case of a villain calling a heroine "my little chipmunk" right before he at-tempted to feed her to crocodiles, and giggled myself into a fit of hiccups trying to imagine myself cooing "Please pass the salt, my little chipmunk," into Taharka's ear.

He had already bathed and was waiting to walk with me down to dinner when I came out of my room that evening. I couldn't help it; when I saw him "my little chipmunk" leaped into the front of my mind and I nearly strangled try-ing to keep a straight face as we went down the private stairs. I was losing the battle with unseemly hilarity when we emerged into the dining hall, and my face was decorated with a broad grin as I slipped into the mantic's chair. I rashly glanced at Taharka as the women began to serve; he was looking at me with a puzzled expression. I composed myself hastily.

"Share the joke, will you not?" he said to me at last.

I struggled briefly with temptation and lost. I leaned to-ward him so that I could whisper in his ear; I was certain that he wouldn't want his men to hear this! "I looked in some of my books to find a pet name," I explained. "There was only one I could find. It was—was 'my little chipmunk'—" Then I gave up my battle to maintain decorum and subsided into a fit of giggling.

Taharka choked. He gave me an outraged glance. Still gurgling with laughter, I pounded him on the back until he was able to speak. "My little chipmunk?" he gasped. "My little—" and then he began to roar with laughter too. That set me off again and we all but rolled in our chairs with gales of laughter. "It suits me not, mean you?" he said at last, ignoring the astounded stares of the assembled populace and wiping tears from his eyes.

I shook my head, still unable to speak.

His face sobered suddenly. "Yet even that would I be glad to be called if it would bring laughter to your eyes again," he said quietly.

Suddenly shy, I stiffened and started to withdraw, then remembered what he had said about the talk. This was the right time to put my arms around him—certainly everyone was here to see it. But it was cruelly hard to force myself to lean over and slip my arms around his neck with all the folk of the castellum gawking. I gave him a quick hug. "Well done," he said in my ear and kissed me on the temple.

For the rest of the meal, he devoted himself to me, ignoring the rest of the company. I made an effort to respond, listening attentively, smiling at him, and even offering him a delicacy from my spoon once, as I had seen a lady do in one of the famed inns of the River Cities. It had seemed to me then, eating alone, an endearing gesture, and Taharka accepted the proffered bite with only a quirked eyebrow of surprise.

As we rose to leave at the conclusion of the meal, I put my arm lightly around his waist, and he put his around my shoulders, and we went through the private door in a fine seeming of loving tenderness.

When we reached our sitting room, I turned to him with a smile, expecting praise for my acting or at least a word of appreciation. The smile died as I saw that he was withdrawn and aloof, pouring himself a larger than usual measure of lifewater. I made my tea quietly. When I came to sit down across from him, in the chair that had become mine by custom, he was staring grimly before him.

"I think your stitches should come out tomorrow," I ventured, after a few moments of heavy silence.

Reminded of my presence, Taharka looked at me. The glowering intensity of his gaze was so powerful that my cup rattled in my saucer as I shivered. I wondered if he had taken offense at my laughter or the name, for I couldn't think of anything else I had done to anger him.

He continued to glare at me. He couldn't have heard what I said, I thought, so I repeated, "I think I should take your stitches out tomorrow, if you feel up to it."

"Very well," he said shortly, and drained off his glass. Rising, he went to the table where the flagon stood and poured himself another glass of the liquor.

I finished my tea and put the cup aside. It was very unlike anything I had seen him do so far, to brood like this, but perhaps my presence was exacerbating his irritation. I would go to bed, I thought, and hope that his mood would be better in the morning. "Good night, Taharka," I said, softly enough that he could pretend not to hear me if he wished.

"Good night, Lady Mantic," he said, and I paused and looked wonderingly at him, for I thought I heard a sneer in his voice. His face was averted, but his shoulders in the embroidered robe were stiff with tension. I left hastily and closed the door quietly behind me.

I was wary of him in this savage mood, I admitted to myself. What had happened? At dinner we had laughed together, and I had done my best to follow his suggestions. I had, I thought, succeeded rather well, too. And then this surly behavior. I had, I thought wryly, forgotten that he was a barbarian, given to inexplicable changes of mood, full of wildness and violence. Only temporarily could a man like that behave like a civilized human being, reasonable and predictable, I thought with a touch of smugness.

The door crashed open behind me. I whirled to find Taharka glaring hot-eyed at me. He strode into my bedroom and slammed the door behind himself. As a wild-beast tamer knows instinctively when his lions are on the verge of attack, I knew that I must not flinch or Taharka would be upon me. I stood completely still, gazing calmly at him, waiting.

"Runa," he said harshly, "patient have I been, but you are my wife and I want you tonight. Now."

I quivered. So this was what came of touching! "I can't stop you," I said as steadily as I could. "I won't use my magic against you again, and you're stronger than I."

"No!" he bellowed. "Wish to rape you I do not!" He took another step toward me and reached out to clasp my upper arms. His grip was tight, but I made myself stand stock still. He gave me a little shake. "Do you fear me still?"

"No, Taharka, I'm not afraid of you," I lied.

"Ugly am I in your eyes? Does my appearance disgust you?"

"No," I answered truthfully. I hadn't thought at all about his looks; he was handsome enough, in his own uncombed way.

"Do you dislike me, then? Are my customs and manners repugnant to you?"

"Sometimes I like you very much. I don't like being man-handled."

He took his hands away from my shoulders. "Among my people, a husband has a right to his wife's caresses, and she to his. Are customs different among your folk?"

"No, they're much the same," I admitted. "And even if they weren't, I wouldn't cheat on you."

He swung his shaggy head from side to side. "Accusing you of adultery I am not! Agreed to marry me, you did. Accepted me for your husband and swore the oath. Do you say to me that you are not bound by the oath?"

My gaze fell. I couldn't deny the shame of that oath-breaking. "I swore the oath," I said with difficulty. "I'm bound by it."

His fists clenched and I straightened to meet the blow. But he did not strike at me. "Then why," he roared, more loudly than ever I had heard him, "why do you deny me your love and your bed?"

I couldn't answer him. I was beginning to tremble.

"Why?" he demanded. "Why? Understand you I do not."

"I intended to keep the bargain," I whispered. "But you

came charging at me and the energy had been building up and I couldn't control it."

"If to keep the bargain you had intended, you could have come to me any night between then and now."

I looked at him, stunned. "Go to you? The idea never occurred to me. How was I supposed to know that you wanted me to?"

He gave his head a baffled shake. "How could you not know that I wanted you to? Your husband I am. Eager enough was I before you struck me with your lightning."

That was true—entirely too eager. "I didn't understand," I said helplessly.

"Perhaps it is that among your people, a wife never goes to her husband when she desires him, but must await his pleasure."

He was making excuses for me. My already tender conscience throbbed painfully. "No, I don't think so," I said doubtfully. "At least those married couples I knew seemed —er, comfortable with each other. I think they sleep in the same bed all the time."

"Waiting for me to come to you, have you been?"

"No," I confessed. "I thought you didn't want me any more because of the way I treated you on the wedding night."

He positively groaned with bewilderment. "Believe that of me you could not have." He reached for me suddenly enough to make me jump, but he only took my cold hands in his warm ones. I jerked them nervously out of his hold. "Is it to be so between us for all time? Are we never to be truly man and wife?"

"You mean you aren't going to insist upon it tonight?" I asked.

"No," he said. "I cannot force a woman who so plainly does not desire me."

"Oh," I said. It was contrary to everything I had heard or read about barbarians, but perhaps there were degrees of barbarity. "I'm sorry, Taharka. You see, I . . . I . . ." It was on the tip of my tongue to confess my lack of experience to him, but I couldn't. In the present circumstances, it would have been funny, at best. And anyway, I was immensely relieved and reassured by his lack of desire. Instead of speaking, I turned to him and put my arms lightly around his neck. He gathered me up in his arms. "When we get to know each other a little better," I said, comforted, "things will be different. I promise."

"With that promise will I be content," he said. "When ready you are, come to me. Patient a little longer will I be." He kissed me, sighing. "But for the sake of sweet mercy, don't keep me waiting too long, my love. Very great, the pain of loneliness is, when a man thinks he has left loneliness behind him." He released me and padded through the connecting door into his own bedroom.

I felt a little lonely myself. If only he had gone ahead, it would all be over with by now. And perhaps he'd have stayed, his comforting bulk beside me all night. Perhaps he would even have held me, as he had done for a few moments, for a longer time. I should have liked that, I thought wistfully.

With all Taharka's faults, and they were many, he was in every way a strong man. He needed my help and support because of the situation we were in, but he was more than willing to pull his share of the load and shoulder his share of the responsibility. I thought back to the slave I had rescued. He had been sweet, charming, accommodating by nature and training. He had been easily dominated. No, he had sought to be dominated. I had never been afraid of Laddie, but neither had I ever been tempted to depend upon him. I had been fond of him, but I had never respected him. I was not fond of Taharka, but I was very, very glad that he was my friend and not my enemy.

I found myself wondering how I did feel about Taharka. I had not lied when I had told him that I liked him very much, sometimes. I was afraid of him, sometimes, not because I thought he intended me harm, but because he was so vital, so intense. I had taken offense at his rough handling of me at our wedding, but presumably the women of his own people accepted that roughness for affection. He had, by his own standards, played fair with me. I wondered what one of the women of his own people would have done. Offered him back buffet for buffet, kiss for kiss, wrestling hug for hug? They must be veritable giantesses, then, I thought.

I determined to quit regarding the hugs and kisses we shared as a distasteful duty and to try to enjoy them. With that virtuous resolve fixed in my mind, I fell asleep.

CHAPTER
9

THE Next morning no opportunity arose for trying my new determination. Taharka was outwardly as cheery as ever, and we invited our one weaving mistress to breakfast at the head table while we discussed spinning and eventually weaving lessons. I had dressed in shirt and trousers—I had a new linen shirt, the first product of our looms.

"Will you ride this morning, my love?" asked Taharka.

"Yes, dearest, my horses need exercise," I replied, smiling.

Taharka took the endearment in stride. "May I ride with you?" he asked.

"Of course," I answered. "Bion, saddle the Margrave's horse too."

We strolled out to the stables to oversee the saddling, chatting of small matters. As we crossed the stable courtyard, one of the tiller folk came running up, holding out his hand as if bringing a message. I turned to take it, realizing as I did so that his face was unfamiliar. Instead of handing me anything, he lunged forward as if to touch me. His outstretched hand passed through my flesh.

Instantly I was snatched out of my body and whirled dizzily into the overmind, that formless place of the collective unconscious. Masters of the art can form and shape it as they like, using a trained will and concentrated effort as tools. Whole little universes can be shaped of the overmind stuff. I had done so many times, for my own amusement and for the ritualized contests of will undertaken by the sorcerers and sorceresses of the Kingdom. I had even built my own retreat there, an idealized farm with welcoming folk, which I could visit when my life of fleeing and hiding and constant wariness seemed too hard.

But that retreat and its lovingly created occupants had been destroyed when I had been captured and I had never rebuilt it. I hadn't visited in the overmind or manipulated its substance since, except for the relatively simple creation of the giant worm that had covered our retreat from the savage camp. Nor had I ever been snatched unready into the overmind at another's will.

I was lost instantly, completely out of contact with my empty corporeal body as I was whirled through impalpable gulfs of distance, dizzily, spinning. When I checked the spin with an effort of will, I plunged headlong down through regions of cold fire.

The fall came to an abrupt end before I could gather my will enough to halt it. I found myself on a barren snow-covered plain, bleak and lifeless, stretching on either side for endless miles beneath the gray sourceless light of the overmind. I looked about me, shivering, wondering why I had been deposited here. The only features of this inhospitable place were random piles of snow—not even firs or spruce thrust through the chill blanket.

I considered how best to find my way back to my body. I was skilled at manipulating the overmind; I could easily create the most luxurious of banquets and the most refreshing of drinks. They would assuage the hunger and thirst that were generated here, but they would not nourish my real body, and without anyone to care for it, it would soon die. Or my essence might die of the terrible cold of this place. In either case, dead was dead.

I was in an unenviable situation. Venturing into the overmind was risky at best, and I had always been careful to maintain a thread of contact with my body. Without that thread, the overmind was directionless and immeasurable. Mere random wandering wouldn't locate my corporeal form.

Another skilled wielder of power might come in after me and help me to find the way out, or a very strong will might lend me strength and direction even if untrained, but there was no one to come to my rescue. I was shivering violently. The cold here was not the chill of a snowy winter day, but a more profound cold. I concentrated and dressed myself in warm furry garments and waterproof boots. There was a powerful will opposing mine; it took a great effort to form the clothes, and they were not the rich splendid furs I had intended, but dirty, mangy hides, ill-sewn and drafty at the seams.

One of the nearest snowpiles stirred and rose. It was a manlike creature, gray of skin, with a fishy dead eye and claws rather than nails on its ungloved hands. Deliberately it strode up to me and cuffed me across the face with force enough to send me sprawling in the icy snow. I licked split and bleeding lips as the creature loomed over me again and delivered a teeth-rattling kick to my ribs. It growled something and pointed.

It is always difficult to manipulate another's construct, much harder than to build one from scratch. But this wasn't funny. I concentrated my will and the creature began to shrivel and shrink. Then it wavered and reformed. That will was opposing me again. No, it was more that one will— several, together very powerful. I could not change their own creation as long as they opposed me.

The creature kicked me again, and I groaned as I heard ribs crack. This time I scrambled in the direction it pointed. With blows and cuffs, it herded me up to another snowpile, which revealed itself to be a sled with a harness on it. The creature grunted and pointed at the harness. When I hesitated, it picked up a heavy short whip. Fixing its claws in the neck of my inadequate fur coat, it ripped it away from my body, leaving me with only the thin shirt I had been wearing, though I still had fur trousers and waterproof boots. Swinging the whip, it struck me across the back. I cried out with pain—I couldn't help it. The blood that welled from the stripe froze almost at once. The creature pointed at the harness again, and I picked it up and shrugged into it. A buckle was fastened across my shoulder blades where I couldn't reach it. Then the creature went away and left me standing in the bitter cold.

Other snowpiles were brutally routed out and harnessed to

other sleds. More of the arctic creatures shook themselves unconcernedly free of the snow, grunting and growling at each other. Then, when the chill had struck into my very bones, the drivers barked and wielded their whips, and with a chorus of groans and whimpers, we draft animals threw ourselves into our harness.

It was not easy to start the sled moving. Its runners had frozen into the crust of the snow, and the whip bit into my skin again and again as I panted and struggled with the unmoving bulk. At last by flinging myself from side to side against the stiff harness, I managed to get the awkward weight moving.

The drivers moved with long loping strides, and if one of the drafters failed to match the grueling pace, they were only too ready to encourage the unfortunate to greater effort. Without sunlight, there was no way to gauge the passing of time, but it must have been hours when at last I stopped, done in and gasping for breath. One of the drivers—they were anonymous in their expressionless uniformity—swung back to administer a dose of leather encouragement.

The women who had imprisoned me here had not counted on one thing. They were themselves mantics (I had long since figured that out) who had lived sheltered and relatively luxurious lives. I was an outlaw who in real life had been imprisoned and brutalized in ways that their feeble imaginations could not begin to visualize. Once I had been a victim; I would be victimized no more. I marshalled any powers as the gray driver stepped toward me, it exploded, its showering pieces dissolving into the gray specks of the substance of the overmind. Obeying their mistresses' shocked impulses, the other drivers and the drafters cowered away, aghast.

Reaching into the deep primitive rage that had been released by the maltreatment I had suffered, I chose the form most congenial to me and to this arctic waste—a lean, scarred, hungry-eyed wolf bitch. Shifting my seeming, I dropped to my four paws, shaking off the human-shaped harness. When one of the drivers, staggering back, would have swung its whip at my stalking form, I launched myself with all my fury at it, tearing out its insubstantial throat. Bitter, smoking blood flooded my mouth. There was a thin scream as the being floundered, and through the red raging bloodlust came the knowledge that this construct, unlike the other, contained the essence of a living human being.

Appalled, I stood over the rapidly expiring body, its rank blood dripping from my jaws. I had never killed before, not a human being. I shifted shape again, to my natural form, and seized the ends of the spouting blood vessels. "To your own body—quickly!" I said. The construct rolled its eyes, blank with panic, at me. Then another will joined mine. The human essence within the driver's body was gone. The construct flickered and dissolved and I was holding nothing. I thought that the essence had probably reached its own body, with my help and that of the quick-thinking other.

I leaped to my feet, to meet another heavy blow across the face. Another and another forced me back staggering, off balance, my ears ringing. From another driver came the lash of the whip, back and arms, ribs, back again. I stumbled and fell into the snow, where an implacable will pinioned me. I struggled to shift my shape, but the will opposed me; I could not. The lash fell again and again, confusing me, and the red blood that stained the snow was mine. They meant to kill me, I realized muzzily as a series of heavy kicks jolted my body. They meant to beat me to death. I had proven that I was stronger than they had expected, and worse yet, I had shown mercy to one of them where they had intended to offer me none. I covered my head with my hands and concentrated desperately, with all my will, on maintaining the viability of the overmind-body in which I was trapped. As the kicks crushed my ribs, I mended them. As my precious warm blood leaked away into the cold snow, I formed more, and as my skin, macerated with whips, burst and parted, I patched it.

My opponents couldn't prevent these measures. At last they seemed to realize it, for there was a growled conference over my huddled form, while I took advantage of the respite to heal ruptured internal organs and cough up a quantity of blood that had pooled within my lungs.

There had been no sound for a time, no movement or indication of life. I struggled to lift myself out of the snow and look around me. There was nothing and no one but the snow and the gray sky. Even as I looked around, a fog began to form and drift in skeins and banks around me. Soon I could see no more than a yard or two, and I understood what my fate was to be. My enemies were not strong enough to kill me by assault. They would take the easier way and let me die of exposure, alone in this hostile universe.

For a while I despaired and sank back into the snow, yielding myself to the cold. I was at the end of my strength and almost at the end of my will to survive. I had little to live for; death would seem an easeful rest to my lonely spirit.

But I would not die to suit my enemies! There had to be a way out. With a terrible effort, wracked with pain, I struggled to my feet and looked about me. There—that way, perhaps. It was as good as any other. I lurched forward, seeking with my mind for some clue to help me back to the real world of warmth and light and life. There was nothing. If there were any clues, I was blind to them. Cruelly, I forced my body onward, step by painful step, as hours passed and I seemed to make no headway against the vastness of this hostile universe. My remaining clothes were shredded and useless against the cold of this place; I looked down and saw that I was leaving bloody footprints and that my fingers were blackened and swelling.

There was something—marks in the snow ahead—obscured by the drifting fog, then revealed. Footprints— bloody footprints! Was there another hapless wanderer here? I wavered as I stood staring down at the marks, and shifted my feet to keep from tumbling into the snow. If once I fell, I would not get up again, I knew. The motion left one of my footprints beside the new one: They matched, and I knew I had been driving myself in a circle. I groaned aloud and sank to my knees.

They would win, I thought. My enemies would know that my essence had died here and in a day or two my body would die too. The life was seeping out of me along with the warmth, and the pain was going with them. There were things I had left undone that would never be completed, an oath I had broken that would never be redeemed, and I cried aloud with pity and terror, "Taharka! Taharka!" I would have liked to bid him good-bye . . .

Like a giant rising sun on a far horizon, Taharka's presence came bursting into the overmind—not his essence, for he was not here, but his will and his strength. I felt his call vibrating in my bones, not the little bones of the ear, but the long bones of the arms and legs, and the skull and backbone, resonating with his wordless summons. Joyfully I bounded to my feet, ignoring the renewed pain, and fled toward the beacon that he provided, spending the last dregs of my strength lavishly in full faith that from his boundless store mine would be replenished.

The snowy plain sped beneath my feet, and the wind of my passage ripped and shredded the fog that had blinded me. I didn't need to see the beacon that was Taharka; I could feel the warmth of him shining on my face. Death and fear and pain were vanquished as I sensed the nearness of my own corporeal envelope. I slipped back into it, glad of the wrenching and the nausea of such transitions—the dead don't feel sick to their stomachs.

"That blanket give me. Hurry up, damn it, she's still cold." I heard Taharka's booming voice—no, I felt it. He was very close. There was a fire near me, radiating a glowing heat, and I was holding so tightly onto my lifeline to the real world that my fingers were cramped into place. I dared not let go.

"Taharka," I said. I wanted to ask him to stay with me. In him alone was my safety. But my throat closed up with fear.

"Here I am, my love. Safe with me you are," he soothed.

Whatever I was lying against moved and heaved. I opened my eyes to find that I was lying in Taharka's arms, covered by several blankets, and the warmth I felt was radiating from his body. "Taharka," I begged, clutching at his tunic, in which my fingers were entwined. "Don't leave me. Please stay with me."

"Stay with you I will. Be easy, my love. Keep you safe and warm I will."

I couldn't convince myself that he would stay, that this was not just another cruel trick. I had to make him understand how important it was that he not let me slip back into the frozen trap he had drawn me out of. "I would have died if you hadn't called me," I choked. "Please don't let me slide back."

"No, I won't. As long as you need me, stay with you I will. And if," he said menacingly, "I find out who has done this to you, an accounting there will be."

"The mantics," I said feebly, catching my breath in a sob. "It was a trick. The messenger was a construct out of the overmind, and when it touched me, I was trapped. Oh, Taharka, it was so cold. I thought I was going to die." I was shivering violently now. "They hurt me so much, and I didn't know the way out. You saved my life."

"I know, my heart. Hush, my love, my sweetness, hush. Rest here. With me are you safe." He was stroking the back of my neck in a steady, soothing rhythm. "I won't let them hurt you again. Rest, my wild little love, be easy." His voice was as gentle as his touch, and I found that my frozen muscles were relaxing inch by inch under his hypnotic treatment.

I sighed tremulously. I was fast slipping into a healing sleep, but I remembered that I was not the only one in danger. The mantics might well choose to strike at Taharka next, and he had no defenses against the deadly perils of the overmind. I roused myself enough to warn him. "Taharka," I said urgently, "you must not let anyone touch you. If you do find yourself trapped in the overmind, stay alive and wait for me to come after you. Time passes differently there than here and it may seem a very long time. But I will come. Do you understand?"

"I understand," he said patiently. "Rest now you must. Cold as the dead you are still."

"Please, Taharka, please believe me. The danger is real and deadly."

"Believe you I do. Is it not I who held you helplessly while wounds and welts and bruises appeared upon your body? Once—once your ribs crack, I heard. And there was nothing I could do to stop whatever was hurting you while you grew colder and colder until dead I thought you were." He shuddered.

"You called me and showed me the way out. You saved

my life," I told him, nestling closer to his comforting warmth.

He took a deep breath, heaving me like a small boat on a great ocean roller. "Glad am I. Rest a bit, my love. Guard you while you sleep I will, nor will I let anyone touch either of us."

Hours later, I woke in a panic. "Taharka!" I cried.

"Here am I," he said in my ear. "Holding you I am."

I opened my eyes, to find that I was still clutching his linen tunic. The fabric was crushed and crumpled by my spasmodic grip. I had to will each finger to relax so that I could let go. I floundered feebly, trying to rise, and Taharka's strong arms lifted me to a sitting position and steadied me. I hurt all over, but at least I was warm.

"Better are you?" he asked.

"Oh, yes," I said.

"Then your injuries we should treat," he said.

"Overmind injuries heal very rapidly," I told him. "They haven't really happened to the physical body, you see. They're just the stigmata of happenings in the overmind."

He looked at me doubtfully. "Perhaps, but injured you are. Look." He lifted me up so I could see myself in the mirror—we were, I discovered, in the mantic's bedroom.

I gasped. I was a gruesome sight. My brand-new linen shirt was a ruin, stuck to a myriad of wounds with crusted blood. My face was a mass of bruises, still purple and black. My hands were swollen and the cracked skin was peeling away from the fingers. From the throbbing of my feet, I could tell they were in like state. I was indeed mending rapidly, but I still had an enormous amount of healing to do. "Ugh!" I exclaimed. "How can you stand to look at me?"

"Wounds I see, and my wife I see. The wounds are not the wife. Your slaves have I had brought up from the surgery, and here are hot water and clean cloths."

I tried to pull my shirt away from one of the cuts left by the driver's whips and yelped as the material pulled away the crusted blood. "Wait," said Taharka. "Soak the shirt free with hot water I will."

He helped me to a stool, dipped a cloth in the hot water

and set to work. I gasped with pain and then, remembering that he had made no fuss when I had sewed him up, bit my lip. Wound by wound, he dabbed away the blood and peeled the cloth gently back from the macerated skin. I heard a rip as he split the shirt down the back for greater ease in removing it. "My new shirt!" I mourned.

"Another shirt you can have," he said with a little amusement in his voice. "No use to you would this one ever have been anyway. What salve should I put on these cuts and welts?"

"Comfrey and goldenseal. There, in the white jar."

He pulled one half of my shirt free and tossed it aside. The other followed it. "Untie this I must," he said uncertainly. He was referring to the band that supported my breasts.

"I will—ah!" The exclamation was wrenched from me when I tried to use my split and swollen fingers. "I'm going to need salve on my hands and feet. You'll have to unlace this, I'm afraid."

Taharka moved around in front of me and fumbled at the lacings. His hands were trembling, I noticed with surprise. Having to undress me must be embarrassing him. "Does it really have to come off?" I asked, hoping to spare him having to remove it.

"Caked with blood it is in the back. Move it to clean some of the cuts I must."

"If it makes you uncomfortable, we could have Tildis do it."

He glanced up and grinned wryly. "Uncomfortable it does not make me. But never before have I been permitted to touch your naked flesh. Having a little difficulty keeping my mind on what I'm supposed to be doing, I am."

"Oh," I said foolishly. I didn't find it stimulating to touch my patients' bare skin in the course of my duties as healer, but Taharka was not a healer. When he got the lacings undone and the band came away, he moved immediately to my back again and began spreading the healing salve on the wounds. "Use it sparingly," I instructed. "Those aren't real wounds, and I don't know when I'll be able to get more goldenseal."

"Real wounds they look like to me, and many real wounds have I seen in my life."

"By tomorrow they'll be healed up and fading, as if they were weeks old, and the bruises will be nearly gone."

"Perhaps. Closed already, they are. Can you lie back so that your trousers I can remove?"

"I'm not hurt under there."

"Easy it is to check and make sure, and you will not wish to sleep in them in any case."

I lay back obediently under his gently urging hand, and he undid the waistband of my trousers and worked them carefully over my apparently frostbitten feet. He salved the feet, then pulled up my covers and tucked them neatly around me. "Your supper I will bring to you," he said kindly. "Rest now." He bent over me and kissed me, and still half under the spell of his gentleness, I lifted my lips to his. He lingered over the kiss, cupping my bruised face in his hands, and when at last he broke away, he was breathing heavily.

How unlike himself he was tonight! He had dealt with my battered body as gently as a woman. No barbarian I had ever heard of would have performed the menial services he had cheerfully done for me. Why, even his voice had been quiet, and his movements, usually so energetic, had been as slow and sure as a skilled trainer moving around a wild colt. I concluded, again, that my education on the ways of barbarians had been woefully incomplete.

He was back with a tray holding a bowl of broth, which he fed me, spoonful by spoonful. The broth finished, he put the bowl aside. Calmly, he began to prepare for bed, removing his gaiters and changing his tunic for a lighter one he brought from his bedroom. "Make you some of that bitter stuff you gave me, shall I?" he asked, yawning.

"I'm not in pain anymore, thank you," I said, watching him apprehensively.

"You just don't like the medicine," he chuckled, blowing out the lamp. He slipped into the bed beside me, settling himself down in the darkness and pulling up the covers over both of us. "Warm enough, are you?" he asked, straightening the blanket. "What's the matter? Shivering you are."

"Nothing," I said.

"Frightened you need not be. Here I will stay all night, and if anyone tries to harm you, my dirk I have ready to hand."

I laughed a little. "With such a guardian who wouldn't feel safe?" I eased over closer to him and laid my face against his left arm trustingly.

CHAPTER 10

TAHARKA Was amazed at the amount of healing that had taken place overnight. The wounds my physical body had sustained from mistreatment in the overmind were as healed as real wounds would have been after a couple of weeks of care. Even the pseudofrostbite on my hands and feet was nearly gone and I had full use of all my limbs.

"I want to take your stitches out today," I told him. "I'm likely to be too busy for the next few days, and I'm sure they're ready to come out. Let me look."

"Busy doing what are you going to be?" he inquired as he pulled off his tunic and turned his back.

I felt my face set grimly. "The mantics have got to be taught that I'm no hedge-witch, but a wielder of power and mistress of the overmind."

Taharka wheeled to face me, jerking the half-undone bandages out from under my hands. "Going back to attack them you are not!" he asserted. It had the tone of a command.

"Yes, I am," I said reasonably. "I have to."

"They nearly killed you. Permit you to take such risks I shall not."

I let one eyebrow drift upward. "There is no choice," I pointed out. "We aren't well accepted by the other mantics and margraves. They don't have to like us, but they do have to respect us. I shall go into the overmind—on my own terms this time—and make them wish they had never thought of setting their treacherous little trap."

Taharka folded his arms across his bare chest. "No," he said uncompromisingly. "Too dangerous it is."

I looked at him, baffled by his attitude. Of all men, he should understand why I must establish myself as an equal among my peers. "Taharka, if the margraves had set an ambush for you, you'd be the first to be battering at their gates and demanding satisfaction. If I seem now to be beaten, neither of us will ever be safe from the mantics again."

Taharka shook his shaggy head like a baited bear. "My wife you are. You shall not, say I, and obeyed will I be. I will protect and revenge you."

"Against physical attack, possibly. But I'm a sorceress. It's my place to protect you and myself from magical assaults. You haven't the weapons. Would I demand to go into battle with you?"

"Surprised I would not be," he replied dryly.

I sighed. "Surely you must see how necessary it is for me to establish myself as worthy of respect among the mantics. I don't want to fight with you. In fact, I was counting on you to lend me your strength and to guard my body until I returned to it. If I must, I'll face the mantics alone—but it'll be twice as hard and three times as dangerous."

Taharka looked at me, taking a deep breath. He seemed to swell a little, as if bristling. Then he hesitated. Turning away from me, he stared down into the courtyard. I waited quietly. This was a pivotal point in our history. Was he so unable to admit that he was wrong that he would jeopardize our whole position rather than concede the issue? If that were so, I would do as I had said—and be gone within the day. I would go back to my deserts, I told myself. Why had I ever left that wilderness that I loved and understood? I could live as I had before, wildcrafting and selling my botanicals in the Republics, perhaps through an intermediary.

He turned back to me. "Lady Mantic," he said stiffly, "you have the right of it. Your pardon I beg. Protect you I would. But I cannot, no more than from the stroke of a sword can you protect me." It was clear that every word hurt him to say.

Without answering I went to him and put my arms around him. Once again, he had shown himself to be more adaptable than I would have suspected him of being.

After breakfast, I removed the stitches from Taharka's in-

juries. Then we returned to my bedroom. I instructed Taharka carefully in his role. Then we lay down side by side
and I took his hand.

I slipped into the formless grayness of the overmind and
began shaping it to the likeness of one of my favorite places,
a mountain meadow beside a swift-running stream. The
peaks towered above, the summer flowers nodded among
the rich grasses. A crisp breeze made the giant pines roar
like some soft and distant surf. A campfire burned at the
focus of a cozy camp. Horses grazed in the meadow, my
faithful Whiskers and Socks, the packhorse I had once
owned.

Then I sent forth a summons. "Cowards! Meet me here if
you dare, in the seeming of your natural form. Meet me in a
contest of wills, to determine fairly and honorably who is the
stronger!" This message I sent forth to the mantics who had
attacked me. Their names I did not know, nor their castella,
but the "flavor" of their essences I knew, and to each appeared a ghostly simulacrum of myself. The specter spoke
those words—spoke them loud and clear, too, so that their
margraves and their whole castella knew they had been challenged. Making a simulacrum of the overmind-stuff that will
appear to those residing in the real world is simple. Making
the insubstantial thing speak, without lungs or voice box or
the ability to control the flow of air, is another matter entirely and requires a master's strength and control.

They came, but not in their natural forms. They burst into
my little universe as a variety of monsters: a dragon, breathing fire; a shambling giant, reaching for me with hands that
could have twisted me into two halves; a coldly beautiful
witch-queen, wielding a wand; and a hybrid monster of hideousness, fanged and clawed, pelted and red-eyed, that
walked upright like a human being.

I laughed as the dragon-fire washed about me, leaving me
untouched. I had suspected that these mantics wouldn't deal
with me honorably. I spoke four words of shaping; the
dragon shrank into a little scuttling lizard, the giant became
a toddling girl-child, the witch-queen aged in the passage of
seconds into a feeble old lady, and the hybrid became a tumbling cub, half bear, half child.

I formed an ornate little cage, caught the stunned lizard, and put it into it. The bars were shimmering force—that mantic would have much to do to escape. The toddler I popped into a shady crib and gave her a bottle of warm milk. The palsied oldster I soliticiously helped into a rocking chair and tucked a shawl around—a shawl that clung tenaciously to itself. The squalling cub I dropped into a hollow stump with a bit of sugar candy.

Separated, the four mantics flailed for a few moments in useless attempts to escape. I brought the old lady a cup of sweet tea. "Here, granny," I said kindly. "This will make you feel better. Don't upset yourself; you know it's bad for your heart."

The lizard, thinking that my back was turned (though vision in the overmind depends not upon the way the eyes are turned, but on the way the attention is directed), was trying to swell itself up to dragon size. I quelled its efforts without looking around, then stepped up to the cage with a tasty fly, which I held out. "Are you hungry, little pet?" I cooed.

Lizard reflexes took over—or at least the mantic's thinking that she should have lizard reflexes—and the little creature snapped up the fly. Then it gagged and flushed a bilious green color all over.

I waited a while longer, alert for any attempts to manipulate my universe. In their places, I could have thought of a dozen stratagems, but I had carefully avoided frightening or hurting them. I had no wish to provoke an all-out war, but wanted merely to convince them that it was far safer to leave me and mine alone. "Well, ladies," I said, at last, "you seem content enough with your new shapes. I can give you the seeming of these shapes in the real world for a few days, if you like. Or we can talk about being good neighbors."

The hag dropped her untasted cup. The toddler began to cry—not a baby's squalls but an adult's slow tears of humiliation and frustration. "Let me out," came a muffled voice from the stump. "If you will permit, I will assume the seeming of my true shape."

I reached into the stump and extricated the cub. When I put it down, it grew rapidly into a middle-aged woman, short and a little stout, with hair dyed an unfortunate rusty hue. "You do indeed have some of a mantic's powers," the woman said grudgingly. "But you can't foretell the future."

"No," I said boldly, "and neither can you. But I can defend myself and my margrave. I will, if attacked again. You and your friends tried to kill me; I shall consider that sufficient justification to destroy you if I have to."

"We meant you no harm," the woman said sullenly. "We intended to scare you away. You are no true mantic. You shouldn't even be allowed to own a horse."

"Ah. The Bearsnake Mantic, if I'm not mistaken," I said.

The woman nodded. "Will you let the others resume their true seemings?"

I bowed courteously. The cage dissolved around the lizard and the crib from the toddler, while the shawl around the old lady relaxed its cozy—but unbreakable—embrace. The lizard revealed itself to be an older woman with a weak, trembling chin. The toddler was younger, a plainfaced girl with watery blue eyes. The grandmother reverted back to the coldly beautiful woman she had been, though I noticed that crown and wand were gone. But if this were a true seeming she was indeed a beautiful woman, flawless in feature and coloring, slender and yet voluptuous.

"The Silvercat Mantic is right," said the beautiful woman, in a voice like ringing ice. "It was we who attacked her and she's justified in defending herself. She has dealt more gently with us than I expected."

I glanced warily at her. I trusted her not one bit.

"She is not a true mantic," insisted the Bearsnake Mantic. "She isn't even remotely related to any of the old families. And that—that savage she's taken for her margrave..." Words failed her.

"That 'savage' is a brave man and a war leader of renown in his own land," I retorted. "Furthermore, he's both honorable and responsible."

"You defend him hotly enough," sneered the ex-lizard, "yet rumor has it that you rule him like a pet dog, not even admitting him to your bed."

There was a sudden rain of green sparks, much larger and more obvious here in the overmind. "Rumor lies," I said flatly. I caught each one's eyes, daring them to say more. None cared to take up the challenge.

The witch-queen watched the sparks coldly. "A wielder of power as well as an adept in the overmind, it seems," she observed. "Sisters, we've overmatched ourselves. Only one of the sorcerers from the Lakes could hope to overcome her."

"We can't afford a sorcerer's fee," protested the youngest mantic.

"Then I suggest that we make our peace with her. Sister," she said to me, "there will be a party at my castellum, the Bluegriffin, in a few weeks. May I send you and your honored margrave an invitation?"

I gave another courtly bow (copied from Taharka). "I'll be pleased to receive an invitation. In accordance with the customs of my people and my husband's, I will of course have to consult with him before I can promise to accept it." I made a mental note not to eat or drink anything if we did go.

"As you wish," the Bluegriffin Mantic said. "We will return to our physical forms now, if you will permit. Will you leave this universe in existence?"

"For a time," I said. "It provides a meeting place."

"May I visit it, then? It's very pleasant here. I didn't know that the overmind could be used to make beautiful places as well as fearful and dangerous ones."

With a gesture, I made her free of the place, wondering at the limitations of their understanding of the overmind. In the Kingdom, many adolescents discover the overmind on their own, and construct their own private retreats. It's a dangerous practice and not one to be encouraged, as untrained minds can easily become lost, but as long as teenagers feel helpless and frightened by the real world, the practice will continue.

My antagonists melted away, and I waited for a time to be sure that no treachery was contemplated. Then I slipped back into my physical body, following the tenuous thread of contact that I had maintained.

When I opened my corporeal eyes, Taharka was leaning on one elbow, watching me anxiously. "No marks I saw upon you this time," he said.

I chuckled. "I was ready for them, and we met upon my ground, not theirs. They aren't really very knowledgeable about the overmind. I'd say that the most they use it for is to make simulacra for their fortune-telling tricks." I told him what had happened.

He shook his head. "Hate us worse than ever now, they will. Oh, the right thing you did. We can't have them casting their spells at us. But secure in the Silvercat we will never be."

"Maybe we should leave," I suggested lazily. I was feeling no impulse to move away from his comforting presence.

"Where would we go?"

"I'd like to go home to the desert. There are no traps there. The desert is a home and a provider for those who understand it." I told him about the sun-washed distances, the tiny paradises of watered canyons, the shy folk, the sudden summer thunderstorms.

He listened to me in silence. Then he reached out and smoothed my tousled short hair. "Leave me then, would you?" He asked with such poignant sadness that I reached out and gathered him to me.

"Of course not!" I cried indignantly (and not very truthfully). "I meant for us to go there together." He came willingly into my arms, nestling his massive head against my breast.

"Forgive me, fooled was I when you spoke so longingly of the solitude and quiet of your desert. Often and often have I seen in your eye the look of one who longs to escape. Trust you I must, for I so swore, yet I dream of wakening to find you gone."

I started guiltily. I hadn't been aware that my occasional attacks of nostalgia for the freedom I had enjoyed all my life were obvious enough to be noticed. Not at least by a—a barbarian? A realization hit me like a flash of lightning. It takes more than neat barbering and conventional clothing to make a civilized man. Taharka, no matter how untamed he looked, nor how loud he roared, was a gentleman. He was kind, and sensible, and honorable, and even if not quite in the fashion to which I was accustomed, cultured. "I give you my word," I said very clearly, "never to leave you without discussing my intention with you and explaining my reasons."

Taharka raised himself enough to look me in the face. "My love, rather would I have your promise never to leave me at all. Yet if you must go, then hold you against your inclination I will not. Follow you instead I shall, wherever you go."

"I don't have any intention of leaving just now." I tugged gently to invite him back into my arms, but this time instead of coming easily, he pulled away a little.

"Don't tease me beyond endurance, my love, for very greatly do I desire you. If you do not intend to accept me as your husband now, cruel it is to take me so lovingly into your arms."

I blushed scarlet. "Oh!" I said in confusion. "I forgot!" I frowned. "But it's the middle of the morning!"

Taharka gave me an exasperated look. "I suspected that thought of that you had not," he said obscurely, kissed me briskly, and rose. I wanted to call him back and tell him that I was willing to accept him, but while I trembled in indecision, he went out the door. I thought he paused for a moment before closing it. Perhaps he waited for the words I couldn't find to say.

The invitation from the Bluegriffin Mantic arrived the next day, brought by the Bluegriffin Margrave and another, who introduced himself to me as the Goldhawk Margrave. I assumed that he was the husband of the younger girl I had struggled with in the overmind, for he was not himself very old. Taharka made a courtly host, meeting the two margraves in the entrance hall, offering them lifewater, which choked them. He studied their attire and bearing carefully.

I had been puzzling over the wording of the invitation. "Bluegriffin bids Silvercat. Full, accommodation. Response."

"What do you make of this?" I asked, handing Taharka the terse note, once the margraves had left upon their old horses.

He looked at it. "Read I cannot," he said quietly, handing it back. "A skill unknown in my homeland it is. Rememberers have we, to hold the genealogies and records of our folk."

I looked at him in shock. A people without writing— without books! Just when I had begun to think that he was a civilized man, this persuasive evidence of benighted barbarity must crop up! I had thought him a gentleman, a kind man, an admirable one; to discover that he was illiterate was almost a betrayal.

I must have been staring accusingly at him; a dull red flush began to climb into view from beneath his beard. "Rememberer am I," he said defiantly. "If you wish me to remember something for you, to tell it to me once only is necessary. Lose it I shall not, as that little piece of paper may be lost."

"But . . . but to have no books . . ." I stuttered tactlessly. "No histories, no works of philosophy or medicine or natural science, no stories to pass an idle hour: how bleak your life must have been!"

"History have we, and stories. After the evening meal I will tell one."

Taharka and I went up to my office, where I read him the note. "Clear enough is the first part," he commented, "but understand what is full I do not, nor whether accommodations are being offered us or whether we are being warned to seek our own accommodations."

"The message was sent this way deliberately," I said. "I suppose one of them would have understood it perfectly. There are so few inhabited castella that all the mantics and margraves must know each other intimately. This was sent in this form to make sure that we know that we're still outsiders, tolerated but not welcome."

"Then to Bluegriffin let us ride, to pay a visit and explain that come we shall not, and to let them know that their treachery we do not fear. Besides, a surprise visit will keep them from conspiring to do us harm. I trust them not."

"Me either. How far is Bluegriffin?"

"Ten miles, perhaps. Runa, my love . . ." He hesitated uncertainly.

"Yes?"

"Neither of the margraves were bearded, and they wore

their hair cropped. Shave my beard and crop my hair should I, do you think? Easier to accept us they may find it if we look more like them."

"Don't you dare!" I said fiercely. "It's your head and your face and you'll wear it to suit yourself, not those sniveling horse-beaters."

He laughed a little. "A firebrand have I wed," he said. "But so attached to my beard I am not. Less repulsive would you find me if I were shaven and cropped?"

"I don't find you repulsive. What kind of a wife would I be if I started dictating to you how you should wear your hair? You don't try to tell me how to wear mine."

"About to ask you to let your hair grow long, I was. Among my folk, cropped hair in a woman is a sign of widowhood. Uneasy it makes me."

I considered. "That seems a reasonable enough request. Many women among my people wear their hair long, too. I cut mine because it was more comfortable and easier to care for when traveling in the desert. I'll let it grow."

"Thank you, my love. Think it an unreasonable request if you asked me to shave my beard and cut my hair I would not either, since here the custom is for smooth faces and short hair and since the custom among your own folk is the same."

"I can't imagine you shaven," I said. "You'll have to consult your own comfort and do as you think best."

"A hard woman you are," he said.

That evening, when we had finished our supper, Taharka pushed aside the empty plates. The northerners clearly knew that he was about to perform, for they gathered around. The tiller folk looked up curiously.

"Attend!" Taharka commanded. Falling into a resonant, carrying voice, he told a story.

A chieftain of a small manor had a son to be proud of, tall, handsome, a fearsome warrior and a cunning hunter. The chieftain had only the one child, for he had come into his inheritance late and unexpectedly. When a daughter had been born to his wife the year after the son was born, he had taken the child into the forest to expose it. But the chieftain had a bitter enemy who was determined to do him great harm. From spies he kept in the chieftain's manor, this man knew that the chieftain's wife was pregnant. When the chieftain had sorrowfully left the newborn girl to die, his enemy took up the infant, wrapping it in his cloak and carrying it to his farm, where it was raised. The chieftain's wife died of mourning for her lost daughter.

The little girl grew up as beautiful and as brave as her brother, and when she reached a marriageable age, the cunning enemy approached the children's father, now a powerful king, and proposed to him that the enmity between them be forgotten and a new friendship sealed by the marriage of "his" beautiful and gentle daughter and the king's handsome son. As an added inducement, he offered a dowry that beggared him. The king took this for a sign of his sincerity and accepted.

The bridal pair loved each other at once, and the marriage was a miracle of happiness. In the fullness of time, the marriage was fruitful of three fine sons as like their father as if they had all been copied by a master craftsman from the same template, and a daughter as like to her mother as one star is to another. So rich were they that they were able to keep the little girl, and they rejoiced in her.

Then, in the very bloom of their happiness, the crafty plotter appeared in their banquet hall and told the horrified assembly what he had done. He laughed and laughed, while the family and their guests stared in shock, nor did he quit laughing until the king snatched the carving knife from the table and struck him dead with it.

With the plotter dead, every eye turned

upon the king's son. No word was spoken, but his sister-wife screamed until blood burst from her mouth. All there knew the law. The four pretty children, the bright and promising boys, so like their father, and the lovely little girl, must die. They were the product of incest, and in a society where there was never enough for all the children to be allowed to live, the tainted offspring of such an unnatural union must die.

Pale as death, the father held out his hand, and the king laid the carving knife in it, his old eyes blinded with tears. The father called the eldest boy to him, and the child came trustingly. He kissed and hugged the boy one last time, then, as deftly as a butcher with a lamb, plunged the knife into his heart. Laying the body tenderly aside, he called the second boy to him. The child was frightened, and would not come. His mother stepped from her place, took his hand, and led him to his father. The execution proceeded as before. The youngest boy was too terrified and stunned with shock to resist; he too went to his death. But the little girl cried and begged her father to be allowed to live, promising over and over never to be naughty again, if only her daddy would not kill her. The father was choked with his terrible grief, and trembling so that he could hardly wield his knife. But for the child's sake, so that she should not suffer, he steadied himself and stabbed her cleanly to the heart.

Last came his sister, polluted by her brother's embrace, cursed by the bearing of kin-children. She knelt before him, and he kissed her upon the lips and slew her.

The four children and the beautiful cold corpse of their mother were laid out as for a splendid funeral. Every guest there stripped himself of possessions to provide grave-goods for the pathetic family, while the bereaved husband and father stood at their heads, as still and cold-faced as a carving of ice; hot tears ran down his cheeks without stopping.

When the bodies had been laid in their barrow, with a store of grave-goods that would have been the pride of a dozen kings, the father turned and walked away, unarmed, dressed still in his bloody feasting clothes, into the forest. No one ever spoke to him again, though hunters would say they had seen him, wandering still in the rags of his festive dress, his mind crushed by the weight of the terrible deeds he had been forced to do. It would have been more merciful if he had died at once, but for many years after the old king died of grief, something seemed to protect him in his madness. Then no one saw him more.

Taharka told this story, with his grammatical inversions and musical vowel shift, with such throbbing happiness, such trenchant horror, such overwhelming sadness, that when his voice died away, I came to myself to find tears wetting my cheeks. A muffled sob beside me and a chorus of sighs reminded me that we were not alone. Gathered around us in the dining hall were most of the Silvercat folk, including Taharka's fellow countrymen, who were as teary as the rest of us, though they must have heard the story before.

"Books we have not," said Taharka. "But as you see, both history and stories do we have." He raised me to my feet and wiped away my tears tenderly.

"I certainly hope that was a story and not a true history," I said fervently.

"As history was it told to me," said Taharka. "Many and many a baby girl has that story saved, for fear of some similar happening."

"Surely your people don't—don't really cast out newborn baby girls to die!" I exclaimed.

Taharka's gaze fell. "There is never enough for the children who are allowed to live. Boys can be sent out to make their way in the world, as all of us were; outliers, such are called. But to send girls out is to make whores and worse out of them. The dowry that a girl must have to hope to marry would destroy any ordinary family. Only the rich can afford to raise and dower even one girl."

"That's terrible!"

"Yes. Cause for much grief and very great sorrow it is. Never enough girls are there for even the men who have lands and manors to marry, much less such as we. The girls we do have are much loved and sought after. Our wives we cherish and protect, and those who do marry, marry for life. No second chance is there. And the parents who must sacrifice their daughter for the sake of their other children—it is said that the memory of the dead baby haunts them forevermore. That this is true, I have seen in the eyes of those to whom it has happened."

The people dispersed to their evening rest, subdued by the mood of the mournful tale.

CHAPTER
11

WE Were not received well at Bluegriffin. The margrave's horse had died, and from the consternation into which the whole castellum was thrown, you'd have thought it was one of the children. The Bluegriffin Mantic received us politely enough, if distractedly, accepted our regrets for the party with no sign of dismay, and begged me to sell her my extra horse, offering a fabulous price. I declined courteously.

As we rode for home, Taharka inquired, "Why did you refuse to sell her the mare? One friend among the old families we might have made."

"I need Biscuit, and anyway, these people don't know how to take proper care of a horse. The poor beast died of overwork and old age. He should have been out at pasture." I sighed. "I tell you, Taharka, it surely feels good to be out of the castellum. That place grows more and more prisonlike every day."

He looked at me keenly. "A rover's soul I fear you have. In your eye again is the look of one who would ride away and just keep going."

"I promised you I wouldn't."

"If your heart was fretted beyond endurance, keep you to your promise I would not."

"My heart isn't fretted beyond endurance. If I look wistful from time to time, well, so do you."

"I don't want to go back to a roving life I'm thankful to have a place in the world and a worthy job to do. With you lies the cure for my wistfulness. There is no cure for yours, I fear."

"Oh, Taharka, it's a glorious day for a ride. Let's not bicker. Let's have a gallop instead. Whiskers has been begging for a run all day."

For an answer he clapped heels to Butterfly's sides. The ponderous stallion leaped into a run, and Whiskers, indignant at being left behind, threw up his head and tail and bolted after them.

We were flying along the road, kicking up a fine welter of dust, when the arrows began to whistle out of a little patch of woods between the road and the river. A yelling clump of men spilled out of the trees. Butterfly was still in the lead; I had been holding Whiskers in a little so as not to pass him too easily. The stallion plowed right through the attackers. But they were ready for Whiskers, who shied as several of them grabbed for the bridle. Another dragged at me, and I kicked at him ineffectually. Whiskers bucked and sidled as one or two of them clung to his head, and I could feel myself sliding off into the attacker's grasp.

There was a familiar bellow and the attackers whirled to face Taharka's overwhelming charge. He rode Butterfly right into their midst and vaulted off, landing on his feet with his battle sword already whirring in an arc about his head. I caught only a glimpse of him as I lost my grip on Whiskers and subsided into the dust of the roadway.

The fellow who had brought me down grinned triumphantly and raised his sword. I gasped; there was nothing to stop him bringing it down upon me. I hadn't had time to gather enough power to form a weapon. I had a little energy, which I flung at him, but though it stung him, it was not enough to slow the fall of his weapon.

A foot of bloody steel appeared in the midst of the man's shattered ribcage, and the triumph in his eyes was replaced with the blankness of death as he was hurled away by the force of the blow. Taharka straddled me protectively, still roaring, the huge battle sword swinging in its murderous circle. I cowered in the dust and closed my eyes, frantically gathering energy from the overmind. In these desperate circumstances, it wasn't long until I had enough for a deadly weapon, and I scrambled on hands and knees out from between Taharka's legs and under the swing of his weapon.

I looked about for the archers. They might stay out of the range of Taharka's deadly sword and bring him down, and in fact I saw one of them, arrow nocked, circling grimly around the edges of the fighting, waiting his chance for a clear shot. Even as I rose to my feet, he drew his bow and aimed, and I muttered a hasty word of sending and hurled the magical bolt at him.

I had never used one of these deadly bolts against a human being before. The man screamed as it struck him and ate into his flesh, and the arrow wobbled out of the bow. Green fire ran along his limbs, withering and blighting them. His chest seemed to implode. He was dead before his blasted remains struck the ground, and I was gathering up my energies and looking for another victim.

The attackers had apparently had enough. Six of their number lay dead, messily hacked about with Taharka's deadly weapon, and another gruesomely blasted by magic. There were a few seconds of uncertain milling about, and the remainder broke and fled along the road.

Taharka chased them a few steps, still roaring with blood-lust. Then he whirled and came trotting back to me. "Are you hurt?" I asked, simultaneously with his "Harm you, did that bastard?"

"No," I said, trembling in my boots. "What about you?"

"Not even nicked a little am I. Skewered I would have been, though, but for you. Small chance has a swordsman against an archer."

"If—if you hadn't come back—I thought I was dead." The trembling was accelerating into deep shudders. I thought I must slide back down into the dust of the road. Taharka hastily sheathed his sword and caught me.

"Where are you hurt?" he said sharply.

I shook my head helplessly. "Not—not hurt."

He scooped me up into his arms. "Away from this carrion we shall go," he said grimly. "For myself I must see if you are hurt. Shake like this when we attacked the cannibal camp you did not."

"I can walk," I managed to say between stiff lips. "Put me down. We have to catch the horses and get out of here before those assassins come back."

Taharka ignored me. He carried me briskly down the road, away from the bloody corpses (and the withered one) around which flies were already beginning to gather. I sighed and put my arms around his neck to ease the burden on his arms, which must have been tired from their exertions. That battle sword was no lightweight rapier.

Once around a bend and out of sight of the carnage, he put me down gently in the grass on the verge and began to examine my limbs for evidence of wounds. "Not wounded are you," he said, sitting back on his heels at last. "Is this caused by some magical attack?"

I shook my head. I was shaking worse than ever, and worse yet, nausea was rising in my throat. "I never ... I never killed ... anyone before," I managed to say, and turned away to vomit out my horror and revulsion. I sobbed hysterically between spasms, while Taharka held my head and murmured soothing nonsense.

When at last the fit had died down, he gathered me up again, moved me away from the mess, and fetched me water from the river to wash out my mouth. "Threw up did I too, when first I killed my man," he assured me solemnly.

I smiled wanly. "Oh, Taharka, what a clanker. You did no such thing."

"True it is, I did. Someday will we visit my father's manor and ask him you can. You'll have to wear a warrior's lock, when your hair grows long enough. A very fierce fighter you are, but glad I am that you're not entirely without a woman's softer feelings."

"I had to use magic," I told him. "There was no other way to stop him shooting you."

"Know it I do! I could feel that arrow between my ribs already."

"But ... but I didn't know ..." I faltered. "I didn't know what a terrible death that magic dealt."

"All death is terrible. Quick and clean your magic bolts are."

I shook my head. "I hope I never have to use them again, but if the same situation were to come up, I'd do the same thing. There are other kinds of magic weapons, but none so quick to shape."

"Do you feel better? We'd best get back to the castellum quickly. Safe out here it is not."

"I'm better. Whiskers won't be far off. He'll come when I call if he wasn't too badly frightened."

"Trained to stay nearby when his rider falls was Butterfly too. I hope he hasn't attacked your pony."

In fact we found the two of them grazing side by side not far up the road. Apparently Butterfly had decided that the company of a mere gelding was more tolerable than being alone with all these frightening events. Whiskers came trotting up good-naturedly when I called him, and Butterfly followed.

"I suspect that the mantics decided that if magical attack wouldn't get rid of us, maybe a little old-fashioned assassination would," I speculated as we rode back toward the castellum, keeping watch for more ambushes. "It would have the advantage of acquiring a couple of horses for them, too. They certainly do seem to be short of horses here. I wonder why they don't just buy some?"

"Not half so much would they mind us if we didn't have three healthy horses," agreed Taharka. "No traders of horses have I seen. Perhaps the plagues have disrupted business too badly to reach this remote spot."

"Horses seem to be awfully important to them, too, as if they don't feel that they are properly mantic and margrave unless they're mounted."

When we rode into the stableyard, Biscuit, who had objected noisily to her two stablemates leaving without her, squealed loudly. A tattoo of kicks thudded against the walls of her stall and her tail lashed nervously. Both Butterfly and Whiskers pricked their ears interestedly, and Butterfly whickered enticingly, giving Whiskers a sidelong wicked look of warning. "Oh dear," I said. "You'd better double-tie Butterfly. Biscuit's in season."

"Why?" asked Taharka. "Let him breed her we should. The foal could we trade."

"Certainly not!" I snapped. "He'd savage her."

Taharka sat on his restive stallion's back and stared at me. "A gentleman he is with his mares," he said at last. Another tattoo of louder kicks rang from Biscuit's stall. "The mare seems favorably inclined. Indeed, kick the stable down she will to get to him unless she's freed."

That was manifestly true. The walls were shuddering now. "Well . . ." I said uncertainly.

"Bring your mare out and hold her. Keep Butterfly's bridle in my hand I will. Then if you think he's hurting her, drag him away I can."

I snorted. "Drag away a stallion in the midst of breeding? Not likely."

"Obey me he will, even then."

Biscuit squealed again and squatted, lifting her tail shamelessly. I shut Whiskers firmly into his stall. Then I put Biscuit's halter on and led her out. Taharka had dismounted and removed his riding pad. Now he brought the stallion up to her flank, where a random kick wouldn't hit him.

Taharka had been right. Butterfly teased the mare gently, nuzzling her flanks and dock, nibbling along her neck, talking to her all the time in little reassuring whickers and grunts. In fact, the mare was more importunate than he was, backing into him, rubbing her hindquarters against him, and squealing. It seemed a very long time before he finally let down and mounted. Even then, though he gripped her neck with his teeth to hold himself in place, he didn't bite as some stallions do.

We put the horses away and went in to our much-needed baths. "A shame it is that it takes so long from breeding to a tradeable riding horse," commented Taharka.

"Yes," I said absently. The germ of an idea was beginning to form and I wanted to think about it.

I took an extra long time in my bath, mulling my idea over and examining it from all sides. I could see no flaw in it. Well, only one; Taharka might object. But surely he could be made to see the logic of it. He had proven amenable to reason before. I dressed with extra care, fluffing out my wet hair to dry with my fingers. I was looking a little haggard, I noted in the mirror, so I used a touch of the rouge Tildis had supplied me with, and chose a gown of a particularly becoming pale green. I had never dressed with a view to pleasing a man before; it was an interesting experience, and not unpleasant.

When I got to the sitting room, Taharka was not there waiting for me as he usually was. I went into my office and began making lists of things I would need to take with me. I was that certain of persuading Taharka to agree to my plan. I was just wondering whether he would lend me his stallion and be content to keep Whiskers for himself—a gelding was not the horse to have on such a trip—when I heard the sitting room door close behind him. I stacked the list of horse gear in the same pile as the list of supplies and the crude map I had drawn to refresh my own memory.

I walked through the door into the sitting room and stopped in my tracks. There was a stranger in the room, a man dressed in the shiny boots, crisp linen shirt, and tweed jacket and breeches that the margraves wore. He looked at me and smiled a little shyly; his cheeks were pale, as if he had been confined indoors for a long time. But what was he doing in our private sitting room, uninvited?

"Taharka!" I called sharply.

"Yes, my love?" said the stranger in Taharka's familiar voice.

I stared at him, my mouth open. "Taharka?" I gasped, when I got my breath back. I stepped a little closer and peered at him. "Is that you?"

"Myself it is, my love, and hard when a man's own wife recognizes him not."

"You look—you look absolutely magnificent," I blurted.

He gave me his courtly bow. "Fitting it is, for a man with such a lovely wife to look magnificent. If I had known that this reaction I would have gotten, shaved long ago I would have."

I was still staring at him. He was clean-shaven, and his hair was cut short and brushed across his forehead. The grizzled effect was much less noticeable; he seemed fairer, almost blond. Perhaps handsome was not the word to describe his face, which was rugged rather than prettily formed, but it was full of dignity and intelligence and kindliness—magnificent indeed. The clothes he was wearing were styled after those the margraves had worn, I could see, and in them he looked completely civilized. No one would take him for a barbarian now!

I felt a little shy of him. I had gotten used to the old hirsute Taharka; this man was still a stranger to me. He reminded me of the Exorcist who had tracked me down and would have hanged me. It was in the air of complete self-confidence and effortless power that the resemblance lay. Taharka, shaggy, might bluster and roar where Taharka, shorn, would act with speedy decisiveness.

He moved with what seemed to be pantherish suddenness to take my hand, and involuntarily I shied away. He stopped and looked at me. "Taharka am I. The loss of a little hair has not changed me, and freely have you given me your hand to lead you down to dinner for many days now." There was a touch of hurt in his voice.

"Of course," I said, blushing and holding out my hand to him. "I hardly feel that I know you."

He took my hand. "More attractive had I hoped you would find me," he said. "Very beautiful you are tonight." His voice was lower and a little husky. The look in his eyes was Taharka's, almost too intense to meet squarely.

"I . . . er, oh . . . thank you," I said, remembering that I had dressed with special care and why.

We caused a sensation when we entered into the dining hall arm in arm and took our places at the head table. During that meal I ate very little. I couldn't take my eyes off my transformed husband, and he, aware of my scrutiny, responded by devoting himself to me with pretty compliments and low-voiced conversation. Yet when we left to return to our quarters at the end of the meal, he was still strange to me. I almost wished he would bellow or grab me and plant a smacking kiss on my mouth. He neither looked nor acted like himself. It was only his voice that I could recognize.

In our sitting room, I put water on for tea, hoping that the familiar ritual would dispel the strangeness I felt. "Make some for me tonight, my love, if you will. Share your tea I would," said the stranger who had usurped Taharka's place and his voice.

"Of course," I said, startled. Taharka would drink the medicinal teas I gave him, but he had always refused to drink tea for the pleasure of it, preferring his fierce lifewater.

As I fussed uncertainly with cups and kettle, the stranger came up behind me. I quivered, wanting to whirl and back warily away, but knowing that such a reaction would hurt Taharka's feelings. I felt him touch the back of my neck, and

I flinched. "A husband's right it is, to give gifts to his wife," he said softly, and draped something that clattered around my throat. His fingers were busy at the back of my neck for a moment, and then dropped away, leaving a cold weight behind. "Even more beautiful you look," he said. "Come and see yourself." His tweed-clad arm steered me into my bedroom and in front of the mirror.

Around my neck was an elaborate necklace of amber, mounted in heavy gold. The metal was formed into the shape of bounding lions and deer, and the amber dripped off it like running honey. It was a treasure, rich and old and barbarically beautiful, and the soft green gown I wore could not have been better chosen as a background for it. I looked at the couple in the mirror. If I could not recognize Taharka in the elegant gentleman who stood with his arm protectively around his wife, no more could I recognize myself in the graceful, bejeweled lady who stood comfortably within his grasp. They were a handsome couple, those two. The lady in the glass raised her hand and touched the necklace admiringly. "It's very beautiful," she said, her red lips forming the words.

"Runa..." Taharka whispered. I turned to him, and he raised his hands to place them tenderly on either side of my face. I saw and felt with wonder that he was trembling. "Stay with you tonight, may I? Be a husband to you, may I?"

I could feel the blood drain out of my face and I swayed dizzily. Yet I did not pull away. Desperately I wanted to say yes, stay with me and tonight I will become a true wife to you. But though my lips moved, no sound emerged. "Savage you I will not," Taharka said wistfully. "A gentleman am I with my lady."

"I'm not afraid," I said, around the obstruction in my throat. "But... but Taharka, my dear... my dearest... I must tell you... I... I..." My throat closed up and I choked.

Gently he slipped his hands down to my waist and pulled me closer. "Tell me what, my love? So terrible that I will cease loving you it cannot be." Gently, he stroked my back.

"I must tell you that... that I've never... I haven't..."

"That have I known since the second day I knew you," he said with perfect composure.

The last time that fact had been discovered had been at my trial, and the courtroom had roared with laughter and sniggers. Even seven years later I could not remember it without a crimson wave of humiliation swamping me. "You . . . you don't think it's funny?"

"Certainly not. It is a sorrow for you, obviously. And very badly did I feel, that I frightened you so much when first I approached you. But a very great privilege it is to me, that I should be the one to teach you the ways of love. Will you trust me?"

"Yes," I gulped. "Please stay with me tonight, Taharka."

He sighed deeply. Turning up my face, he kissed me, long and searchingly, seeking and begging a response, and awkwardly I tried to respond. Being kissed by a man without a beard and mustache, I found, was much more comfortable that being kissed by one with those adornments. "Come," he said, "let us drink our tea. No hurry is there. The night is ours."

My hands were shaking as I poured the tea and carried it to him where he sat on the sofa. I gave him his cup and sat down uncertainly next to him, in the inviting curve of his arm. He snuggled me closer, and so we sat for a time, cosily sipping our tea. "What is to happen, I will tell you," Taharka said. "It is the unknown that frightens you." Quietly he talked to me, explaining step by step what he would do and what responses I could expect within myself and from him. I blushed often and hid my face in my cup, but I was grateful to him for his kindness. As he had foretold, much of my anxiety had been caused by ignorance, and as I understood the matter better, my trembling ceased and I relaxed softly against his side, willing to follow his lead.

Draining his cup, he put it aside, and taking mine, set it down also. Turning to me, he laid me across his lap and began to kiss my face and throat, while he gently touched me with his free hand, lightly at first on belly and hip, then firmly on breast and thigh. I stiffened when he began to take liberties that I had never permitted anyone before, but he had explained to me what he was doing and why, and he continued to tell me that most women liked to be touched so, and to ask me whether this caress or that felt more pleasant, and soon I was sighing and stirring beneath his hand and lips.

It was all so tenderly pleasant that I wanted to share the experience with him. I reached shyly up and began to stroke his jaw and ear and shoulder, about all I could reach of him, and he told me as I did how very nice it was to be touched, and guided me to more intimate caresses that I would never have thought of myself, not realizing that men found such things pleasurable. He seemed to find them pleasing, quivering and saying my name with such longing that I felt tears stinging the insides of my eyelids. It had never occurred to me that the greatest joy of love between man and wife would lie in the giving of pleasure.

At length he rose and drew me to my feet. "Ready now we are to move into the bedroom," he said, smiling tenderly at me. "Now, Runa, my love, don't jump so. You found what we did here pleasant, did you not?"

Blushing, I nodded. "A hundred times better will you find what follows. You have trusted me this far. Will you trust me a little farther?" I nodded again. He released me and walked alone to the door of my bedroom and opened it. "Then come, my love." I understood. He would force me to nothing. If I panicked now as I had before and refused to go farther, he would accept it—but how deeply he would be hurt! I went quickly across the floor to him, before my courage should fail.

In going to him, I went unsuspecting into great joy and found a comfort I had never thought to find. In becoming my lover as well as my husband, Taharka became also my dearest friend and companion.

CHAPTER
12

THE Next few days were so filled with Taharka and exploring the new sensations and feelings he had evoked that I thought little about my plan. In fact, I more or less forgot it until I began tidying my desk. Since my husband was illiterate, all the paperwork of the castellum fell to me, and I had neglected it recently. I was humming cheerfully, if not very tunefully, as I sorted and stacked, when I came across the lists of supplies and equipment and the crude map I had drawn. I stopped in midnote, my plan for integrating the two of us and the Silvercat firmly into the economic structure of the plains society recurring to me with twice its former persuasive force.

After dinner that night, as Taharka and I sat cosily together sipping tea, I broached the idea. "Taharka, dearest?"

"Mmmm?" he said lazily.

"I think I know how we can make ourselves so important to the mantics and margraves they'll never even think of attacking us again."

"Good hearing is that. What plan have you now?"

"Well, what the Burdened need the most—or think they need—is horses. They want young, strong horses. They don't care much about the quality of the animals, but they want them broken to ride. Correct?"

"True. But young, strong horses, broken to ride, have we none to spare them. Biscuit, especially now that in foal she is, you won't wish to sell."

"No. But I know where there are hundreds of wild horses, free for the catching."

There was a long silence. Illiterate he might be, but my husband was not stupid. "Then why are these horses not caught?" he asked suspiciously.

"They're in an isolated place in rugged terrain, and there are a few small difficulties that tend to discourage ordinary horse-hunters but needn't concern a wielder of power very much."

He sighed. "Where are these horses? Back in your own land?"

"No, the Kingdom's too far away. It took me two years to ride this far. It must be three thousand miles or more. These horses are only five hundred miles or so."

"A mere holiday outing. Tell me."

"After I left the ox-nomads, I rode more or less due east for a long time, and came to a range of low hills. They were very dry and the ox-nomads had warned me not to try to ride across them, so I veered north. I came to a land inhabited by a race of peaceful savages who lived in roving family bands, living on what meat the men could kill and roots and fruits the women could gather. Often such primitive peoples are infested with various supernatural predators and parasites, since they're easy prey as they go about their food-gathering, and these people were no exception. I found and cleaned out several nests of night stalkers myself, and killed a couple of rock ogres."

Taharka pulled me closer. "To think of you exposing yourself to such dangers makes my heart cold. Before I ever met you, you might have been killed."

I chuckled fondly. "Then you never would have known you hadn't met me. Besides, I wasn't in any danger. You keep forgetting that I'm not helpless."

"Forget it I do not," he claimed. "That I could forget it I wish. Frightening it is, being married to a wild witch. Is it these poor people who have the horses?"

"No, the horses don't belong to anyone. There are bad-lands to the north of the Dust People's land. I had thought I had seen badlands before, but never have I seen anything to compare with this. It's all rocks and gullies and gorges and cliffs, not in neat lines like cliffs are supposed to run, but going this way and that without reason. In those badlands there is a race of small, sturdy wild horses. They must have been let go there by some human agency, because they come with every color and marking you can imagine. There are piebalds and bays and grays and chestnuts and red duns, and many of them have blaze faces and white stockings."

"What has color to do with their wildness?" interrupted Taharka.

"Real wild horses, those whose ancestors were never tamed by humankind, are always dun with a black stripe down their spines. They have short bushy tails and their manes stand on end," I explained. "I want to go catch five or six of those horses and bring them here. I'd have them broken by the time I got back, and we could sell the colts for a fair price. We'd keep the mares and fillies. That way, we'd be suddenly very important to the mantics and margraves as the only source of horses in the plains."

"Caught and tamed wild horses before, have you?"

"No, but I've talked to those who have, and read books about it."

"All alone you want to go five hundred miles, into a country infested with vampires and such, capture five or six wild animals whose only thought will be to stamp you into rags, and drive them five hundred miles back, breaking them as you come."

"Yes, that's it exactly," I said eagerly, though I sensed that Taharka's attitude was not wholly approving.

"Runa, my dear love, misunderstand me I hope you will not, for your indomitable courage is one of the things about you I love the most—but over my dead body you will have to ride to go on this mad expedition."

"Taharka!"

"Wait. Before you point out to me that stop you I cannot, listen to me. Months you would be gone, months in which the castellum and I would be against the mantics wholly undefended."

"You can take care of yourself. And if word were spread to the mantics that I was bringing horses, they wouldn't molest you."

"Allow you to go the Silvercat would not."

"Oh, that," I said scornfully. "It couldn't stop me."

"Shock you I do not want to, but has it occurred to you that even now you may very well be pregnant?"

That gave me pause. It hadn't occurred to me, or at least not in the context of my proposed journey. "All the more reason why I should leave at once, if I am," I said at last. "I won't want to be out riding half-broken horses when I get big and awkward."

Taharka groaned. "And what about me? Should I not worry about you? Wouldn't I miss you? What kind of a man must you think me, to let his wife—his pregnant wife—ride off on such a dangerous and exhausting errand? Does it not matter to you that I would be afraid for you, that all who knew of it would snicker behind their hands and say, 'There is Taharka, who sends his wife into deadly danger while he stays snug at home'? What if off into the west you ride and never return? What am I to think then? Shall I think, 'My love died alone and uncomforted when I who should have cherished and protected her was not there'? Or shall I think all the rest of my days, 'My wild witch loved me not enough to come back to me'? Runa, my love, if you would destroy me, take up my dirk and cut my throat! It would be the kinder end."

I eyed my husband with some bewilderment. "But I've been riding about the world all by myself for years."

He gave me a stern look. "Approve of it I do not. If I had known I would have hunted you down and protected you."

I giggled at this absurdity. "I don't say there weren't plenty of times I could have used your help," I admitted. "But whether you approve of the risks or not, you have to admit that the plan would work."

"Mmmph," he said noncommittally.

"And you have to admit that there isn't much of anything else that will work. The mantics hate me because I'm a stronger sorceress than all of them together can handle. The margraves hate you because you're a greater warrior than all the fighters they can send against you. The next step will be to bring in a hired sorcerer to attack me and to band together to lay siege to the Silvercat."

"Possibly you're right," he grudged.

"We can't stand alone against the entire plains. As I see it, we have two choices: either we make ourselves necessary to them or we pack up and get out."

"Maybe so, but allow you to go off horse-hunting alone I will not."

"No, I see that. I wasn't thinking when I suggested it. Forgive me, dearest? I've never been half of a pair before."

"I forgive you," he said, eyeing me warily.

"So I guess you're going to have to come with me."

There was a long silence. "Think of that I should have," said Taharka ironically. "Flattered I am to be invited."

"Well, you said you were ready to settle down and didn't want to go roving anymore."

"Said that, did I? Before I knew you very well, it must have been." He gathered me up in a rib-cracking hug. "Fine, horse-hunting we will go."

Since I was already close enough to be within easy reach, I kissed him. "I've got the lists ready, but I want to bake some journey bread, so we won't be able to leave until day after tomorrow."

"Day after tomorrow! A couple of weeks it will take me to get ready."

"Nonsense. We can live mostly off the land."

"Hard it is to hunt for thirteen people while traveling."

"Thirteen! We aren't going to take that many. The two of us are plenty."

Taharka looked at me dubiously. "Two of us? Taking the warriors we are not?"

"Of course not. They couldn't keep up, for one thing, and for another, who'd guard the castellum while we were gone?"

He shook his head. "Wild witch indeed! Nor tamed a bit are you yet."

"Tamed!" I sputtered indignantly. "I'd like to remind you just who the civilized one of this pair is. Not," I conceded magnanimously, "that I hold it against you for being a barbarian. I like you the way you are."

"Barbarian! Regret that slur you will," he said, and kissed me into breathlessness, from which the evening progressed to its logical conclusion, and neither of us thought any more about our journey.

* * *

Riding Butterfly and Biscuit, saddlebags full, Whiskers whinnying indignantly in the stable at being left behind, we left the castellum when the dawn light was still only a pink suggestion in the far east. I was bubbling over with good spirits, pleased to be once more going somewhere, and in company. I set a good pace, and before the shadows stretching enormously before us had shrunk appreciably, we were nearing the western border of the Silvercat March.

With a swish the Silvercat materialized out of the hip-high grass. "You may not leave my lands!" it snarled. "You are my food."

"We're coming back," I told it. I was gathering energy quietly.

Nervously it lashed its tail. "You may not leave," it repeated.

Carefully I arranged the energy into a shield, one powerful enough to stun a natural creature the size of the Silvercat. What it would do to a supernatural, I wasn't sure, but it would certainly jolt the creature if it tried to attack. "I promise you we'll come back," I reassured it. Nudging Biscuit with my heels I sent her on past the snarling guardian. Out of the corner of my eye I could see Taharka, battle sword drawn, urging Butterfly to follow.

The Silvercat squalled and struck at the air with a massively clawed forepaw. But it did not leap. I checked Biscuit to let Taharka take the lead, and I watched carefully as we rode beyond the creature's territory. It winked out and I remained on the alert for telltale swishes in the grass for several miles. It didn't reappear, however, and I assumed that it must be magically bound to its territory.

When I felt safe enough, I urged Biscuit up beside Butterfly. The big stallion was lagging along in a draggy walk. He had traveled before in the company of those afoot, and had never been forced to develop a snappy, ground-covering walk, such as my own horses assumed automatically. Taharka didn't seem to realize that his mount should be traveling at a better pace. "Dearest," I said diplomatically, "may I ride Butterfly for a while? When we're chasing the wild ones

I'll need to ride him and it's better to get used to him now without all the excitement of chasing horses."

Taharka looked mildly surprised, but vaulted off readily enough and gave me a leg up. I wouldn't say the stallion was comfortable to ride—he set his feet to the ground with a solid determination to drive them in up to the knee—but I discovered that like many "hard mouthed" horses, he simply had never been schooled to respond to a light touch on the rein. Within an hour he was as responsive as the half-trained Biscuit. He was also stepping along at a much better pace. His first response was an irritated tail switching when I began to urge him to lengthen and quicken his stride, but gentle persistence and carefully timed squeezes with the calves of my legs soon overcame his resistance. Biscuit, of course, fell automatically into a brisk traveling walk. By no means the seasoned traveler that Whiskers was, she had still been with me for nearly a year.

"I'm going to miss Whiskers," I remarked to Taharka.

"Why didn't you bring him?"

"A wild stallion will attack any male horse that intrudes on his territory. Another stallion will defend himself, but a gelding won't. A mare won't be attacked, though a herd stallion might try to steal her."

"But fast enough to catch a riderless horse is Butterfly?"

"You don't chase them down and catch them. You push them along until they've gotten used to you and you can drive them where you want them to go. Then you can ease up alongside them and drop a loop on one, or if the lay of the land is favorable you can move them gently into a trap."

"Will the herd stallions not fight to protect their mares?"

"Oh, yes. We'll catch horses out of the young bachelor bands mostly. If we watch carefully, we may be able to pick up a few fillies, too. The herd stallions whip all the young-sters out of their families, but the fillies are usually picked up immediately by some other stallion, while the colts need a few years to mature before they'll be ready to take on a family of their own."

By noon, we had traveled a good twenty-five miles. The horses were in need of a rest and a little time to graze, and it was getting hot, sticky, and oppressive. I suggested to Taharka that we have our lunch and rest for a couple of hours in the shade of a grove of trees I saw near the banks of a little creek. He agreed readily.

"Phew, I'm ready for a rest. We covered a fair amount of ground this morning," I sighed, keeping my back turned to Taharka's stiff-legged gait. I hadn't realized that he was so unused to long-distance travel on horseback. I rummaged in the saddlebags and brought out the picnic lunch.

"Too old am I to travel with you," he groaned as I handed him his meat and bread. "Too far and fast do you ride for one as delicately raised as I."

"Better eat. This food is the last you'll get that isn't trail rations. You ride Butterfly this afternoon. You're more used to his gaits than you are to Biscuit's."

"You mean done for the day we are not?" He threw himself on his stomach with a truly heart-rending moan. "Saddle sores all over my body I have."

"Shall I make you some poplar tea?" I asked with concern. I hadn't realized that he was in such pain.

"No, my love, but rest a while I must."

"Oh, we'll stay here for a couple of hours. The horses need to graze. You could have a little nap if you liked."

He took me at my word and was asleep within minutes. I sat with my back propped comfortably against a log and thought tender thoughts about Taharka and how very much I still had to learn about him. And he about me, for that matter. We were still strangers to one another, and yet we had established a trust between us that overcame our lack of common knowledge and experiences, and even the incompatible expectations that our two different cultures led us to hold. I hadn't thought of it, but maybe this trip was the best thing we could have done. It would give us a chance to get to know each other as we couldn't have in the press of business at the castellum.

I was glad too that I hadn't continued to deny him his husband's rights. The tenseness between us, along with much of the misunderstanding, had evaporated once that barrier was overcome. The long, quiet talks in the dark comfort of our shared bed were more precious than the lovemaking that often preceded them.

I hadn't realized what a cruel blow I had dealt to Ta-harka's masculine self-esteem by rejecting him with what had seemed to him such loathing. Only now did I see what a difference there was in him. Much of the loudness and rough horseplay that had frightened me had been the result of sheer nervousness. He had wanted desperately to impress me with an ardor he didn't feel (after all, I was as much a stranger to him as he to me) but had thought I would expect from a bridegroom. Secure now in his possession of me, he was content. Believing himself desired, he no longer felt the need to impress me by noise and an expansive manner. He had sheepishly confessed all this to me one night when I had told him how much more comfortable I was with him when he was gentle and soft-voiced.

I knew that he very much wanted to believe that I was pregnant, although I was reasonably sure that I wasn't. Whether he wanted a child for its own sake, or to establish his manhood, or even as an additional tie to me, I didn't yet understand. But there was no doubt that he wanted a child. He had brought up the possibility of pregnancy to dissuade me from undertaking this trip alone, but he had thoroughly convinced himself that it was not only possible but true that I was carrying his baby. He was going to be bitterly disappointed if I wasn't.

My eye was caught by a movement on the horizon—just a flicker, but both horses raised their heads and looked, ears pricked. I gave the surroundings a quick survey; there was nothing amiss but in that one quarter. Then I settled back to watch. There was another movement. A head peeking over the brow of a little rise of land? A few minutes later, a sideways slipping of what should have been a stationary shadow followed. "Taharka," I said quietly. He awoke instantly. "Someone's sneaking up on us. Northeast—look along the skyline of that hill over there."

Moving with casual ease, he sat up and stretched, but his eyes were searching the horizon keenly. "I see. Fetch the horses."

I rose and without haste brought the horses from their pickets. Quietly, though both animals were snorting uneasily now, I saddled them and replaced the saddlebags. There was a rustling nearby, and Biscuit sidled nervously. I formed the energy I had been gathering into a weapon. Taharka was on his feet, his stance relaxed, but his left hand loosened the battle sword in its scabbard and his right was resting easily on his belt only inches from its hilt.

There was a crashing and a chorus of yells as four or five scruffy bandits burst from hiding and came charging. Taharka's bellowing warcry sounded; there was a whistling as he hefted the huge weapon, ready to cleave the first man to come within his reach.

The bandits plowed comically to a halt, just outside the range of Taharka's sword, and milled about uncertainly. They were a starveling, ragged bunch of ruffians, armed with nothing but daggers, and no real threat to us. Almost I could have felt sorry for them, even though they had clearly planned to murder us. I left them to Taharka and scanned the landscape to his back and sides; if the bandits had been at all clever, they'd have sent at least one of their number to attack from an undefended angle. Apparently they weren't at all clever.

"Aw, sir, we weren't going to hurt you and your lady," whined one of the bandits. "If you'll give us a bite to eat, we'll let you go on your way, free and clear."

Taharka laughed. "And if I give you nothing, you'll let us go on our way."

"We're hungry, sir. You've got plenty. Spare us a bit," begged the man.

"If there was any honesty in you, go and work for one of the margraves you would," Taharka said contemptuously.

"They won't have us. We aren't tiller folk, and we have no weapons."

I pulled one of the bags of journey bread out of my saddlebag. "Taharka, may I give them something to eat?" I asked. "They look hungry enough."

"Stab you in the back they would," he said.

"They won't, because I won't turn my back on them."

"Please, Lady," said one of the other bandits. He stepped incautiously forward, hand outstretched in supplication, greedy eyes on the bag I was holding. I thought he was going to be decapitated as Taharka's mighty sword sang

sweetly though the air—and so did he. Squeaking with
alarm, he scrabbled hastily backwards, and Taharka checked
his swing inches from the man's neck.

"Mount up, then you can give them your alms," said Taharka quietly, never letting his attention waver for an instant.
I climbed quickly onto Biscuit and led Butterfly up beside
his master. I tossed the bag to the one who had asked me,
and the others gathered around him eagerly clutching for
their share. While they were occupied with squabbing over
the food and cramming it into their mouths, Taharka vaulted
onto Butterfly's riding pad.

We rode away at a lope, ignored by our would-be attackers. "Very well you did, my love," remarked Taharka,
when we had put several miles behind us and drew the
horses to a walk. "Argue with me I was afraid you would."

"I might be a contentious wife," I said, "but I've got better sense than to argue with the war leader in the middle of
combat. When we're in that kind of situation, you're in
charge. I'd hope you'd do the same if the danger were magical or supernatural."

"Without hesitation," he said. "When you were traveling
alone, how did you deal with situations like that one?"

"Illusions, usually. If illusions were not enough, I'd use
enough energy to shock or stun. But mostly I stayed out of
trouble. We were careless to rest in so open a place, so near
to human habitation. I didn't even put out wards, as I would
have if I'd been alone."

"Wards?"

"Magical guards against supernaturals. Here you shall
not pass signs for the commoner sorts of dangerous supernaturals. They can also warn of the approach of human
intruders. But I traveled for the most part in uninhabited
lands. Human beings are the most dangerous predators of
all, and I stayed away from them as much as possible."

"An excellent policy and one we'll adopt. A mighty warrior I am, but I would avoid a fight if I can. Fights enough
come a man's way in his lifetime without seeking them out."
He yawned hugely. "Interrupt a man's naps, too, they do."
He glanced at me sidelong, grinning slyly. "Or his enjoy-

ment of the sweet adoring smile on his wife's face when she thinks him asleep."

We traveled at a good pace for the next few days. We were never again so careless. We spent our noon rests in swales or thickets where we were not easily visible. At night, I set wards around our camps. Taharka did much of the hunting with the bow he had brought along for the purpose, though I also showed him how to set the snares and traps I had always depended upon. The plums and berries were ripe in the thickets along the creeks, and there were always various greens that could be cooked into the soup or eaten raw as salads. The perch and sunfish that lived in the sluggish streams were delicious broiled over the coals. We fared well.

The nights were the best. We put our blankets together upon a mattress of dried grass or springy twigs. It was too hot to snuggle together, and we were usually too tired to make love, but all through the night there was the comforting touch of his shoulder or hip or knee, his steady soft breathing beside me, the delicious little reminders that for the first time in my adult life I was not alone. They were golden, those nights, and those days riding side by side across the unmarked prairie.

CHAPTER
13

"T AHARKA," I said without moving my lips, "sit still. Don't move."

He froze obediently. We were taking our noon rest under one of the straggly trees that were dotted around a little pond. This was the land of the Dust People, and I knew these folk. If we were to pass in peace, we had to contact them. They were consummate masters of concealment, and the greatest general of the civilized nations had nothing to teach them about the art of ambush. That they were all around us I knew, but only by magical means. There was neither sight nor sound of life in a monotonous dun landscape that wouldn't have hidden a moderately prosperous lizard.

Moving slowly, I laid out piles of dried fruit from the prairies—a treat for the Dust People. Then I sat quietly down beside Taharka and folded my hands. Time passed.

A man materialized silently out of the ground and sat down crosslegged across the campfire from us; he moved with an absolutely fluid grace, as if he were boneless and weightless. He was short and stocky. His face was full of the stillness of great distances. I didn't move or speak, nor did he; neither of us looked at the other.

"Runa," he acknowledged my presence.

"Lud," I responded, adhering to the local notion of propriety. We sat in silence for another time. "Eat," I said, waving at the nearest pile of fruit, when I judged that enough time had passed that I wouldn't seem unduly hasty. I must have miscalculated, for Lud's eyes flickered and he almost looked at me.

Finally, having paused long enough to reprove me for such crude haste, he picked up a dried plum and ate it delicately. There was a further wait. "Good," he said.

The word was a signal. The people of Lud's band rose up out of the landscape and poured into the camp. They moved like wraiths, with the same grace Lud showed. Beside me, Taharka stiffened in amazement. They were very alien and very beautiful—the color of the ocher landscape, skin, hair, lips, and eyes. Except for a thin cord of twisted hair about their waists from which dangled various small possessions, they were completely nude. When I had visited this land before, the people had been thin and frail, subsisting upon grass and insects; but they had had a good year, and were sleek and full of life, skins gleaming, white teeth flashing in shy smiles. Each went to a pile of fruit, and I looked around. Some of my friends of the year before were missing. There were two young women, as alike as twin fawns, whom I didn't know. Lud's chief wife Bee had a new baby.

Soon they were all eating fruit, still silently, with the same delicacy Lud had shown, but eagerly, nevertheless. Bee gave her baby a firm round breast while she ate.

When they had eaten, Lud, still gazing into the distances beyond me, asked, "Friend?" with the tiniest tilt of his head toward Taharka.

"My husband, Taharka."

Lud almost glanced at me. "Good," he approved, having thought that over. Among the Dust People there is no such thing as an unwed woman past puberty. I had shocked them severely the year before when I had politely declined to belong to any male among them, even though times were so poor they could not possibly have supported another person. They found it unnatural and offensive that a woman who might be productive would choose not to be. They were a dwindling people; never enough babies lived to replace the adults who died or were killed. Lud's band had been formed by the amalgamation of two bands that become too small to offer their members safety. The two strange girls were probably the last remnant of some third band.

Bee handed her baby to one of the other women—Rainbow, her name was—and walked over to Taharka. "Don't move," I hissed at him. He sat quietly while she examined him, touching and exploring his clothes, his hair, his body. The two strange girls edged nearer, clearly fascinated.

"Good," Bee approved, stepping back. "Baby?"

"Not yet," I said, blushing.

She frowned and turned to look at Taharka again, clearly wondering if there was something wrong with him. The two girls came forward and began to touch him in turn, and I felt him start as their explorations became a little personal. One of the girls giggled softly. I reached over and gently but firmly removed the hand of one of them which had wandered where it ought not to have. Taharka shot me a glance I chose to interpret as gratitude.

Lud had observed these activities with benign detachment. "Hunter?" he asked now, nodding at Taharka again.

"Yes, indeed," I answered. "A mighty hunter who has killed his bear."

This impressed Lud. A corner of one eyebrow twitched. He sat in silent thought for a time. Glancing at Bee, who nodded, he gestured. The two girls and a boy about sixteen —just entering puberty—stepped forward. How they knew it was they who were summoned, I didn't know, nor what message had been exchanged between Lud and Bee. "Bird," he said, tilting his head toward one of the girls. "Mist," he indicated the other. "Om," evidently named the boy. "Yours." He pointed at Taharka. "Babies," he said, indicating the girls. "Hunter." This was toward Om, the boy. Lud stepped fluidly across the space between us and took my wrist. "Runa," he said. "Baby." He pointed at himself.

Evidently considering the bargain to be settled, the rest of the band stood and began to move out of the camp. Lud pulled on my wrist, and though he was no taller than I and probably not as heavy, he was immensely strong; I was being towed along with him.

"Just a moment," said Taharka sharply. "My wife, Runa is. Very beautiful your—er—daughters are, and a fine hunter the boy will be, but by the customs of my own people, trade my wife I may not." He stepped forward and put his left hand on Lud's forearm just above the grasp on my wrist.

Lud turned and looked at Taharka, his amber eyes suddenly blazing with catlike intensity. "Runa is mine," he said, with a ring in his voice I had never heard from one of the Dust People before.

Taharka lowered his head, the great cords in his neck swelling. "Mine Runa is, by her own choice. Let go of her," he roared.

"The strongest takes the female in her season," said Lud.

I tried vainly to twist my wrist out of Lud's grip. "I don't wish to go with you, Lud. I want to stay with my husband." Neither man paid me the slightest attention.

Taharka drew his dirk. "Sorry I should be to hurt you, Lud, here in your own lands and following your own customs. But let you take Runa I shall not."

Lud simply looked at Taharka and spoke a single meaningless word. My husband dropped to the earth limply, making no move to catch himself. He lay randomly as he hit the ground, all a-heap.

"Taharka!" I choked, and twisted frantically to free myself and go to him. Lud simply held me. Reaching out with a foot, he stirred the lax body. There was no response, but I could see that Taharka's mouth had fallen open and that his eyes were open and staring.

Wild rage surged through me. I reached into the overmind and began gathering a deadly bolt of energy. I fully intended to blast Lud into rags, who had dared to hurt or kill—I feared that he was dead—my roaring, exuberant, brave, loving Taharka.

Lud turned his amber gaze upon me and spoke—and the energy was gone, beyond my reach. I couldn't even find the overmind, though I searched frantically. There was nothing, no energy, no magic, no help for me. A frightened cry rose to my lips as my feet began to walk of their own accord, dropping obediently in behind Lud as he let go of my wrist and strode gracefully off into the dun hills.

Frantically I fought to control my own steps. I tried to stop myself, to swerve to either side. I might as well have been attached to Lud with unbreakable steel; I walked behind him as tamely as a cow being led to the byre. I closed my eyes and struggled with my own body. My feet kept going as though sight were irrelevant. I didn't even stumble. My mind was as free as ever, but my body obeyed another's will.

"Do not fight against Lud. If you go to him willingly, he will be a kind lover and a good provider for your babies. And we will be sister-wives."

I opened my eyes to find that Bee had fallen in beside me. She was looking at me with gentle concern, smiling tentatively. There was nothing I could say to her. Every fiber of my being was intent upon the destruction of her mate, whom she loved. Perhaps she read as much in my eyes or heard it in my harsh panting breaths, for she turned away.

I contested with my whole will every step my feet took, but I might as well have contested the passage of the sun. For a time, I strove to quicken my step, meaning to attack Lud's imperturbable back; that was no more successful than my efforts to free myself. Then I abandoned my feet to their walking and concentrated upon altering the swing of even one hand. The effort proved futile. I closed my eyes again and sought for the overmind. The way into that place was as undiscoverable as the path to paradise, though I had formerly moved in and out of the overmind as freely as I moved about in the physical world.

At last, exhausted, I ceased my efforts to escape and withdrew into myself to think. There had to be a way to free myself from the spell Lud had cast over me. And if I could free myself, perhaps I could help Taharka. Maybe he wasn't dead but ensorcelled; the word that had captured me had sounded very similar to the one that had felled him. But time—I lacked time, if I was to help him, and every unwilling step took me farther away from him.

Delving into the farthest recesses of my memory, I went back to the times when I had listened to my mother and her friends talking about the different species of magic. I was very young—my mother had been hanged as a witch when I was just twelve—and I hadn't understood all I had heard. But a child's memory is retentive, and my mother had numbered among her friends not just sorceresses like herself, but magicians, necromancers, summoners, witches, wizards, loremasters, and illusionists.

I was myself a wielder of power and mistress of the over-mind, as well as an herbalist. None of these skills would serve in this extremity. My sources of power were denied me and my access to the overmind was blocked. Herbal medi-cine is a gentle art, suited rather to soothing the distresses of humankind than to violence and escapes.

Some of the arts I would not use, not even if it meant the death of Taharka and myself. Necromancy, for example, is a black and evil art, one best left alone. Rare is the necro-mancer who can avoid being tainted by the death and cor-ruption he deals in.

But the summoner's skill, now, that might be useful in my present plight. Summoners studied the ways of humankind and of animals and used their knowledge to counterfeit the imperatives that move men and other creatures to act as they do, thus enforcing their own will upon them. Wild creatures could be brought by such means to easy striking distance of the hunter's bow, or people lashed into a mob frenzy. To my mind, the art was at least a little suspect, though I knew a few of its ways—enough to set a snare where the rabbit wouldn't evade it, for example.

It seemed to me that the spell that had been placed upon me had something in common with the spells that brought the game to the hunter, though I had never heard of one so powerful that it would force an unwilling victim to obe-dience. If it were an aspect of the summoner's skill, it should be breakable.

My thoughts were interrupted by the cessation of travel. All afternoon the various members of the band had gathered edible plants and small game as we walked, except for Lud, who was concentrating on keeping me under control. Now each member brought whatever he or she had gathered and put it in a pile by Bee. The rest of the women gathered around and began preparations for the evening meal.

The sun was setting, and for a moment my thoughts flew back to Taharka. Was he alive? I took heart from the fact that the two girls and the boy Lud had traded for me were

not with us. Surely they wouldn't have remained with a lifeless corpse.

Lud startled me. He had come up to me where I stood, my
muscles awaiting another command. Now he tugged at my
shirt. The buttons defeated him. "Take these off," he ordered. "The women of the Dust People do not wear clothing."

I ignored his order. I had not the slightest intention of
removing my clothing, and Lud, not understanding how the
fastenings worked, couldn't force my fingers unwilling to
the task.

His eyes narrowed as he realized that I didn't intend to
obey. For a few moments he stood looking at me, and then
turned away, abandoning the issue for the time. I knew that
he would avoid a confrontation if there was any doubt of
victory; he maintained his control over his folk by force of
personality and his skill as a hunter. As he left, my body
seated itself, much to my relief—my feet and legs ached
fiercely.

The crude preparations of the food completed, Lud sat
down and ate. He ate sparingly, and I guessed that the meal
was the poorer for his not having hunted that day. When he
had picked out the choicest morsels, the rest of the adult
males moved in and ate what they wanted. The women ate
next, while the children hung about, watching the diminish-
ing pile of food with hungry, mournful eyes. Not until all the
adults had eaten were they allowed to scrabble through the
remains of the food.

It seemed cruel to me, and it was one of the reasons so
few of the children lived to adulthood. Yet I could understand, if not sympathize, with the reasoning behind the customs. The hunters had to be strong and well fed, or all
would starve. The women too contributed to the food supplies of the band, carried the burdens, and underwent the
stresses of pregnancy and nursing. The children were non-
productive, and if one died there was always a chance of
another to take its place.

Even so, the Dust People loved their children dearly, even
the men often cuddling one, playing little guessing games

with it, or carrying it when it tired on the trail. Theirs was a harsh life.

I wasn't invited to eat with any of the groups. I wouldn't be fed, I guessed, until I had proved that I was a useful member of the band. I would not have eaten the mess of ropy half-cooked roots, lizards baked in their skins, and fat white grubs roasted upon long thorns that the members of the band consumed with relish, but the grace period before I must act to free myself was shortened. If I became too weak from hunger to return to Taharka, both of us might well die.

It was nearly dark now. I was more than a little apprehensive. Lud might well decide to seal his possession of me that very night, and my determination not to undress wouldn't prevail against a sharp flint knife and a few brisk tugs. The time had come to throw every last bit of strength and will and knowledge into the effort to free myself.

"Lud!" I said clearly, looking directly at him. Everyone in the camp paused, startled. "You're a coward." My direct glance alone was a challenge. My words were a deadly insult.

Even in the fading light, I could see a coldness pass over Lud's face. The rest of the band whispered together. "You're afraid to face me in honest wizard's combat," I continued. "I'm only a woman, but you must use such spells on me as you use to bring the game within reach of your spear. You haven't the courage to stand up to me in the overmind."

"A male may challenge another male," said Lud. "A female awaits the male's pleasure."

"A true shaman doesn't fear a sorceress. I call you coward and challenge you to meet me in the overmind."

Lud gestured impatiently. "Combat is for males."

"I will never bear the child of a male who can't overcome me in wizard's battle."

Lud hesitated, glancing about at the avidly interested faces of his people. Then he looked straight at me, accepting the challenge, as he had to if he were not to lose face. "When I have shown you that I am the stronger, you will remove your clothing and accept my baby into your womb."

"If you can show me that." I shrugged. I had to get him to meet me in the overmind. It was my only chance. If I lost the battle, I wouldn't care what became of my tenantless body. "When I show you that you are no fit mate for a sorceress, you will not hinder my return to my husband."

He nodded brusquely. Abruptly, the barrier blocking me from the overmind was gone, and I slipped instantly into it. Lud arrived there simultaneously, and in that instant we were locked in a desperate battle of wills. Lud was striving to form a little universe very like the ocher hills and plains that made up all the world he knew. I was intent upon forming the likeness of one of the great cities of my homeland, an environment strange to Lud, where I might readily confuse and disorient him. But he was powerful. I had never measured wills against one so strong and at the same time so alien.

The ocher hills flickered around us, heaved themselves up and formed themselves into stone walls and blocks of buildings inhabited by insubstantial wraiths. Then the city shuddered and slumped toward the roundness of weathered hills, the blocks running together as if made of sand. The city shimmered and reformed, superimposed. The hills shifted and strained to absorb the buildings. Hills—buildings; pavement—plains. Back and forth they wavered, dominated by neither Lud's images nor mine.

The incredible forces we were hurling at each other's creations couldn't remain balanced for long. There was a cosmic groan that crazed the shifting universe across. I was flung sprawling by a mighty upheaval, and I saw Lud go tumbling. There was an endless instant of noisy chaos, and the overmind settled into a bastard simulation, not what either of us had been seeking to create, but an unnatural amalgam.

I sat up and looked about. I was sitting on a sand-strewn stone floor. Barren walls enclosed me, shattered and roofless to the brassy sky. Dust drifted in the corners and blew on the keening, acrid breeze, rattling thinly against the worn stonework. Lud was near. I sensed his "flavor," but the feeling was directionless. I could neither see nor hear him.

I scrambled to my feet and clambered through the broken walls, over piled building stones. That led only to another chamber, as bleak and uninhabited as the first. I peered about. There had once been a door in the right-hand wall of the room; I edged up to it and looked through. A long narrow room was beyond. This one was partially roofed at the far end, and disappeared into cavelike darkness. I didn't much relish stumbling about in the dark, so I concentrated upon forming a lamp. It took an immense effort, and the resulting light was a feeble ray that penetrated only a few feet.

I had to find Lud and continue the battle. But where was he? He must be seeking me as earnestly as I was looking for him. He couldn't be far. I edged warily into the black tunnel. It would be very dangerous if he surprised me, and equally as great an advantage if I could come upon him unawares.

Chamber followed chamber. Some were roofed and dark; others were open to the sky. Once I found a trace of bare footprints in the dust, but lost them in the next dark stretch. Another time, I crossed a line of my own booted prints—in a place where I was almost certain I hadn't seen any openings to either side.

Time passes differently in the overmind than it does in the real world. Instead of a steady progression of minutes, each equaling the next and adding up to hours, minutes may vary in length. Hours may add up to minutes, and weeks sometimes pass in an eyeblink. I wandered through the universe of ruins. When I felt hungry or thirsty, I created a fruitful orchard or a gushing fountain, and occasionally I found places where Lud had created a spring or a patch of roots. I saw him once, far away, teetering upon the top of a crumbling wall and peering about. I melted back into the shadows. When I saw him scramble down, I hurried toward the place, but either I lost myself in the mazelike rooms or he was gone when I got there.

I was beginning to feel weak, a sign that my physical body was suffering from my prolonged absence. Lud had eaten in the real world more recently than I had, and his corporeal body was more adapted to cycles of privation, so the advantage there was his, but I was more widely experienced in the overmind and more adept at manipulating it.

I became aware of Taharka's presence gradually. I thought

of him often as I wandered, and at first the faint traces of his "flavor" seemed only a part of the deep anxiety I felt for him. The feeling that he was near grew more and more strongly upon me, until it masked Lud's spoor, and I realized that he was trapped in this ruinous universe with us.

I had to find him! He was utterly unused to the overmind. He might not even be aware that he was in it. He would certainly be unable to manipulate it against the strong inhibitions both Lud and I had laid down. He might die of hunger and thirst, and death in the overmind is just as permanent as physical death.

I knew that calling him would alert Lud to my location, but there was no alternative. Seating myself on a gritty stone floor, and paused to gather all my energy, and sent out a summoning call to Taharka.

He felt it. I could sense that much. But he was not coming. He was resisting the call with all his proud and stubborn will. Untrained though he was, he was a formidable opponent. I strengthened the summons, and still he refused to yield to it. He was suffering, I could feel, and weak, and I could have crushed his resistance and forced him to come to me. However, if I had the ability to do it, I lacked the will. He didn't realize that he was struggling against my efforts to help him; he thought he was fighting against an unknown force that was trying to coerce him into an action against his will. It would do him incalculable harm to be mastered so.

I realized that he didn't know my "flavor." How could I communicate to him that it was I who summoned him? What feeling could I put into my call that he would receive from no one else in the world?

Reluctantly I answered the question I had asked myself. There was one feeling that I could project that he would know could come from me alone: love. However, in the overmind, such a thing cannot be counterfeited. If I didn't love him, I couldn't project the feeling to him.

Did I love him? I liked him, certainly. I respected him and enjoyed his company. He had taught me to take joyous pleasure in his lovemaking. I was willing, I realized with some surprise, to spend the rest of my life with him, to accept his weaknesses as freely as I accepted my own, and to understand and rely upon his strengths. Did all these together add up to love?

I knew what I knew of romantic love only from reading. The books I had read indicated that "true love" was a cosmic experience. Women in books seldom *liked* the men they loved. They were more apt to fear their displeasure than to enjoy their company. They were breathlessly helpless in their adored's presence. I felt none of these things. I no longer feared Taharka, and I felt more rather than less capable when he was around, as if his company helped me to transcend my own limitations.

Well, I couldn't say, then, that I loved Taharka, nor that he loved me (again relying on the books I had read). But the feelings I did have for him were flourishing and growing. Could they be formed into a "flavor" that Taharka would recognize and respond to?

I had to try. Already I had remained in place too long and risked revealing myself to Lud, for whom my summoning call would have blazed like a great beacon. Once again, I gathered all my energy, but this time I wove into the summoning all my feelings for Taharka, my admiration for his courage and intelligence, the near awe I felt for his beautiful singing voice, the joy we had experienced together, the tenderness I felt for him. This complicated call I sent forth with desperate strength.

Lud was near—very near, and coming closer. I dared not break my concentration to look around, or even move. *Taharka, dearest, come to me. It's I, your wife. Come, oh, come, hurry.* My lips shaped the words but I didn't speak them aloud.

Taharka heard me! He recognized my "voice." He was coming as fast as his weakened condition would allow. I had to keep my concentration intact to guide him to me. Where was Lud? I had been striving so desperately to reach Taharka that I had lost track of him. He must be close, perhaps in the very room, behind me, stalking me. I dared not move.

There was a clatter of tumbling blocks. I heard Taharka's voice—the overmind analog of his real physical voice—calling my name, and intensified my summons. Then I almost lost my concentration when there seemed to be a whisper of sound—bare feet on stone?—from behind me.

There was another crash of falling stone. The tottering, ruinous wall before me suddenly shook, trembled, swayed, and came tumbling down, blocks rolling and sliding. Taharka, dusty, bloody, staggering, came scrambling through the rent in the wall.

"Runa!" he croaked through cracked, dry lips. "Called me, you did, my love? Here am I."

"Taharka!" I leaped to my feet and ran to him, gathering him against me. "Oh, Taharka, I was afraid you were dead!"

"Thirsty am I, but not dead. That you would come after me, I knew. I waited. Is there no water in this place?"

I concentrated, and a fountain burst forth from the one remaining whole wall, splashing down into a little basin that the paving stones obligingly heaved themselves up to form. I gave Taharka a little push toward it, and he cupped his hands and drank thirstily.

As I fondly watched him drink, I remembered Lud. Even as I did, and wheeled to scan the chamber, he stepped out of the shadows. Taharka, glancing up, saw him. With an inarticulate roar of anger, he flung himself across the room, seizing Lud in a bear hug before he could dodge. The slighter savage was borne across the room, and they both went tumbling over some of the blocks that littered the floor. Hastily I reached out with my will and quelled Lud's attempts to shape the surroundings. With his magic suppressed, the battle was between the overmind strength of each man—and each had imbued himself with nearly the same physical attributes as he possessed in reality.

Lud was wiry, the more agile of the two, but Taharka, even weakened as he was, was much the stronger, and his strength was fueled by his anger and directed by all his warrior's skill. He was squeezing Lud to death. I could hear bones creak. "Taharka!" I called. "Don't kill him. His folk need him."

Taharka was no berserker. He glanced at me. Rising to his feet, he dragged the ineffectually struggling Lud with him and cast him aside, sending him rolling across the floor to bring up against the far wall with a crash. "Hurt you, did the little savage?" he demanded.

I shook my head. "We've won, dearest. He can't fight the two of us. Let him go back to his body now. Give me your hand." I wanted to keep close contact with him. Since our physical bodies were so widely separated, I would have to send him back to his before I tried to get back to mine, with which I still maintained contact in the midst of Lud's band. It was going to be tricky.

I explained what I intended. Taharka scowled, but agreed. I closed my eyes and reached to the limits of my ability to reach from my tenantless body to his unconscious corporeal form. Locating it, I gave his selfness a push with my will, and he was gone from beside me. I opened my eyes. Lud was gone, and for one horribly frightening moment I was alone in a dissolving universe. Then I wrenched myself out of it and back to my body.

I opened my physical eyes to find the last of Lud's band walking away into the coolness of the early dawn. Lud stood across the camp, staring into the distance. I dragged my shivering, nauseated body to its feet. Without speaking or looking at me, Lud hefted his spear and strode off, paralleling the path taken by his folk.

I trudged back toward the pond where Taharka had been left. I hadn't gone more than a mile or so when I heard galloping hooves, and Taharka came riding out of the dun hills on Butterfly, Biscuit on a lead line. He vaulted off, and I was gathered into a warm, real, physical hug.

CHAPTER
14

TAHARKA And I sat upon our horses watching the three young stallions watching us. "These are what we're looking for," I said with satisfaction. "A bachelor band of colts. Looks like two two-year-olds. The gray may be a little older. They've never been chased and they're young and inexperienced. Let's move in on them and see which way they run."

Butterfly was regarding the three wild ones with less enthusiasm. He knew deep in the genes that those colts coveted his mare, and he was bristling all over. Biscuit, pregnant and uninterested in the posturings of the male of her species, chewed a mouthful of grass as she placidly surveyed the strangers.

"Attack us to try to get Biscuit, will they?" asked Taharka.

"If they even think about it Butterfly will change their minds for them in a hurry." I urged Biscuit to a sedate walk and we eased up on the colts. They held their ground, the older gray arching his neck and stamping with a forehoof, before the strangeness of it all overcame them and they moved away, not panicked but uneasy and willing to maintain their distance from these strangely burdened horses. Again we eased up to them and again they moved on, until they accepted the pressure of our nearness and fell into line to travel on. We rode quietly after them, never crowding then enough to spook them, never backing off enough to let them completely relax.

The country hereabouts was rough and rugged, and we

were often out of sight of the little band, but they left an easy trail to follow in the dusty soil, and before long we found that we were swinging in a huge irregular circle, perhaps twenty miles in diameter.

"They've stopped to drink," Taharka said suddenly.

I glanced at him, surprised. The light was fading as evening settled over that wild and broken land, and I could hardly see the horses, never mind make out what they were doing. "You must have eyes like an eagle," I remarked.

"Reading it is that spoils your vision," said Taharka with a grin.

"No doubt," I said, and kicked Biscuit into a trot. "Move them on. We want to keep them a little thirsty."

There was a startled snort and a thud of hooves as the colts spooked away from the little spring-fed pond. I pulled up and stepped off. "Let's camp here," I said. "We'll have to take watches to keep the colts away from the water."

"A little cruel it seems," objected Taharka. "Thirsty they must be."

"The wild ones are tougher than domestic horses. We won't let them get thirsty enough to suffer, just thirsty enough to know that we control the water and they only get a drink by obeying us."

"Then will we set traps around the pond?"

"No, we drive them up to the pond and away from it as we choose. We keep them moving, like we did this afternoon—relay them. Gradually we move in closer and closer until we can ride right up to them and turn them wherever we want them to go."

"Slow it is."

"Chasing them won't get us anything but tired horses. This reduces the chances of one of them getting hurt, or one of us. By the time we drop a noose on one, they'll be so used to us they won't go crazy with fear."

Taharka considered this, and nodded. "Why no one catches them, I begin to see. Much patience it takes."

I rode out at the first pink hint of dawn. The colts had tried to come back to the water twice during the night. The second time they had remained so close to the camp that I could hear the occasional thud of an unshod hoof and the swish of a tail.

The colts were feeling frisky in the dawn chill, and flung up heads and tails and raced away over the steep and rocky trails when I approached. I didn't succumb to the temptation to chase them, but kept Butterfly to a steady, ground-eating walk. There was another half spooked, half frolicsome stampede when I rode up to them again, but as the sun rose higher and the heat grew more oppressive, the colts' spirits flagged and they began to allow me to move to within a hundred feet or so before they moved doggedly on. The smaller of the two-year-olds, a sorrel, was beginning to lag.

Early in the afternoon I recognized the vicinity of the pool where Taharka waited for me with Biscuit. I trotted up to the colts, forcing them on past the pond, even though the sorrel tried to dodge past me to the water.

Taharka was holding Biscuit as I rode up and slid down from Butterfly's back. "I used her a little this morning to drag logs," he said. "Building a fence I am across the mouth of a box canyon a quarter of a mile that way. Use it for a holding pen, I thought we could."

"Leave the gateway nice and wide and we may be able to ease them into it. Remember that wild horses can climb like cats. You might have to block off anything that isn't absolutely vertical." I gulped down the soup he handed me and swung into Biscuit's saddle.

The sorrel colt had almost sneaked back to the water, the dun hanging behind him. The gray was nowhere to be seen, but I heard him whinny for his friends from farther up the trail.

The colt held his ground until I was almost within touching distance, gazing wistfully past me at the water. Then his nerve broke and he scampered back to his companion. They both moved off obediently when I rode nearer.

It was nearly dark when we returned from the second long twenty-mile circle. All three of the colts tried to crowd past me to the water, but Biscuit was having no sauce from these youngsters and laid her ears back, baring her teeth, and they reluctantly gave way. I could have reached out and touched the gray.

Taharka stood watch over the water while I ate my supper

and rested. While he ate, I prepared three thirty-foot nooses, each securely fastened to a good-sized log. I hoped that at the end of the next day's circles the colts would be so tired and thirsty that I could ride right in among them and rope one, who would then have the log to drag all the next day.

The moon was up when I went on watch around midnight. "The little one keeps trying to get past me," Taharka informed me as he passed on his way to his blankets. "I had to push him away with my hands the last time. Very thirsty he is, poor little fellow." There was a note of reproach in his voice.

When I went to my post between the colts and the water, I picked up one of the nooses and opened it out. It was unlikely that the colts were enough tamed yet for me to be able to catch one, but it was as well to be prepared.

In a short while the sorrel colt came edging up the trail, blowing nervously. I held my ground, standing with a relaxed posture, not looking directly at him. He hesitated, weighing his chances of dashing past me. He blew at me, and I blew back at him, in the manner of one horse greeting another. He pricked his ears, and we exchanged another huff of greeting. The colt tried to pass me; instantly my bearing changed from friendly greeting to indignant menace. I straightened abruptly and stamped my foot.

The colt shied back, startled that I had taken offense. Then he lowered his head and clamped his tail placatingly. I relaxed and blew at him again. Reassured, he moved forward, and I stepped backward as he did so. Step by step we moved back to the edge of the water. As soon as he reached the pond, the colt forgot all fear and plunged his head in to drink, and as he did so I began to rub his rough-coated shoulder. He quivered when I touched him, but was too absorbed in his drinking to offer serious objections, and I continued to rub his withers as he drank, the noose held in the hand that rubbed. Soon I was able to slip the rope around his neck and secure it so that he wouldn't choke.

I continued to rub him until he raised his head, water dribbling from his lips. His sides were as round and taut as a barrel. He turned his head to sniff doubtfully at me. But he was too full of water to spook as I eased away from him, intending to get out of the way of the royal fit he would doubtless throw when he found himself tied. I was surprised when he followed me trustingly. I moved far enough away to be out from between him and the log, but not so far that he couldn't stand beside me, his head almost against me, which he seemed to find reassuring, for he heaved a sigh and cocked a hip.

I looked up and saw the gray coming down the path. It seemed almost as if they had sent the smallest and least valuable of the band in to spring the trap, and seeing that he had had his drink and seemed content, they were coming in for theirs. I picked up another noose and laid it over the little sorrel's back, which he accepted calmly. He made no objection when I shoved him over beside his water-gulping friend, and when the gray raised his head, I just reached across the sorrel's back and dropped the noose around the gray's neck.

There was an uproar then! The gray felt the rope around his neck and spooked, shying away from me. When he hit the end of the rope, already at a dead run, the log was jerked so suddenly that its inertia kept it as solidly in place as if it had been three times its size. The gray was flipped right over and came down on his side with a terrific whump. The log, yielding to the forces upon it, came sailing through the air. Fortunately, both Little Sorrel and I had scooted out of the way, and the log went crashing into the gray, who went down again, winded and thrashing.

Taharka, alarmed by the commotion, came dashing up. "Keep back!" I yelled at him as the groggy gray staggered to his feet. Taharka skidded to a stop and watched as the gray bolted into the night, the log bouncing along behind him, catching in rocks and bushes.

I stepped aside so that Sorrel could run with his friend if he wanted to, but he seemed to regard me as the only haven of safety in a terrifying world and followed me. When he came up against the rope, he stopped, bewildered by the sudden tug on his neck, and when I moved away, he whinnied pitifully. "Made a friend, there, have you?" Taharka chuckled, as I walked slowly back to the colt.

"Evidently this little fellow has just been waiting for someone to come along and catch him," I said, moving slowly and easily as I untied the rope from the log.

"That you intended to rope them tonight, I didn't know,"

said Taharka severely. "Several days I thought you said it would take."

"The opportunity offered, so I took it. It won't be this easy another time." We took the colt around—he was innocent of any knowledge of leading, of course, but content to follow me—and cautiously introduced him to our two horses. He humbly saluted each one, yawning his mouth as a foal would, and even Butterfly condescended to accept him. With a little coaxing and rubbing, we got a halter onto him, and left him with the other horses.

"We might as well get some sleep. The other two won't be back tonight. The gray won't get too far, dragging that log, and we can find him tomorrow. The dun has probably been spooked clear out of the badlands," I said.

"Good! Together we have not slept for far too long a time," said Taharka promptly, and I grinned at him. Unfortunately, though, I fell asleep before the matter could be further pursued.

We were awakened in the dawn light by Butterfly's bugling challenge. I pulled myself out of my husband's sleepy grasp and sat up to see the dun colt knee-deep in the pond. When Taharka would have risen, I held him back. "Let him drink," I whispered. "Then get a rope and get mounted up. He won't be able to run with so much water in him." The dun was drinking and drinking, his sides swelling out, as he made up for the thirst of the last three days. When he moved away, he fairly waddled.

Hastily we saddled and mounted. Then we set out at a good lope to follow the dun. He led us right to the gray, who hadn't gotten far before his log had tangled in some brush and stopped him. He was sitting back against the end of the rope, doing his best to choke himself to death. As we loped past, I swung by and popped him on the rump with my rope, causing him to leap forward and ease the pressure on his windpipe.

The dun had nearly foundered himself. He broke into a clumsy trot as we rode up to him, then dropped back to a dispirited walk, his belly sloshing audibly as it swung uncomfortably from side to side. It was no great matter for us to ride up one on either side of him and drop the loops around his neck. Then we played him from either side, like a fish, until he gave up and came meekly back to the camp, though I mistrusted his eye.

Sure enough, when I tried to get a halter on him, he made an effort to bite my leg off that would have done a crocodile credit. We had to throw him, and when we let him up he was not only haltered but hobbled and sidelined as well, and Taharka had made a gentleman of him with a few quick strokes of his razor-sharp skean. Even as a gelding, though, I feared that he would never be a reliable riding horse for any but the wariest of riders.

The gray was older and bigger, but by the time we got back to him, he had choked himself into semiconsciousness, and halfway halter-broken himself as well. We got him haltered and back to the camp with little difficulty, and he too was hobbled and sidelined and gelded.

We stood back and looked our catch over. The dun was next to worthless, with his outsized, coarse head, crooked legs, and vicious temperament. He might make a packhorse. The gray had the makings of a decent horse. He had already learned that fighting a rope was futile. He was about four years old, old enough to be a useful animal, and I resolved to break him to saddle right away.

Little Sorrel came timidly up to me, unsure of his welcome, and I spoke soothingly to him. He was very small, no more than thirteen hands, but he had the best conformation of the three, with a nice head, and I thought he had the potential for a good deal more growth. Doubtless he was a late foal, always the lowest in the pecking order, the last to feed and the first to have his food taken away from him, and had wintered over without enough growth. He was barely two now, I thought. He still had many of the mannerisms of a yearling.

"Shall we cut the little one, while we're at it?" asked Taharka.

"No," I said consideringly. "He's just a baby and he needs to get a little growth on him. He doesn't seem to need to be hobbled, either."

"Somebody's pet that got away, do you think he is?" The colt was leaning his head against me.

"No, I suppose he's just naturally gentle. You find them

that way sometimes. Too bad he's so young. He's the best of the lot."

Taharka gave me a startled glance. "Best he is? I would have said the gray was best and the dun better than this one. Bigger they both are."

I laughed. "Size has nothing to do with it. Look at how straight his legs are, delicate but well tendoned, and how nicely his shoulder lies back. Give him time, dearest. Remember how Whiskers ran your Butterfly into the ground? Little Sorrel might well be just such another."

"Sorry for him you are. He knows a soft heart when he sees one, and how to make up to it."

"Maybe," I admitted, scratching the colt under the chin, "but you mark my words. In three or four years you'll be trying to trade me out of him."

We spent the next three days halter-breaking the three colts and breaking the gray to saddle. Butterfly was an enormous help. It was necessary to exercise both the new geldings to keep their wounds from swelling, and Butterfly soon learned the trick of using his vastly superior weight to control the skittery wildlings. He disciplined them instantly if they crowded him or became rowdy. All three of the colts held him in awe, and when I eased onto the gray's back for the first time while Taharka held him from Butterfly's back, one wicked slantwise look from the stallion was enough to quell any rebellion.

By the morning of the fourth day, the gray was far enough along in his education to be useful. Little Sorrel of course was no trouble; he only asked for the opportunity to follow me about, and learned quickly and sensibly to respond to the halter. He made no objection even when I sat on his bare back for a few moments, but he was really too small and immature to be of use. The dun submitted to the halter only after all of us had lost a good deal of skin, and Taharka flatly refused to let me ride him—not that I was reluctant to be dissuaded.

Taharka's box canyon pen had proved of immense value in the breaking process. It would have been incredibly more difficult and dangerous without it. I was beginning to realize that I really couldn't have done much by myself. I needed

Taharka, needed his help as much as I was discovering that I needed his companionship.

Several other horse herds had used the pond for water, but our presence had driven them to other water sources. The next morning Taharka and I set out to discover another band we might catch. We rode many miles that day, but the landscape was as devoid of horses as the surface of the moon. The only benefit we gathered was a better knowledge of the lay of the land.

We were discouraged and weary when we got back to our camp. I cooked supper while Taharka brought the colts in to water. "Running out of grass for the horses here, we are," he reported as I gave him his bowl of soup.

"I hate to move on. We've scared all the horses out of this area; I don't want to scare them away from all their waterholes. Besides, we've got your pen here."

"True, but grass we must have." We had brought as much grain as we could carry—not enough, for horses that were working as hard as ours were—but we had to dole it out sparingly.

"You're right. Tommorrow as we look for horses we'll keep an eye out for another camping place."

"Come back here after a while we can. These horses don't seem very wild. Harder to catch have I seen domestic horses, and harder to break, too."

"These must never have been chased. They obviously don't count human beings among their enemies. I've had horsebreakers tell me that a horse that has never been handled is often easier to break than someone's spoiled pet. They've picked up no bad habits and they pay attention."

The next day I rode the gray, with Taharka and Butterfly keeping a close watch on our progress and leading from time to time by the halter the gray wore over his bridle. We intended to make a short day of it, out of consideration for the colt's tender back, which was unaccustomed to the rubbing of the saddle. He let us know when we crossed out of the territory that the three colts had considered their own. He knew perfectly well that a colt found roaming in a herd stallion's territory was begging for a beating.

We almost rode into the midst of the herd. We came

around a blind corner and saw a family of wildings looking curiously at us. The patriarch was closest, a big chestnut with a high crest and a woolly mane, who scented Butterfly immediately and bugled a warning that shook the pebbles loose from the sides of the draw. He was perhaps ten years old, at the height of his powers, confident, the scarred veteran of many a battle. But we hardly noticed him.

Most wild stallions can keep a family of only two or three mares and many have only one. After all, there are as many colts born as fillies, and the effort of keeping a larger number of mares from marauding bachelors would soon wear out an ordinary stallion. This one was clearly not ordinary. He boasted a harem of six mares, matched in color. Each was a lineback buckskin with faint stripes on her hams. They were as handsome a herd of brood mares as any human breeder could have gathered. Along with the mares were their foals and yearlings—and every one was a gloriously flashy red dun!

I had never seen horses quite that color. Their body coats were a clear gold, like their dams'. But the manes, tails, and stockings were the fiery red of their sire's coat. The manes of the little foals stood up and flickered like flames, and the yearlings gleamed like fire. I was instantly possessed with a lust for a herd of those youngsters. I wanted the mares and the stallion too, but common sense informed me that a mature breeding stallion was hardly a practical quarry. Nor were the mares likely to take kindly to domestication. No, I would settle for the yearlings and foals.

I suddenly realized that the chestnut stallion was edging up on us, his glittering eye fixed on Butterfly, whom he identified as a rival. Butterfly was more than willing to accommodate him, if a fight was what he wanted, and the air was shivering with the furious challenges being flung back and forth between the two. The gray colt was indicating his urgent desire to be elsewhere.

"Hi, you," I yelled at the top of my lungs. "Get on out of here!"

The mares spooked and bolted away, but the chestnut clearly considered my noise of little significance. His business was with Taharka's stallion. He stopped and shook out his mane until it stood up like a crest, pawing the earth and squealing. Butterfly surged forward. Taharka was pulling back so hard on the bit that the horse's mouth gaped open, but he too had no time for humans at the moment.

"Taharka," I called, alarmed.

"Yes, my love?" he panted.

"This is getting serious. Get off." My gray was dancing around in circles. The only thing that kept him from bolting was the fact that I had his nose bent around almost to my knee.

"If I get off, they'll fight."

"I don't think you can stop them. Butterfly won't run now."

Taharka vaulted suddenly clear of his mount. As he did so, the two stallions charged. There was a horrendous squealing, and a flurry of dust that obscured the scene for an instant. "Catch Butterfly!" I heard Taharka bellow.

Before I could do anything to prevent it, he stepped into the melee and vaulted onto the chestnut stallion's back. The wild stallion, startled out of his battle madness by the sudden weight on his back, reared, crashing over backwards. My heart leaped into my throat. But Taharka jumped clear of the horse and then back onto him as he struggled to rise. Butterfly, disconcerted by the sudden shift in action, was circling around the outside, and I grabbed his bridle and dragged him away from the monumental battle going on in the soft sand of the draw.

The chestnut, wilder than any deer, more savage than a wolf, was determined to throw his clinging rider. He reared and bucked and spun, twisting his great ugly head about to try to tear Taharka off with his teeth. Taharka, looking small and crouched on the enormous beast's back, clung to the flamelike mane. When the stallion tried to bite him, he doubled up a fist and punched him on the end of the nose. He must have been enduring a beating from the battle sword that was hung from his baldric, for he shrugged out of it and let it go spinning away.

Red madness was in the plunging stallion's eyes. He went crashing into the face of the gully wall. My breath choked in my throat. The creature would kill himself gladly if in so doing he could destroy his tormentor. He would never submit to a rider. Taharka would be killed! I swayed on the gray's back, dizzy with terror, strangled with the clamor and dust of the titanic battle.

The red stallion reared up and up into the air, pawing at the sky, springing off his powerful haunches to leap up and dive down through the sky like some great eagle, bawling with mad rage. Again and again he flung himself down, striving to crush his rider beneath his great weight, and always Taharka leapt free as the stallion went down and vaulted back on as he lunged to his feet. Foam was flying above the roil of dust now, and the beast's bawls of rage were insensibly changing into groans of despair. Taharka's yells were becoming hoarser, too.

Suddenly, when it began to seem that the beast he bestrode might exhaust himself, Taharka flung himself forward, literally climbing the huge creature's neck until he was clinging to his head. I gasped as I saw my gentle husband take a solid bite into the stallion's ear.

The stallion screamed in real agony, shaking his head and pawing at his tormentor with his forefeet. But Taharka's legs were clamped around the beast's neck, his mighty arms were wrapped around his head, half blinding him, and his jaws were set firmly into the creature's ear.

Slowing and staggering, the reeking, dripping stallion came at last to a spraddle-legged stop.

Without releasing the ear between his teeth, Taharka rolled his eye at me. "Mummph!" he commanded urgently.

Coming to myself with a start, I climbed hastily off the trembling gray and pulled the halter that he was wearing over his bridle and off his head. Snatching the rope from the saddle, I ran to the red stallion and hobbled and sidelined him. Ropes of bloody foam dribbled from his jaws as I worked the halter onto his head. Then I ran to Butterfly and scrambled on, taking a tight grip on the halter rope. I jerked the stallion to the side as Taharka dropped off and rolled away in the opposite direction.

The stallion tried to lunge, tripped himself on the sideline and went to his knees, groaning. Floundering, he struggled to his feet, and stood, head down, defeated and subdued. From a magnificent, savage, wild king, he was reduced to a rough-coated, nondescript, dull-eyed nag. I could not but feel a pang of sadness for ruined beauty and freedom. The very color of his coat was dulled.

I slid down from Butterfly and went to Taharka, who was still kneeling in the sand, head bowed. "Taharka, dearest love, are you all right?" I cried anxiously.

He raised his head and looked at me. He was bleeding copiously from his nose, and there was even a trickle coming from his ears. He spat out a mouthful of blood. "Better I have been," he admitted. "A fit horse for a warrior, that one is, a real fighter."

I felt him all over, but could find no broken bones, nor did he complain of pains that might indicate internal injuries.

"Whatever made you do such a crazy thing?" I inquired at last. "You might have been killed."

"Let him kill Butterfly, I couldn't. Quite a stud horse the old fellow thinks he is, but he's never had to fight for his mares."

I sighed and put my arms gently around him, mindful of his many bruises. "It was the bravest thing I ever saw," I admitted. "I was scared to death."

We had quite a time getting back to the camp. The red stallion, hobbled, could move only slowly. Taharka was reeling in his saddle from the cruel battering he had absorbed. Butterfly required constant watching or he would have taken shameless advantage of his erstwhile enemy's defeat and fettering. The gray colt was worked harder than I would have preferred to use him.

When we finally reached camp, I put Taharka to bed with a cup of poplar bark tea and set grimly to the many chores that had to be done. It was long after dark before I dropped into the bed myself and instantly into sleep.

CHAPTER
15

THE Next day I rode out on Biscuit and located the red stallion's mares and foals. I followed them once around their circle and found their watering place. But I dared not press them too hard, since the old lead mare was too crafty to stay in the territory if she were harassed. Besides, some of the late foals were too small and young to be driven as hard as we had driven the bachelor band; their dams would abandon them if they were unable to keep up and we had no milk to give them. Nor did I feel that it was right to deprive nursing mares of water.

When I got back to the camp, Taharka and the red stallion were not there. My heart pounding, I hurried to the pen, where I found the stallion, saddled, with Taharka standing quietly by. From the lather on the horse's flanks, he had been fighting the saddle, but Taharka was cool and dry.

"Not so easy to break will this one be," Taharka called as I rode up.

"Do you think he's worth it?" I asked. "A mature wild stallion hardly ever makes a good saddle horse."

"This one will be good," Taharka answered stubbornly. "Sell him we will not. Keep his mares when we catch them and breed more little red and gold colts, we will."

"All right," I capitulated. "I'll take Butterfly tomorrow and work the herd again. You can keep on with your prize catch there. But be careful. He might be slightly less dangerous than the Silvercat, but I'm not sure of it."

Taharka threw me an exasperated glance. "Careful I always am," he said. "Be careful yourself."

Taking Butterfly proved to be an inspiration. He considered himself the victor in the battle of the stallions and the mares had still not been taken by another herd stallion. By lying along his back, I was able to ride right in among the mares. I was an amused spectator as the black stallion strutted about "his" new herd, flattening his head almost to the ground, ears back and a mean sneer on his face as he snaked the mares into a tight bunch and headed them back toward the camp.

When I found the pen standing open, I assumed that Taharka had seen us coming and had wisely removed himself and the stallion. With a little guidance from me, Butterfly put the mares right into the pen. I shut it after them and rode back to the camp. Taharka wasn't there either, nor was the red stallion, nor Biscuit. The three colts were there on their picket lines. I was even more astounded when I walked into camp and found that the supplies and equipment had been divided scrupulously. Half was missing, half was neatly stacked by the cold fireplace.

Dumbfounded, I looked around. Every evidence indicated that Taharka had taken half the supplies and two of the horses. There was a line of hoofprints, one shod and one barefooted horse, leading east. But I simply refused to believe it. Why would he do such a thing? It was absolutely inexplicable, knowing him as I did, that he would abandon me without a word of farewell.

Then the doubts began to set in. Did I know him? We had been wed a very short time, after all, and he had never pretended that it was a love match. He had told me that he loved me, but always in the moments when we were together as man and wife, when a man may say any extravagant thing without the expectation of being believed. An abysmally lost feeling washed over me.

Then Butterfly whickered and I realized that even if Taharka would leave me so unceremoniously, he would never leave his favorite horse. The whole thing was a confusing puzzle. I would simply have to follow him and find out. If he did indeed mean to leave me, then I would be free to go my own way. If there were some other reason for his departure, some unimaginable reason that he could explain, then we would be together again. At the very least, I could go back to the Silvercat and get Whiskers. I missed the little gelding. At the moment it seemed to me that he was the closest thing in the world to a friend that I could claim.

But I couldn't leave at once. There were the mares to be thought of. I wasn't going to free them. I had been phenomenally lucky to catch them so easily; such luck would certainly never come my way again. They would have to be haltered and hobbled and herd broken. Then I would have to drive the unwieldy herd—mares, foals, yearlings, geldings, and stallions—all the miles back to the Silvercat. I groaned at the immensity of the task.

It took me several days to halter and hobble the six mares and the four yearlings, since I could do it only by roping them one by one, using Butterfly's great weight and strength to control their terrified plunges and hold them while I cautiously eased the hobbles into place. I sidelined only the lead mare. If she were controlled, the rest would be reasonably docile; even the three wild colts would be content to accept the leadership of a wise old herd mare. The foals I left unhobbled, though I caught each one while its dam was secured and rubbed and petted it all over, beginning the gentling process.

The hobbles I put on the wildlings were traveling hobbles, long enough to permit a walking stride, not long enough to allow a trot or gallop.

On the fourth day after Taharka's disappearance, I packed my gear on the dun gelding, mounted up on Butterfly, and lined my herd out to the east. That first day was pure hell. The mares were not in the least willing to leave their familiar territory. I rode Butterfly into a lather trying to keep them rounded up and headed east, switched to the gray, rode him until he was staggering with exhaustion, and finished the day on Little Sorrel, who proved to have more stamina and to be more able to carry my weight than his diminutive size would have suggested.

At the end of the day, we had covered no more than ten

miles. I wove a powerful spell to hold the herd, the illusion of a distant wall of fire surrounding them. I rolled up in my blanket without bothering to eat, so exhausted was I, and slept like the dead. The next day was a little better, as we left the lands familiar to the mares and they gradually ceased to try to bolt and scatter.

Never in the time that followed was I able to travel more than fifteen miles a day. The foals were just not strong enough. Every now and then, when I found a particularly rich pasture or good watering place, I would hold the herd for a day and let the little fellows rest and recuperate, while the mares filled up on the richer grass of the plains, making milk for their foals at heel and nourishing the ones that were growing within them.

Without Butterfly I couldn't have done it. He seemed to understand what I wanted, and to lend his intelligent aid to herding the other horses along. Even when I rode Gray or Little Sorrel, he continued to drive the mares, and to hold them at night while I slept. He was a vigilant watcher against the wolves that followed us occasionally, hoping to pick off a weak foal or a cripple, and repeatedly I was roused by his ringing challenge in time to ward off an attack by the predators.

I found that more and more I would talk things over with the black stallion, and he would bend his great head and listen as intently as any reasoning creature. Into that sympathetic ear I poured all my fear and loneliness and the ever-increasing certainty that Taharka, many miles to the east and drawing farther ahead every day, had left me deliberately and callously. I believe that the horse knew his master's name, for whenever I spoke it he would lift his head and look out to the far horizon. He, no less than I, had been abandoned.

My days were filled with concerns of feed and water and a good place to hold the horses for the night. By the time darkness came each evening, I fell exhausted into my lonely blanket and slept, though not dreamlessly. In the earliest dawn light, at that half-dazed stage between sleep and waking, I would reach out my hand to touch the comforting bulk of my husband beside me, and find nothing but cold emptiness.

At last I drove my herd into the Silvercat March. I almost expected the beast to appear and greet me, but it did not. I bunched the herd on a good stand of grass on the riverbank, out of sight of the castellum, and rode cautiously ahead on Gray, leaving Butterfly to guard the herd. The animals in my care represented fabulous wealth.

All seemed normal at the castellum. The fields on the river bottom were deep in ripening grain. The Silvercat banner flew over the gate, which stood open to the usual traffic. I rode up the switchbacks on the bluff. Partway up, I passed some of the indwellers, who stood and stared in amazement as I rode past them. I nodded and spoke, but they were too thunderstruck to respond; clearly my appearance here was completely unexpected.

As I rode through the gate and into the courtyard, Tildis came hurrying out of the building onto the porch. "Hello, Tildis," I said. "Is Taharka here?"

She hesitated, her eyes darting about as if seeking guidance. At last she said, reluctantly, "The margrave is here, Lady Runa, but he's with the mantic and cannot be disturbed."

"With the mantic?" I stepped off Gray and tossed the reins over the porch railing.

"Yes. If you wish to see him, you must come back later."

I gave her a level look and walked past her into the entrance hall. She followed me worriedly. "If you want to wait, Lady Runa, I'll have a cup of tea brought to you here. The mantic and margrave will be free to see you after supper." She hurried past me and stopped as if to block the foot of the stairs.

Without pausing, I walked forward. She hesitated, but yielded, and I climbed up the grand staircase. I was dimly aware that she scuttled through one of the side doors, the one that led to the warriors' quarters, but I opened the door to the mantic's private rooms and walked in.

There was no one in either office or in the armory. I opened the door to the sitting room.

Taharka was there, bathed and shaved and elegantly dressed, leaning over a woman. When I entered, they both turned to look. I had never seen the woman before. She was a silvery blonde, with huge melting-violet eyes and pouting pink lips. She was slender as a girl just entering upon womanhood, mantled in her own flowing hair, dressed in clinging blue gauze, her hands as soft and delicate as flowers.

"How dare you enter here when I and my husband are together?" she said imperiously. Her voice was low and musical, with a husky vibration deep in her throat.

I ignored her and turned my eyes upon Taharka. If I were to be dismissed from here, he must be the one to do it. At first I thought he was drunk or drugged; his eyes seemed blurred, and the fine powerful line of his chin that I had loved to stroke was softened. Then he recognized me, and his glance sharpened. "Runa!" he said. "What are you doing here?"

"I thought I lived here."

The woman's eyes narrowed. "Runa? Is this the false mantic?"

Taharka glanced down at her—she came only up to his shoulder. "Yes, my pet," he said fondly. "But never did she want to be mantic. She will not maintain her claim, I'm sure." He turned to me. "Ailinis is the true mantic, Runa," he said proudly. "The last descendant of the true blood of the Silvercat family she is. And she has chosen me to be her margrave!" The last he said with an exaltation so unlike anything I had ever heard him say that I wondered again if some spell had been cast upon him. I glanced at the woman speculatively, and discovered that she was wearing about her neck the gold and amber necklace of running deer and lions that Taharka had once given to me and I had left behind for safekeeping, hidden in a place that only he and I knew about.

As I watched, he raised her tiny hands to his lips and kissed them reverently. I think he must have forgotten me, as he caressed her fingers tenderly, his grizzled head bowed over her hands. She glanced triumphantly at me out of the corner of her eye. I had never before seen the triumph that a woman feels when she takes another woman's man. I had never before felt the searing, helpless rage of a woman whose man has been taken. "I don't seem to be needed here," I said curtly.

Taharka actually started. He had forgotten that I was there. When he raised his head, I saw that his eyes were all blurry again, and I realized that I was seeing the effects of overwhelming love. Taharka was dizzy with desire. I turned to leave.

Before I reached the door, four of Taharka's northern warriors came bursting into the room. "Throw her out of the castellum," ordered Ailinis.

"Wait!" said Taharka, and I felt a brief flash of hope. "Did she come on my black stallion? I want him back." The hope died in my throat, nearly strangling me.

"No, she came on a gray gelding I never saw before," said Satha, who had ridden upon Biscuit.

"Fine," said Ailinis. "Take the gray gelding and put him in the stables. Then throw her out."

"I'll take my horse Whiskers," I said, hoping desperately that the tears which were stinging my eyes would refrain from spilling over until I was away from the place.

"Give Whiskers to her," ordered Taharka.

"Oh, darling," pouted Ailinis. "I'll be so unhappy if you give away my sweet Whiskers. You know how I love to ride him."

Taharka looked a little troubled. "But, pet, he belongs to Runa. She brought him all the way from her own land."

"She doesn't deserve to own a horse. For posing as mantic when she was no true mantic she should be hanged from the battlements. Losing her horse is a very small price to pay for her crime."

"We can't send her out to wander in the world without even a horse."

The silken woman leaned back and gazed up into Taharka's eyes winsomely. "Oh, darling, if you give her my horse, I'll be so . . . so unhappy . . ." Her breath caught and huge tears welled into those enormous eyes. "In my condition, it wouldn't be good for me to be unhappy."

Taharka looked down into her eyes and I actually saw him

sway. Tenderness and passion swept over his face. "Of course not, my dear, sweet little love." He beamed.

"Take the horse and throw her out," ordered Ailinis again, shooting me another of those triumphant glances.

For an instant—only for an instant—utter bloody destruction trembled upon the tips of my fingers. I was a wielder of vast powers. I could have brought the whole castellum down about me in my red rage. How sweet revenge would have been! I could almost see the honey-tongued little bitch lying crushed beneath the stone blocks, the faithless Taharka smeared into rags beside her. Tiller folk who had followed her and turned from me—where would they have been without me?—the northern warriors who obeyed the behest of the usurper, all would be crushed and ground together, and in the moment of their dying would my terrible hurt and humiliation be soothed as by a balm. . . . Then I recollected myself. Once before I had been tempted to turn to evil, when I thought a horribly painful and degrading death was my only other choice, and then I had resisted. Could I not resist now, when only my pride was damaged? I could.

In that instant I turned from evil once again, and vowed with all my being that never again would I trust or befriend any man or woman. From this moment forth I would be sole and alone, as I had been all my life. Always had I hoped that someday there would be a place for me, a companion, a lover. Twice now had I been miserably deluded in that hope. I would hope no more, but go into the wild places of the earth and make my life apart from humankind.

So quickly had all this transpired that the warriors were still reaching for me. The only remainder of my internal battle was a shower of green sparks that sent them reeling back, exclaiming. Ailinis, eyes wide, shrank against Taharka, who closed his arms protectively about her and glared at me.

"War leader!" said Satha suddenly. "Your wife Runa is. By our customs were you wed. Put her aside just because your fancy has changed you cannot."

Ailinis shot him a vicious look. "Throw her out!" she

ordered shrilly. "She . . . she's upsetting me." She looked wistfully up at Taharka.

"Take her away, but don't hurt her," said Taharka, hoarsely, his voice thick with passion. I turned and walked proudly out the door, but as I went I saw him bury his face against her bosom. Satha and the three warriors walked with me.

In the courtyard, I saw Bion leading Gray through the gate that led to the stable courtyard. The warriors closed up around me, herding me—they didn't try to touch me again—toward the gate of the castellum.

I went. There was no possibility of regaining Gray, and less of getting Whiskers. If I tried, these warriors would try to stop me, and either I would have to kill them or I would be ignominiously thrown out. But I could no longer suppress the tears, and they rolled down my cheeks as I walked along. I ignored them, hoping that the warriors wouldn't notice.

They escorted me all the way down the road to the foot of the bluffs, and when they stopped there I kept on marching.

"Lady Runa!" called Satha. I resolutely kept walking. He hurried after me. "Lady Runa, I'll go with you. It isn't right, sending you out like this without anything. I'll fight for you and hunt for you."

"No," I said brusquely.

"But—"

"No. Go back to the castellum. I want nothing of your master." I spoke in bitter contempt. He stopped and I kept on walking. Then I hesitated. Satha had offered what he thought was right. I didn't want his aid, but I had been ungracious. I turned, to find him still staring after me. "No," I said again, more gently. "But thank you for offering. The Silvercat is your home—stay and be happy. I need no protection, nor want any company."

He raised a hand in silent farewell and acknowledgment. I turned away again and marched resolutely down the road.

It was well that some instinct had warned me not to bring the horses with me when I rode up to the Silvercat. I was not so destitute as Ailinis supposed. Taharka had evidently forgotten Butterfly and the three colts, and he had never known that I captured the red stallion's herd. I held in these horses a considerable treasure.

They were still where I had left them, and Butterfly raised his head and whickered when he saw me coming. I went to him and gathered up his lead rope. "Do you want to go back to Taharka, old fellow?" I said. He raised his head and looked far away, searching the horizon. "You miss him, don't you? But Little Sorrel can't carry me as far and as fast as I mean to go, and none of the mares are broken to ride. He has stolen my Whiskers and Gray. Wouldn't keeping you be fair trade?" The stallion breathed softly on me and lowered his head, touching me with his soft muzzle. "I should send you back, I suppose," I said. "But I need...I need you, old fellow."

The stallion didn't understand my words, but he understood my anguish well enough. He nuzzled me sympathetically, and I sobbed into his curly mane.

When at last I had regained command of myself, I scrambled up onto his back—Taharka and Ailinis had stolen my saddle as well as my horse when they had taken Gray—and herded the mares toward the town. If Taharka meant to carry out my plan of providing horses for the Burdened Ones, the mantics and margraves, he was going to find his market sadly undercut.

The pens at the livestock market were empty, and I turned my herd into them, separating mares and foals from yearlings and putting Little Sorrel and Dunny in a third. Then I went to find out to whom I should pay my market fees.

By the time I returned, a considerable crowd had gathered. I had hardly dismounted when I was besieged by eager bidders; I could have sold three times the number of horses, even at the exorbitant prices I demanded. I insisted upon easily portable wealth—gold, jewels, and the like—rather than donkey-loads of cloth.

I reserved Butterfly, of course, as he wasn't really mine to sell, and Little Sorrel, of whom I was becoming increasingly fond, and one of the younger mares whose colt was old enough to wean. I meant to carry a good quantity of grain with me, and to travel far and hard. I would have preferred not to subject a pregnant mare to the coming ordeal, but neither did I wish to take Dunny. With horses as with people, there are some individuals to whom you take an instant and abiding dislike, and so it was with Dunny and me. We loathed each other, and parted company gladly.

In a remarkably short time, I was a wealthy woman. There was little to savor in the realization. I had no use for the treasure I had amassed—I even found myself, in a forgetful moment, thinking how pleased Taharka would be and how we could trade for various items we needed at the castellum. Then the bitterness of memory soured the smile upon my lips into a wry twist. I bargained for a good saddle, two packsaddles and three hundred pounds of grain sewn into fifty-pound sacks. As soon as I had had all three horses shod and obtained an extra set of shoes for each, I loaded four of the sacks onto Butterfly and the rest of my possessions onto the mare. Then I put my new saddle, padded with several blankets, onto Little Sorrel, mounted up and rode out, heading west.

I knew where I was going. With the sure instinct of a mortally wounded animal, I was heading for my home territory. I longed to hide myself in the secure vastness of the deserts south of the Republics. Three thousand miles away, they were but the distance meant no more to me than if it had been an afternoon stroll. There I had once been happy. If I could not be so again at least I would be safe. I yearned after the solitude of the desert with all my being. It was, at least, a solitude I had chosen.

I rode on into the night, pausing once to water the horses and give them a generous feed of grain. I intended to feed them lavishly as long as it lasted, and then perhaps I could find a place to buy more, for I intended to swing far to the south. To head directly west would take me back into the badlands, where I would be in danger of losing my horses to the wild bands, and then among the ox-nomads. They were an interesting people, but unpredictable and without the redeeming features of civilization; it had taken all my cunning and magic to pass among them the first time. To attempt to traverse their lands a second time would be begging for trouble.

Then there were range upon range of mountains, through

which I knew only one path, a trail that had taken me the better part of a year to travel. Furthermore, the trail ended at the borders of the Kingdom, where it was worth my life to venture. The terms of my exile had been most specific.

I meant to roam to the south, in the hopes of turning the southern flank of the vast mountain ranges. There were, from what vague reports I had heard, civilized people there from whom I might be able to purchase supplies. Stories of powerful supernaturals were told, of kinds unknown to those of us who lived in the more temperate lands between the jungle and the endless fir forests and cold marshes of the north, but these were not dangerous to one of my power.

What were my chances of surviving such a journey? Not good, I ruminated; but I could not bring myself to care very greatly. As long as I lived, I would press on, and if I died, I would sink gratefully into easeful death.

I rode until I was so exhausted I could hardly drive myself to care for my animals. Then I slept, to awaken in the earliest dawn and ride on, doggedly. I walked much of this day, to spare Little Sorrel, but he seemed not to feel my weight and pranced along as gaily at the end of the day as he had at the beginning. Fueled by the grain, the horses traveled well, and I rode until nearly midnight.

My own rations were more sparing than those I gave the three horses. A handful of dried fruit in the morning, a pot of soup and a cake of journey bread in the evening, were all I could bring myself to eat. Little Sorrel needed no great strength to carry me. Soon I was almost as thin—though nowhere near as weak—as I had been after I had spent five years in the hellish women's prison of the Kingdom. I had fallen into nearly as black a mood of despair, too, and I drove myself and my horses hard trying to outrun the pain and humiliation I had experienced in this treacherous green land.

CHAPTER
16

THE Time came when the grain was nearly exhausted. If I were to keep up the punishing pace I had set, I must find a source of supply. I had passed through several inhabited areas, as well as the wilderness, in my long flight to the southwest, but I had avoided human habitation. That was both the most sensible, and in my dark mood, the most preferable course.

Here in the south, summer had some weeks yet to run, and the crops would still be in the fields. In the Silvercat March, fall would be setting in. The harvest would be gathered and the trees along the river would be dropping their golden leaves into the smooth brown water. For a moment I wondered if the harvest would be sufficient for the winter. The supplies of the castellum were the business of the mantic, and I thought bitterly that Ailinis hadn't the look of one inured to hard work and responsibility.

Then I set the memories aside. It was still too painful to think of, and in any case, it was no longer any concern of mine. Taharka had chosen.

I began to watch for signs of civilization. But I seemed to have entered into a land of peaceful small villages, each with its surrounding fields of coarse grain and beans. What I wished to find were large cities where a stranger might enter unremarked and purchase feed and supplies without arousing curiosity. When I found a road, I turned into it.

This road led only to another of the little villages. I halted Butterfly—I had taken to riding him since the grain was nearly gone and the mare was easily able to carry my little bundles of possessions and supplies—and looked uneasily at the little town.

It was attractive enough. The cottages were scattered in groups around a central park. Trees of many kinds were planted in the park and along the streets, which wound pleasantly among the low-built cottages. The houses were painted in harmonious pale colors, and each cluster of houses was shaded by its own little grove of flowering trees. It seemed peaceful and welcoming, but I knew that among the few hundred inhabitants of such a place, a stranger would be remembered and remarked on for many a day. Nor was it likely that there would be any stores or shops where I might barter some of my treasure for the supplies I needed. Each family doubtless grew enough for its own needs and little surplus.

"Shall we go in there and ask about a larger city?" I asked Butterfly, who flicked his ears back to catch the sound of my voice. "They'll remember us if we do. On the other hand, we aren't being hunted and we could wander around for weeks and never find the cities. If there are any. What do you think?"

Butterfly indicated that he had had enough of standing and would like to move on, the direction being entirely up to me. "All right," I said. "If they turn out to be cannibals or horse-meat eaters, it's all your fault." I sighed. "And maybe there'll be a little inn where we can get a bite to eat and a hot bath. Perhaps I could even sleep in a bed."

I was right about being noticed. There was no wall around the town, and I rode into the streets unimpeded, heading for the park, which I thought would probably be the commercial center of the town. I had not passed between the first two clusters of cottages before I had collected a following of big-eyed whispering children, and by the time I reached the park, a dozen adults had joined my entourage. I nodded and spoke a pleasant "Good afternoon" to each person I passed. They all responded with a shy smile and a murmured phrase.

In the park there was a watering pond for animals, an attractive thing arranged in levels interlaced with little splashing waterfalls. I dismounted and watered the horses, then turned to a pleasant-faced woman who stood nearby.

"Excuse me," I said politely. "Is there an inn in this town where a stranger may arrange for food and lodging and stabling for beasts?"

"No," she said, in a slow, flowing accent. "We see very few travelers here. But any branch would be proud to have you stay with them. My own would be glad to welcome you if it would please you to honor us." There was a murmur from the listening crowd, in which I thought I detected several offers of hospitality.

"It is I who would be honored," I said. "Forgive me if I unknowingly offend against the customs of your people. Are there places where one might buy feed for animals and supplies for traveling?"

"No," she said again. "Possibly the elders of the branch where you choose to stay could make arrangements for your needs to be met. If you will come to my branch and stay with us, I'll speak to our elders about it."

She was genuinely eager to have me come, and had answered my questions kindly enough. These seemed a gentle and harmless folk. I bowed a little. "Thank you for the kindness of your offer. If such generosity to strangers is indeed the custom of your folk, I would be proud to accept. I'll ask one more kindness of you, if I may. Will you advise me if I transgress against your customs?"

The woman smiled the sweet shy smile of the villagers. "It is for us to discover your customs and make you comfortable among us. My name is Lii. Will you follow me?"

"Thank you," I said. "My name is Runa." I gathered up the reins and the mare's lead rope—Little Sorrel was fastened to her packsaddle. "What a beautiful little town you have here," I observed, as we walked down a shaded street. Each cluster of cottages was set in its own lovingly landscaped setting, and every house was both individual and a harmonious part of the whole hamlet. The land around was sun drenched, but each grove was cool and dim and scented with spicy plants.

Lii smiled and turned to me. "I'm so glad you like it," she said, laying a hand on my arm. "We all truly hope that you'll be happy here."

Before I could answer, she indicated one of the clusters.

"This is my branch. Treat it as your own." We walked into the grove amid bushes that were masses of huge pink and white and lavender flowers. Smaller patches of aromatic herbs scented the air. Here it was both cooler and quieter than the street. People began to emerge from the cottages and join us, and as each one came up to us, Lii introduced us. I soon lost track of all the names.

The whole troop of them came with us to the stables. There was plenty of room for my three horses, and a plethora of willing hands to help unsaddle and groom them. They were given more sweet hay than they would eat in a week.

When we left the stable, I was escorted to a cottage. "This will be your stem," Lii told me, giving me a hug. The other adults of the stem, a dozen or so, gathered around.

"Thank you," I said. "Is it in accordance with your customs to take a bath?"

"Oh, yes," said one of the men, a tall fellow about Lii's age, with the same sweet smile. "We'll show you where the bathhouse is."

"My clothes should fit her," said one of the women, who had been standing beside me comparing our heights. "I'll fetch some." She sped off before I could protest.

The tall man put his arm confidingly about my waist. Lii took my hand on the other side. We proceeded to the bathhouse in a group, all crowding in upon me and upon each other, and I saw that all of my numerous escort touched and embraced each other. It was not a sexual sort of touching; the men and women were as likely to hug or hold each other as one of the opposite sex. It seemed more that they were uncomfortable unless they were touching and being touched.

People differ concerning the amount of space they like to have about them. I had found that I made the ox-nomads very nervous by "crowding" them, until I learned to keep a distance that seemed to me almost insulting. The folk of the Republics, on the other hand, stayed just within the area that made me feel I ought to step backward. These people seemed to prefer to have no space at all around them. I could see those on the outside gravitating to the inside of the group as we walked.

Their companionability didn't end with walking, either, as

I discovered when we arrived at the bathhouse, which had a lovely big rock-lined pool of gently steaming water. As we went through the door, everyone shucked off his or her clothes, helping each other and me liberally. Then we all went to a little room with a large basin in the middle, where a great mound of frothy white suds was being whipped to an even stiffer consistency. Everyone took handfuls of this foam and began washing his or her neighbor with it; since I was the newcomer (and needed it more, no doubt), I came in for more than my share of gentle scrubbing. But no one was neglected.

Seeing that everyone was busily lathering everyone else, I took a handful of the cleaning foam and dabbled it tentatively on an elbow that was projecting from the slippery mass of bodies. The owner of the elbow, a fair-haired man some years Lii's junior, was clearly delighted with the attention, and began a strongly rhythmic chant. Soon everyone was chanting, and scrubbing in time with the rhythm.

It was a strange feeling, being washed by so many hands all at once, nor were there any areas of the body these folk felt it was improper to wash on an utter stranger. But it did feel good to get the dust and sweat of the trail off! My hair, too, was treated to many scrubbings.

When we were all white and dripping the foam off in gobbets, we made our slippery way back to the hot pool, sliding and giggling and clutching at each other. Into the water we went, with an enormous splashing and laughing and a great roil of disturbed water, as everyone was sloshed clean of the foam. There was, I noted, a considerable current that carried the floating islands of foam away, but where the hot water was coming from I could not discover. If it was being heated by a fire there must have been a mighty conflagration under unimaginable boilers somewhere!

There was a lot of laughing and ducking and horseplay. Then we all scrambled out—I was lifted out by at least a dozen hands—and we dripped our way into a third room, where there were huge creamy piles of drying cloths. I wasn't surprised when I found that everyone dried someone else, but caught up a cloth and applied it vigorously to the torso of an older man with a cheerful grin and a laughing, knowing eye. Then we dressed each other, and I was dressed in an impossibly gaudy and indecently tight long slim dress with a jingly belt and slippers that laced up to my knees.

Supper was simmering on low brick stoves. When we got back to the cottage, we joined forces to set the food out. As singular as the bath had been, the meal was even stranger. The dishes themselves were simple and good. On several tables placed about the floor, a huge round flat piece of bread had been put upon a great tray. Upon this bread was heaped piles of different viands—soft cheeses, spicy pastes of beans and onions, salads of mashed boiled eggs with tiny green seeds, heaps of nut-flavored grains with herbs, piles of juicy fruits—several upon each foundation loaf.

The trick of eating, I found, was to tear off a piece of the thin bread, roll it into a scoop, put a mixture that seemed especially toothsome into it, and feed it to someone else. When you found someone whose touch with the food was to your liking, it was as well to hang around him or her in hopes of being fed often. By the same token, when you found someone who liked the way you combined foods, you fed them frequently.

Supper over, we all cleaned up. Then Lii came to me. "In the evening is our time to worship the good gods who provide us with the bounty of the earth and sky. Will it offend your own gods if we invite you to participate?"

"My gods would be offended if I declined to offer thanks to the deities of such an hospitable people," I said, a trifle owlishly—the meal had been accompanied by a lot of heady beer.

The folk of the stem murmured in pleasure, and we proceeded to another of the cottages of the branch. As we entered, I found that it was one big open room, the multitude of shutters thrown open to the glowing pink sunset light. The other stems were assembling there, too, and each gathered in its own place around the perimeter of the room.

Presently the assembled folk began a soft wordless chant. Each stem linked itself into an even closer embrace and swayed with the rhythm. Soon the people of the whole branch were swaying all together, each stem offering its own harmonious note to the chant.

The chanting and the swaying ceased when a dignified old lady stood up and advanced to the center of the open space around which we were grouped. She stood to face the last gleam of the setting sun and spoke in a sweet, resonant voice. "Gods of the sky, we thank you for the blessings you have showered down upon us. Gods of the earth, we thank you for the blessings your soil has yielded to our tillage. Gods of the waters, we thank you for the blessings that you have poured out for us. Gods of the people, we thank you for the blessings of health and happiness and harmonious thoughts that you have placed within us. Unknown gods, we thank you for those blessings of which we are not aware." She lowered her hands and turned to face the people. "Who has news of a blessing to share?"

A man rose from among one of the other stems. "Elder, we have had a child born among us today. It is a girl, and her mother will call her Dei."

The folk chanted softly, "All gods, thank you for this blessing!"

A woman stood up. "Elder, one has gone from among our stem to reside in the Divine Home in the bosoms of the gods. Old Viw has died."

The folk repeated their chant, and I thought to myself that a death was not my idea of a blessing.

One by one, men and women rose. Each told of some happening—a harvest of fruit, a calf born, even a lost article found, and each was hailed as a blessing.

Then Lii was standing and the Elder nodding to her. "Elder, we have been blessed by the coming of a stranger to abide among us. Runa is her name."

Again there was the chant of thanks, and then, seeing that no one else stood, the Elder raised her arms again. "Children, the gods give us only one command, and that a right joyous one to obey. They say to us, Cherish one another. Therefore, obey you this command."

Instantly the stem began to mingle, hugging and touching one another. "The custom is to cherish as many as you can who are not of your own stem," Lii whispered to me, before disappearing into the affectionate melee.

Before I could do anything about it, I was swept into the

crowd, hugged, patted, stroked, cuddled. I was bewildered, almost dizzy. Mine had been an austere life. My mother had held me; my slave Laddie had hugged me a time or two; and Taharka, whom I had thought was my husband, had cuddled me several times. But I had never been subjected to such a storm of affection.

When at last I found that I was hugging the blond young man whom I thought of as Lii's younger brother—Kev, his name was, he whose elbow I had scrubbed—I clung to him almost frantically, and he must have sensed my distress, for without releasing me he swung me into a corner and shielded me from the crowd with his body. "We'll go back to the cottage soon," he whispered reassuringly.

Sure enough, the members of Lii's stem precipitated out of the crowd as if by magic. They gathered tightly around me—I was as glad to see them as if they were familiar old friends—and we drifted out of the group and down the now darkened trails back to the stem cottage.

Sleeping arrangements were informal. The large main room of the cottage was furnished with several long couches, each heaped with small pillows. There were cupboards along one wall which were opened to reveal piles of neatly folded blankets. The folk each procured one of these and carried it back to the couches. There they fell into disordered tightly snuggled groups, like puppies in a basket, and went to sleep.

I found myself tightly held in Kev's arms with my head pillowed on his shoulder and someone else's head on my thigh. I was too tired to do anything more than fall asleep. But I think that even as I slept the undemanding affection of these gentle people began to work a healing upon me.

The next morning the whole stem trooped out to work in the bean fields. There was one that was ready to harvest and I spent the morning helping to strip the vines of the dried pods. Even as they worked, the people of the stem stayed together, moving up and down the rows in concert, often touching each other, wiping the sweat from someone's brow, dropping handfuls of beans in others' sacks. We returned from the fields for a lunch of fruit and cheese and milk, feeding each other as before.

I met the elders of the branch that afternoon. They were as kindly as the people of my own age, and promised to try to gather up as much of the large-kerneled grain of their people as could be spared. They gently refused all offers of payment, and hardly seemed to know what the gold I offered them might be good for. It would take several days to gather up the grain, they told me, for they would have to negotiate with the elders of other branches of the trunk, which I took to mean village.

Of course, all the adult members of Lii's stem had come with me. My interview with the elders over, I wanted to check up on my horses, and they fell in with the suggestion cheerily. We found many of the children of the branch gathered at the stables, feeding tidbits to my horses on enormously outstretched hands, their voices hushed. Butterfly, I knew, could be trusted to behave like a gentleman, though few stallions are safe children's pets. The wild mare, Rabbit, I was less sure of. She timidly accepted the treats that were proffered her. Little Sorrel was glorying in the attention, slobbering affectionately all over the little hands, lowering his head so that it could be petted, whinnying after any child that strayed away from his court. Knowing how naturally gentle he was, I opened the stall door and led him out. Choosing a calm-looking child, I placed him on the colt's back and led him a few sedate paces, while Little Sorrel placed each foot with care and the child glowed with incredulous joy. When I swung that child down, another came up, holding up arms to be lifted, and I spent the rest of the afternoon giving rides to the children. They were amazingly well behaved, never pushing or disputing about whose turn it was, hugging me in thanks when I lifted them down.

The pattern of the next few days was much the same, and day by day, even hour by hour, I felt my wizened spirit open out under the beneficent influence of the warm affection and gentle kindliness of the villagers, especially those of the stem I was beginning to think of as my own. I was as thoughtless as one of the children, and as carefree.

I awoke one morning in the midst of a pile of warm and comforting bodies, stretched luxuriously as those about me began to stir, sat up and looked out at the gladness of the dawn, and realized that the time had come for me to go.

There was great sadness and many protests from my friends when I told them. The elders offered me a permanent place among the people of the branch, and made me promise to return to them if ever I thought to settle among any folk.

"I've been very happy here," I admitted. "But there are things I must do in the world. I . . ." I hesitated for a moment, ashamed to admit my cowardice. "I fled from a great responsibility because my feelings were hurt. I broke two oaths, and the fact that one of the oaths was first broken by the other party does not release me. I have to return and redeem both."

The elders looked at me, and one said, "If you must do this, then you must. We knew that there was some great sorrow upon you when you came, and we knew that here you could find rest."

I nodded. "Not just rest, but healing. If I may, I'll leave Little Sorrel here for the children. He loves them and they love him." There was a delighted murmur from the children. "I must speak to you of something serious," I continued. "You and your folk are the kindliest and warmest folk I have ever met. But you're sadly unprepared for invasion from the rest of the world. I must warn you that people elsewhere are wild and dangerous. They may come upon you and slay you for your goods or for the fun of it. I urge you to prepare to defend yourselves in case such people as that find you."

"We thank you for your warning, Runa. We are defended. Are you not yourself very dangerous, and far wilder than most of the bandits and raiders against whom you warn us?"

"I?" I said, a little offended. "I'm a meek and quiet traveler. I harm no one who offers me no harm."

"And those who do offer you harm soon regret it. Nor does the thought of going back to face a terrible struggle on many levels—physical, emotional, magical—cause you to feel a qualm. You are perfectly confident, and with reason. Yet you were easily tamed, and if we chose not to let you go, not only would you stay but you would be happy with us. Kindness is a very powerful weapon."

I stared uneasily at the elders. How did they know all

that? I hadn't talked about myself. I knew that I left only with their permission; if they chose to keep me I would find it a sweet captivity. These were not the unsophisticated innocents I had thought them. "Nevertheless," I said at last, "kindness is a less immediate weapon than a sword. Please be wary of strangers."

They thanked me for my warning and for blessing them with my company, and I went out to Butterfly and the mare, loaded and ready to travel. There was a good deal of hugging and a few tears. I was lifted onto Butterfly's back by many hands. I rode out the same way I had come by and pointed Butterfly's nose to the northeast.

I had been terribly hurt and shocked by Taharka's defection—so hurt and shocked that my brain had quit working and the only think I could think of was to run and hide. I had assumed that Taharka had known Ailinis before and that he had pretended to wed me only to become Silvercat Margrave.. Then, I had thought, or felt, he had dumped me for his true love and installed her as mantic.

When my brain began to function again, as my starveling soul was plumped by the gentle affection of the village folk, I realized that there were several logical flaws in these assumptions. If he had known Ailinis before, why had he bothered with me? Apparently she was the last of the true Silvercat line—or close enough to be accepted by the tiller folk, anyhow. All they would have had to do was to open the castellum themselves and set up as mantic and margrave. Or, if they had been unable to banish the supernatural guardians of the place (but surely the true mantic would be able to do that!), they could have presented themselves to me. I would have been easily convinced, for I was wary of the responsibility and had certainly not been immediately attracted to Taharka. By now I would have been hundreds of miles to the east and Taharka and Ailinis would have been firmly ensconced in their position.

Supposing on the other hand he had met her after he had wedded me—when and where was a problem I would leave aside—why had he ridden off with me after the wild horses? If he had intended to take and keep the animals, why had he left the three colts behind? Why hadn't he waited until we caught the mares and taken them too? No, he had to have met her after we were already in the badlands, where she could not possibly have been, or after he returned, and in that case, why had he left me as he had?

There was only one reasonable conclusion: magic. A powerful summoning spell had been laid upon him. The Bluegriffin Mantic had mentioned the "Sorcerers from the Lakes." Ailinis must be one of those wizards-for-hire, and had cast the spell upon Taharka. Unschooled in magic, he had been irresistibly drawn. Even so, he had stayed to divide the gear and supplies with me. They can't have liked that, the jealous mantics who had arranged the spell. They no doubt meant me to perish, not realizing that the wilderness was far more home to me than the habitations of humankind.

I remembered the dazed look in his eyes, the difficulty he had remembering things, the way Ailinis had bent him to her will against his own sense of rightness. Taharka was far from perfect, but he was always keenly alert, and his character was as strong as mine.

There was only one honorable thing to do, and that was to go back and break the spell that had been laid upon Taharka. Only then would I (and he) know whether he truly loved Ailinis or whether he was merely ensorcelled. Ailinis may have taken Taharka away from me, but she would not keep him unless it was truly his wish, uninfluenced by any magic.

Furthermore, I had never been easy in my mind about taking Butterfly. Oh, I could recite the argument that Ailinis, with Taharka's acquiescence, had stolen my Whiskers, along with Gray and my saddle, and that Butterfly was a fair exchange. But as fond as I had become of the great awkward curly-coated beast, he was not my horse. He missed Taharka yet, and he knew we were headed back toward his master—I had to keep a constant pressure on the reins or he would have accelerated into a trot. Taharka missed the stallion, I had no doubt, as much as I missed Whiskers.

I hoped that the Silvercat would manifest itself to me before I arrived at the castellum. It bothered me that I had not seen it before. If the creature recognized Ailinis as the true mantic, I would be about my business as soon as the spell was broken. If it still hailed me, then she was going to be bounced out on her rounded little bottom. I didn't particularly want to be mantic, but what was mine was not going to be stolen from me—man or horse or home.

CHAPTER
17

I Was being followed. There was a faint haze of dust hanging in the air some miles behind me, and occasional high-flying flocks of disturbed ground birds. There was a trembling in the overmind rather like the dancing heat haze on the summer desert floor.

I doubled back, circling widely. My pursuer was too wily for me and eluded my scrutiny, though I found the tracks of two shod horses.

I rode in the streambeds and on the rocky ridges, hiding my tracks, hoping to lose the follower. He or she was a skilled tracker, and my tricks only delayed the pursuit.

I made a series of forced marches, relying on the coarse yellow grain of the village folk to sustain my two horses. All I accomplished was nearly to exhaust the mare.

At last, in desperation, I laid an ambush. Leaving clear tracks into a low swale, I rode on through and concealed the tired horses in a thicket with a liberal smear of aromatic ointment up their nostrils so they wouldn't smell the hunter's horses and give away my position by calling to them. I readied a potent globe of destructive energy and set myself where I could see the pursuer before I could be seen. I didn't want to hurt anyone, but neither did I intend to be harassed over all the long miles back to the Silvercat March.

I waited almost motionless all that afternoon, tormented by flies, scorched by the sun, every sense straining to catch a hint of the coming of the follower. When the sun at last slipped behind the horizon, I sighed and rose, dusting myself off and letting the energy dissipate. Outfoxed again, I thought ruefully. What now? The horses were rested by their afternoon's wait in the shade, and I should ride on. But if the horses were rested, I was not, having been at a quivering pitch of readiness for instant battle for hours. I was weary and stiff and more than ready for a bowl of hot soup and my blankets.

Tomorrow, I thought, as I trudged down the swale, the hunted becomes the hunter. I'll track whoever it is down and demand to know why he's following me. And he'd better have a good explanation or he'd bitterly regret bothering me. After all, the elders had called me "dangerous," hadn't they?

I rode a couple of miles and made camp on the bank of a meandering little creek. I debated the wisdom of a fire. After all, whoever had been following me was still out there somewhere and the light of a fire might give away my position. On the other hand, if he'd been close, he would have ridden into my trap, and I had nothing which could be eaten without cooking. I decided to make a small fire to cook a porridge of the yellow meal and dried fruit mixture I had brought from the village, which the villagers ate for breakfast. The horses would warn me soon enough if there were prowlers about. I even felt secure enough to leave the setting of the wards until I had eaten.

It was full dark by the time my porridge was boiling, and I was nodding where I sat crosslegged before the tiny fire, feeding it an occasional twig. I heard a sudden thump of hooves and Butterfly's low whicker. The disturbance woke me up in time to keep me from dropping my half-cooked supper, and I listened intently, but there was no further noise. I shrugged. Butterfly was teasing the mare again, no doubt. He never gave up hope.

I was leaning forward to poke another twig into the fire when the hair on the backs of my arms ruffled up into an atavistic bristling and a chill brought out the goose bumps. I was no longer alone. I leaped to my feet, reaching blindly for energy.

"Frighten you I did not mean to. It's only I." Taharka stepped into the firelight.

I stood staring at him. I could think of nothing to say. After the way we had parted, a calm greeting would have been hypocritical. Besides, I felt a little foolish. I had been riding hundreds of miles to come to his rescue and he was clearly in no need of my help.

"An old friend of yours I brought with me," he said after an uncomfortable pause, tugging on a rope that he held. A small bay head, a little grizzled about the muzzle, came poking into the firelight. Whiskers! He had brought my horse. Had he come all this way and chased me for days just to return my horse?

"Your supper you've spilled," he said. "Some venison steaks I have in my pack. Ripe persimmons I found while I was waiting for you to give up your ambush, too." He led Whiskers a little farther into camp and began to unload the pack he was carrying.

Automatically I stooped and built the fire up. It would have to burn down to a more considerable bed of coals than the few twigs it had taken to boil the porridge would provide, if it were to broil the steaks Taharka put down on a tin plate.

He unfastened the halter rope and Whiskers came over to me, whuffling a greeting. I scratched the itchy place behind his ears before sending him on his way to the green grass.

In the newly refreshed light of the fire, Taharka and I stood facing one another. He reached out a hand uncertainly.

"Runa, glad to see me you are not, nor do I blame you," he said. "When you came to the castellum, I . . . I must have been mad . . ."

"Or ensorcelled," I said coolly. "Tell me exactly what happened, beginning with the day I rode out on Butterfly to scout out the mares."

His proud head sank between his shoulders. "I hardly know," he said, shaking his head massively from side to side. "Working with Red, I was, when it seemed to me to be the right thing to do to hurry home. I thought that it was my duty to be at the Silvercat, and remiss had I been to have ridden so far away on an errand I only half understood. Back at the camp I hurried and gathered together my things. I knew that none of the horses there were really mine except Red, and bad I felt about taking Biscuit, but it was so desperately important to get back that the theft was excused."

I flinched a little. It was much the same argument I had used about stealing Butterfly. "Why did you leave half the equipment and supplies?" I asked.

He rubbed hands over his face. "Did I? Glad I am, but remember why or how I do not. I must have realized that not all the gear was mine."

"Go on. Then what happened?"

"Like traveling in a dream, the trip back was. At first I rode Biscuit and packed Red, but then it seemed better to ride Red. It seems that it took only a few days. All I remember is that vitally important it was that I get back as fast as possible. When I got there..." His voice faltered. I waited quietly for him to go on.

"I seemed to know her. In the mantic's quarters she was living, and the tiller folk treated her as if she belonged there. She greeted me as if she had known me all my life, as if she forgave me sweetly for wandering off, since I had hurried back so promptly. Never have I seen any woman so wickedly beautiful." He sighed. "These things I tell you as they seemed to me."

There was a long silence. The fire crackled, sending sparks soaring into the darkness.

"Nothing do you ask me of her," he observed heavily.

"There are choices that have been made," I said, "and decisions that have to be made. Go on with your story."

He seemed to fumble for words. "Half-mad with passion for me, she was," he said. "Skilled in the ways of love as the most expensive whore in a great and corrupt city. Get enough of her, I could not. To me it seemed that she was my rightful wife and that my marriage to you was some forgotten dream. Then... then you walked in, and almost I didn't recognize you. She had been teasing me, as she often did, seeming to yield and then withdrawing, making me beg for her. She had told me she was pregnant.... Wanted a son, I did. It seemed a very great gift."

"How could she have known?" I asked. "I wasn't more than two weeks behind you."

He looked at me with misery in his eyes. "Time had no meaning for me. It seemed many days."

"I see. Go ahead."

"I more than loved her," he said, hanging his head. "Adored her, I did. You see, lie to you I do not."

I almost wished he would. I was of two conflicting minds. The wielder of power was listening to the story with keen attention to the details that could tell me what spells had been used on him, for it was clear to the dullest intellect that he had been at least partly ensorcelled. The woman listened in agony to his recital of his feelings for another woman and her skills and excellencies. I struggled to keep my face expressionless. "How did you escape from the spell?" I asked.

"To me Satha came after you left. He had found out that you had sold horses in the town, and figured out that you must have driven those wild horses all the way back by yourself. Listen to him I would not—could not. Angry I was at him, for I was on my way to Ailinis when he stopped me. Then angry he became, and told me . . ." he faltered. "He reminded me of the oaths I had sworn and the injustices I had done you. Then he left, saying bitterly that he would follow no dishonored oath-breaker. He said that he meant to find you, to defend and protect you in my stead."

The fire was burned down enough now, and I put the meat to broil and a larger pan of the meal to cook. Taharka watched me, brooding. "Then what happened?" I asked.

"As he left me I was standing, when he rode past me upon Biscuit, and I realized that he meant what he said. To the stables I ran, meaning to get Red and chase him down, to stop him. But as I was there Ailinis came in, in great haste, and moved to touch me, and I nearly forgot what I had come for. Whiskers it was who reminded me, for as she came near he laid back his ears and tried to bite her, and she grabbed a pitchfork, meaning to strike him with it. Stopped her, I did, and remembered that your horse Whiskers was, and why you had not taken him, and remembered too that I had seen her mistreat him. Yet she had claimed that she loved to ride him so that I would take from you and give to her what she had no right to. I put her aside, saddled Red, and rode to catch up with Satha."

I stirred the porridge and turned the steaks while the night birds called in the silence. The fall air was cooler than the summer had been. I took a deep breath of it. "Was it difficult riding away? As if you were being called back?"

"It was as if my heart were being torn out of me, as if I were turning away from all happiness and all joy forever."

"Yet you went on."

"If a thing is right, done it must be."

"I see," I murmured. "Go on with your story."

"When I caught up with Satha I told him I would come after you as was my duty and that he was to stay and guard the castellum. Then we returned. I packed Whiskers and set out to follow you. Only a day ahead of me you were, and yet you traveled so fast that I lost ground every day. I came to the village where you left Little Sorrel and saw the children riding him or never would I have known that you had turned back. They told me there that you spoke of oaths and a task to be done and rode back the way you had come. I found your tracks and followed. The rest you know."

I slid the broiled meat onto a plate and spooned some of the thick mush beside it. Handing it to him, I asked, "Do you still feel drawn to return to the Silvercat?"

He accepted the plate, but didn't dig in with his usual hearty appetite. "More than ever. Always I remember Ailinis, and longing for her is a fire in my bones. Under a spell do you think I am?"

I shrugged. "You were drawn back to the Silvercat the first time by a summoning spell, and when you arrived there you must have been placed under a very powerful love charm. But from what little I know of such things—I don't use them—a love charm is a temporary thing, easily broken by one who sets his will against it. Such things are more than half dependent upon the consent and cooperation of the victim. So you must tell me: Are you ensorcelled, or do you genuinely love Ailinis?"

He threw back his head. "Do you, my rightful wife, ask me so calmly if I love another woman? Among my own people, no woman would be so cool. If I say 'Yes, I love Ailinis with all my heart,' will you strike me dead with your magic as you meant to do this afternoon? Will you cry, or shout, or scream? Or will you sit there as cold as a witch?"

I regarded him steadily. "If you tell me that you love Ailinis, and that the Silvercat has accepted her as mantic, then I'll give you back Butterfly and take Whiskers, and in the morning I'll ride west—alone. If you tell me that you don't love Ailinis, but only desired her for a time, and that the Silvercat hasn't recognized her, then in the morning I'll ride east with you, and we shall see what we shall see. So I ask you again, and you had better think carefully about your answer: Do you love Ailinis?"

He trembled where he sat, but whether it was from anger, or indecision or some strong emotion, I could not tell. "Understand you I do not," he said harshly. "My wife you are, and your husband I am. The oaths were sworn. They must be honored. Leave me you may not. Take another woman, abandoning you, I may not. Angry at me for being unfaithful, you should be. Berate me, slap my face, or demand some fine present in reparation, and understand I would. But as cold as ice you sit there and say, 'Say this and I ride west alone, say that and I will ride east.'"

"Do you think I want you if you want someone else?" I asked scornfully. "Am I a vine that will wither and die if its support is removed, so that I must beg you to stay with me if you love Ailinis? Are you a child, that I should reproach you for what you've done? As for oaths, the oath is broken, broken, broken. It was broken when you took Ailinis in your arms. It does not bind me now. Do you expect me to force you to abide by an oath you regret, and stay with you while the years pass and you come to hate me more bitterly every day?"

Taharka looked steadily at me. "Sorry I am to hear that the oath does not bind you. It binds me. The truth will I say to you. Yes, I love Ailinis. I long for her every moment. She is beautiful and passionate and demanding, and I would give my life to lie once more in her bed. My life would I give, but not my honor. My wife you are, and if you ride west in the morning, and if I can't stop you, then west with you I will ride."

"You shall not."

"The truth I have spoken, and I will do what I have said I will do. You do not consult my wishes in this, I shall not consult yours." He looked at me, studying my face. "Nor will you use magic to deter me. Your notions of honor are different from mine, but no less strong. You will battle this out with me on grounds where we are equals, not those where I am unarmed."

I glared at him. "You call it a battle. I say that you wed me to become Silvercat Margrave, and once that was attained, put me aside for the first flirty tail you found. This is no battle, but a betrayal of trust. I'll ride west to the deserts, and I'll tolerate none of your company."

He laid his congealing food aside. "So, anger there is, indeed. That you did not care, I had begun to think." He stood up and I rose too, not liking to have him towering over me. "Wed you I did to become Silvercat Margrave, and because I wanted a wife. No ambition to take a sorceress to wife had I, especially one untamed to a man's loving touch. Wed me to get the use of my warrior's skills and my followers you did. Deny it if you can! At least you I found attractive as a woman. To you I was loathsome and unclean, yet wed me you did."

I shook my head. "You were not loathsome. You frightened me, or I never would have resisted your advances that first night. Once the bargain was made, I at least would have kept it to the end of my days."

"My advances? A husband should not have to make advances to his wife. She should show him that she wants him, not flinch away from his touch." Suddenly he stepped forward and grabbed me by the upper arms.

I stiffened, but I didn't permit myself to either draw away or respond in anger. I coolly stared him down. "I'm not to use magic, because the contest would be too unequal, is that it? Yet you may use physical strength against me."

He dropped his hands and stared at me, breathing harshly through his nose. "Then use your magic," he said. "Lash me with your green fire. No? Then here." He stopped to the pile of tack and freed the quirt he carried, more as a decoration than for use. "Here is a physical weapon. Take your revenge for my unfaithfulness." He held out the whip.

I stepped away from it, averting my eyes. "I have no wish to hit you, Taharka."

He sighed heavily, tossing the whip down. "Do you care

so little for me that nothing I do has the power to affect you? Nothing is there that will be punishment enough that afterward you can forgive me?"

"Punishment?" I said, trying to understand him. "Do you think that if I take that whip and hit you with it, the whole incident will never have happened? How many blows does it take to turn time back?"

"If when I walked into your firelight, you had rushed into my arms and clung to me in happiness that I had come back to you, it would have been as if it had never happened."

"Rushed into your arms! Did you think I would?"

"If I did, sadly mistaken I was, was I not?"

I subsided into silence, trying to think. Clearly his view of what had happened and the effect it would have upon our relationship was different from mine. But he had said that he loved Ailinis. Why then didn't he want to be free of me so that he could be with her? Why did he seem to accuse me of coldness? Tired, confused, hurt, I couldn't puzzle it all out. Finally I raised my eyes to his. "Very well, Taharka," I said. "I forgive you. I cannot rush into your arms. I can't believe that I would be welcome there in Ailinis's place. But I'm willing to listen to what you think should be done now."

"Ailinis's place it is not. In my arms is your rightful place. My wife you are."

I shook my head. "I won't debate the point with you. Let it stand that neither one of us quite understands the other. Setting aside all hurt feelings, what are we to do? We have each made demands upon the other that we can't or won't fulfill. We can't go back to the way we were before. What now?"

"I shall not permit you to ride away alone."

"What will you permit, then?"

He made a helpless gesture. "What revenge you wish to enact upon me, I will permit. Harm to Ailinis I will not permit—that she is carrying my child is possible."

"I don't want to enact any revenge upon you. I don't even want to do anything to hurt Ailinis."

"What do you want, Runa?"

"I want to be in my desert, far away from anyone who can hurt me ever again," I cried passionately. "I never want to be afraid again. I never want to have people thinking that it's all right to practice whatever cruelty they wish upon me because of what I am. I never, ever again want to be tempted by anger or pain or fear to turn to the evil use of my skills!"

Taharka stood staring at me, as if what I had said had been so totally unexpected that he was unprepared to assimilate it. At last I was driven to break the silence, to cover up the naked feeling I had revealed. "You say you love Ailinis, that you wish to protect her. I want to go home. Why can't you go to Ailinis and let me go my own way?"

He shook his head. "No," he said positively. "Such a coward as that I am not, nor are you. Wedded we are, together we will stay."

"No matter how miserable we both are?"

"Miserable we shall not be. Permit it I will not."

I turned away. "What can you do to prevent it?" I asked, wholly heartsick, exhausted, and defeated.

"Refuse to be miserable, I can. Refuse to do anything to make you miserable, I can. If you make the same choices, then neither of us can be miserable. And this at least can I do, no matter what you choose," he said, and pulled me into his arms.

My immediate reaction was to wrench away from him. Against his great strength, my efforts were useless. "Let go," I said furiously.

"Harm you I shall not," he said. "But your husband I am. The right to touch you I have. As the right to touch me, you also have. No rights at all has Ailinis. A thief she is, who has tried to steal from you your husband, and from me the good opinion of my wife. Will you allow her these thefts?"

I didn't answer, but I quit struggling against his hold, to find that he immediately relaxed his grip, encircling me still but not squeezing or restricting me. I stood passive. If he were in truth determined to go wherever I went—and I saw no reason to doubt him—then I was being unpardonably foolish to cultivate my hurt feelings. We could not, perhaps, be happy together, but we could be comfortable. And in simple truth, what had happened was not entirely his fault. Magic had been used to lure him away and to ensnare him in Ailinìs's trap—at least at first. He had not deliberately betrayed me.

I sighed wearily and let my head fall against his shoulder. "I'm a coward, Taharka," I said. "I suspected that magic had been used to ensnare you, yet I took your words and actions at face value, and ran away to hide. I had gotten clear to that village before I realized that I owed you at least the chance to make up your mind freely."

His arms tightened comfortably. He drew a deep and shuddery breath. "More than that, you owe me," he said severely. "To fight for me, to remind me of my honor if I stray, and never even to offer me the chance to change my mind, you owe me. My choice was made when I spoke the words of the oath, and so was yours. The option of freeing me you have not got."

"How very . . . permanent," I said, in some awe.

He chuckled. "So it is. Completely permanent. For the wrong reasons we wed each other, perhaps . . ." He hesitated, and then went on, "Or perhaps not. I would never have chosen to wed Ailinis, not if fifty noble titles lay in her gift. Nor, I think, would you have chosen to wed an evil man, not if he brought a thousand soldiers to be his bride price."

"I hope not," I said. "Then what do you want us to do? Do you advise us to ride west, leaving behind all this and starting over somewhere else, or do you counsel attack for the sake of regaining the Silvercat castellum?"

"If riding west you insist upon," he said carefully, "with you I shall go. If my counsel you seek, back to the Silvercat would I ride, and challenge Ailinis. Recognized by the Silvercat have we been, and the castellum is rightfully ours. But be warned, an easy life of it we shall not have, even if we succeed in sending Ailinis about her business. Powerful enemies we have, nor will they give up for one setback, and our plan to make ourselves important to them by selling horses is a lost opportunity, since you sold the mares to all those who would have been our best customers." I stirred protestingly in his arms and he added hastily, "Exactly the right thing you did to sell them. When I think of you driving them alone over all those hundreds of miles, I wish that you had taken the whip to me. I deserve it, for riding off and leaving to you that task."

"You didn't know I had the mares," I excused.

"Waited to find out whether you had the mares, I should have."

"Next time, see to it," I said severely, and we laughed (a little shakily) as if it were a great joke.

CHAPTER
18

"**W**HY Haven't we seen the Silvercat?" I fretted, peering through a screen of leaves at the castellum, perched upon its bluff.

"I don't know," admitted Taharka. "Seen it I have not since we rode west to catch horses."

"Well, where is it? It should be here. Look, who is that man? He's too big to be one of the tiller folk. Is it one of your warriors?"

"Where? Ah, yes. Unknown to me he is." Taharka, peering intently at the castellum, frowned. "The gates are open, but none of our folk do I see. Those who sent Ailinis have consolidated their position, I should say."

"You're the tactician. What do we do now?" I asked.

"Help us it will not to lurk about out here. Into the castle we must go. Our northern warriors will back us. Take care of the magic you can and I have my battle sword."

"The warriors will back us if they're in the castellum, free and armed. They may be dead. They may be elsewhere. They may be locked up or ensorcelled."

He grinned at me. "As the warriors say, a good life it is which is ended by honorable death."

I studied him. There was an intensity about him I had not seen before. He had something to prove, I realized, to himself and perhaps even to me. I nodded. "Very well. Give me a time to summon my energy and then we'll ride into the dragon's lair."

He caught his breath. "Name yourself coward again and

me you will have to reckon with. Summon your energies, wife."

"Taharka?"

"Yes?"

"You'll see Ailinis. She might even be hurt or killed. If she tries to use magic against you, I can protect you, but if the hold she has over you is real, I can't help you. I don't want to ride into that castellum and find myself fighting you."

He let the leaves fall back into position. "Runa, my wife, sworn the oaths are. A usurper and thief Ailinis is, and she takes the risks that all such folk take. I will ask you not to harm her if you can help it. But don't endanger yourself to obey that request."

Still I hesitated. "I wish I knew where the Silvercat is," I said. "If it has recognized her, it is I who am the usurper."

"No usurper you are," he stated.

I turned to peer up at the castellum. Taharka laid his hand upon my shoulder and turned me to face him. It was the first time he had touched me since the night he had walked into my camp. Having established his right to touch me, he had chosen not to exercise it, and I hardly knew whether to be glad or sorry. I couldn't help shuddering at the thought of his touch, as if he were somehow polluted, yet he was my husband—wasn't he?

"Not sure of me yet?" he asked.

My gaze dropped and I colored. He was shrewd enough to read my conflicting feelings in my face. "Blame you I cannot, perhaps, yet wish I do with all my heart that you loved me enough to trust me."

"Love—it's the whole crux of the matter, isn't it?" I said wryly. "We married without love, and yet you can't help wanting me to love you and I can't help resenting that it isn't I whom you love but"—I nodded toward the castellum— "her. It must be a very important thing, love, and yet I hardly know what it is."

"When lost I was in the overmind in that maze of ruined buildings and drifting sand, you called to me with love. Like a beacon it was, burning so brightly that it blazed even through many stone walls, and I could follow it to you."

Startled, I glanced at him. "I remember," I said. "I had to send something that you'd recognize as coming from me."

"It was the only sign or token or word of affection that I have ever had from you. Took it for more than it was meant for, perhaps I did." He glanced provocatively at me.

"Taharka," I said severely, "when we get back to the Silvercat Castellum and we're sitting around on some long winter evening with nothing to do, I'll be glad to debate the nature of love with you, and trade insults about who trusts whom less."

He laughed softly. "A sorceress I would wed, would I not, and one untamed into the bargain? Yet no other woman, no, nor any man either, in all the world, would I rather have beside me at this moment."

I felt a surge of warmth. It lasted until we galloped up the winding trail, he on Butterfly and I upon my old reliable Whiskers, and burst through the gate.

"Ho!" he bellowed. "The margrave returns! Northern warriors, to me. Usurpers, look to yourselves!" Bending low over Butterfly's neck, he drove the stallion through the door of the main building and, without pausing, shod hooves slipping and clattering on the stone floor and striking a shower of sparks, up the grand staircase. There he leaned down and pounded upon the door of the mantic's quarters with the great hilt of his battle sword. "Ailinis! False mantic, come forth!"

I left Whiskers outside and followed more quietly, glowing with latent energy. In the gloom of the hall, I cast a light about me that illuminated the room, and the indwellers who had been staring after Taharka shrank away from me. Above, Taharka vaulted off Butterfly, wrenching the door open. I formed a pulsing, whining ball of energy, ready to be used as weapon or shield, and followed him.

Within was a milling crowd of people. I saw the Bearsnake Margrave, staring amazed at Taharka before he loosed a rattle of orders. Ailinis stood facing Taharka, a confident smile upon her lips. Taharka hesitated in his charge, shook his great head as if clearing it, and stumbled. Ailinis negligently raised a hand as if to cast some impalpable object she held at him.

I raised my arms and spoke one word of guidance and another of shielding, and a vast sheet of green fire erupted from my outspread fingertips. It shimmered and coalesced, forming an almost invisible curtain between Taharka and Ailinis, and the tiny clot of magic that she had thrown hissed and vanished like a moth in a bonfire as it struck the magical shield.

As if freed from clinging hands, Taharka sprang forward, bellowing a warcry in which I heard my name. Ailinis swung around to face me, lips thinning, and I stepped through the door, wearing the awesome power of my magic like a cloak. Never had I invoked the full strength of my power before, and the savage joy of it surged through my heart as I began the chant which would nullify all lesser powers.

Yet was Ailinis a lesser power? I had balked her attempt to ensnare Taharka again. Even now, he was hewing a path through a gaggle of strange men-at-arms. But now she turned her attention on me. Her silken beauty dropped away from her as she released the illusion spell that bound it and diverted the energy into a violet lance of flame that stabbed against my shield with the destructive force of a bolt of lightning. A groan burst from my lips as I poured more and more of my gathered power into the shield, for if her crackling, spitting javelin reached Taharka it would not gently enspell him, it would blast him limb from limb, fry his brains, and burst him like an overheated egg.

The energy lance surged forward, and I poured more of myself into holding it. The protective force was too wide, too diffuse. The lance, concentrated on a spot no larger than a coin, would penetrate the shield unless I could shift its form to oppose the lance directly. In the instant between dropping the shield and seizing the lance, both Taharka and I would be horribly vulnerable. If Ailinis recognized her chance, we were dead . . . unless . . .

Releasing my body, I leaped away from it, letting it fall disregarded and tenantless. It was helpless, but I was freed of the necessity for manipulating energy by spells. I could do so directly, through my mental control of the overmind substance. Ailinis gasped as my body slumped awkwardly to the floor. Then, her eyes narrowing ferally, she leaped forward, slim dagger raised to strike my defenseless envelope. For that instant, she forgot her energy lance, and I dropped my shield, reforming my energy.

Reaching out with hands made of green fire, I grabbed the bolt that would have seared my physical hands into blackened stumps. Wrenching the energy lance from Ailinis's momentarily slackened magical grasp, I turned it away from Taharka's broad back and held it, jolting and bucking against my precarious control.

Ailinis, feeling her own magic wrenched away from her —the sensation was much like having a limb wrenched away—screamed and whirled. I could feel her struggling to take her energy back, and like some monstrous beast longing to return to its beloved mistress, the lance hissed and writhed as though to escape me and return to her. Oh, she was strong, and the spells she mouthed were unknown to me, strange and potent. She was a summoner indeed, no mere lurer of rabbits, but one who might charm the wandering planets from their courses. Yet even as I struggled to master the fiery spear, I was the stronger; she could not take it back from me.

The physical world was fading away as I drifted farther into the overmind. I could see the struggling fighters only as fading wraiths. But I saw Ailinis turn with new determination to approach my fallen physical self. She meant it harm. I sensed that her dagger was raised. She must have been beside herself with rage, for if she plunged the dagger into my helpless body, the sudden release of control over our conjoined energies would blow the castellum off the bluff in a shower of fragments and she would surely perish with the rest of us.

I turned and dived deep and blindly into the overmind, dragging those seething, surging forces with me. If I must die, and there was nothing I could do to stop Ailinis from murdering my helpless body, then at least Taharka would not die with me. But hope was not entirely gone; I attached a tenuous thread of energy to my lax body even as I spent lavishly of the remainder to drive myself far into the formless depths.

Far into the overmind I fled, tailed like a comet with blazing fires, until I came up against a familiar presence, a raging feline aura. Here was the Silvercat! I braked my headlong flight, regarding the creature with amazement as it squalled and flailed against its immaterial prison. It was no creature of the overmind; what was it doing here? Then I understood. Ailinis, knowing that it would not recognize her claims as mantic, had thrust it here. It was not a creature of the overmind, but neither was it, stictly speaking, a material being either, and thus it could pass into the overmind as it was.

It too was a victim of Ailinis's plots, fueled no doubt by the envy and spite of the other mantics. Why I was not yet dead, I didn't know. Though time passed differently in the overmind, Ailinis's little dagger had been only inches from my heart, and those inches would not, even in the overmind, take forever to traverse. But while I lived, I meant to undo all of her works that I could.

"Silvercat!" I projected with such force that the overmind reverberated. "Stop fighting. I mean to free you and send you out of this place."

The wild gyrations of the creature ceased, and it peered about it, as I formed a substratum for it to stand upon and the sketchy semblance of the plains that it knew. "My mantic!" it rumbled. "One came who would claim your place, but it was not my meat, and I went to cast it out. Then I found myself here."

"I'll send you back where you belong." Plucking away some of the energy I held, I used it to shove the Silvercat back in the direction of reality. To my amazement, it resisted me.

"You must come too. You are my meat."

"If you hurry, you might get to that meat while it's still fresh," I projected wryly. "When I saw it last, that one who wished to claim my place was trying to stab it to the heart."

There was a roar of wrath that shook the overmind and split the half-formed simulation I had created like rotten cloth. "It shall not! You are my meat! Show me how to go!"

I pointed the Silvercat in the direction from which I could still feel a faint tug from my corporeal body and shoved.

Then I found myself swept along in its wake as it burst into the mantic's office. The struggle I had left still raged. Only one thing had changed. Instead of stooping over me, driving a weapon at my heart, Ailinis lay sprawled across my body, a dirk standing out from her fair, slender back. I was jammed back into my body with such force that the world heaved and lurched nauseatingly around me.

There was an ear-splitting squall of rage and the Silvercat went bounding into the thick of the battle, scythe-clawed forepaws swinging in huge arcs as it reaped a human harvest. I scrambled out from under the slack body and rose to my feet. The men-at-arms nearest to me, silent with terror, were tumbling over each other in their haste to flee from the saber-jawed monster that sprang among them, batting them aside like toys. Taharka was wearily blocking thrust after thrust from the clustering enemies about him.

But there were too many of them! They had not all been in the room when Taharka had burst through the door. Where were they coming from? He had to have help. I reached to form an energy weapon, and found that my reserves were all but gone. I could make a weapon enough to stun two or three of my gallant husband's assailants, and then my energy would be spent. He staggered, nearly failed to block the thrust of a spear—he was almost exhausted. I shrank back as the fighters around him howled and surged forward, ignoring the Silvercat, which was itself sore beset now, batting at a dozen spears and swords and swinging its head with its foot-long fangs vainly at its tormentors.

I watched in horror as the usurper's forces surged suddenly in a human wave over my husband. Some of them died, but there were too many—the great, bloody battle sword went flying, and then Taharka rose from the living mound, shaking himself and roaring as lesser men clung to him. The mound subsided again; Taharka was buried under it somewhere, helpless. The Silvercat snarled as it retreated through the door into the armory.

Someone screamed hysterically, "Take him to the battlements! Hang him! Hang the false margrave!" I gasped in horror as the struggling pile of bodies parted to reveal Taharka, bloody, torn, semiconscious, being dragged by a score of willing pairs of hands toward the stairway to the battlements.

I tried once more to gather energy. There wasn't time—there were too many of them, and already they were binding his hands behind him as they dragged him up the stairs. They had forgotten me, and I turned and ran. The northern warriors! They had to be here somewhere. They had to be. My mother had died by the noose. My only love would not die that horrible death also, not if I had to spend every crumb of my life's energy to prevent it.

I pelted down the stairs, seeking. Precious seconds fled as I flung open every door, shouting for Satha with a voice cracked by fear. In the surgery I went cannoning into Bion, who was cowering behind the slab. "The northern warriors!" I gasped. "Where are they? Quick, damn you!" In my urgency I grabbed him and shook him so that he could hardly answer. Choking, he pointed, and I flung him aside and dashed down the hall to the locked storage rooms that Tildis had discovered. There was a thunder of blows coming from the heavy wooden door of one of them.

"Stand back," I yelled, and gathered every spark of energy I could reach. I would have only one chance at it. There would be not time nor power enough for a second try at the stout wooden door. By the time I could find a key, my love Taharka would be dead and dangling. Speaking the words of shaping and aiming through dry lips, I flung my wad of energy at the door. It was enough! The centuries-dry wood exploded into a shower of splinters and sparks, and Satha and the rest of the northern warriors erupted through it while the pieces still clattered to the floor.

"The battlements!" I screamed. "Oh, hurry, hurry! They mean to hang him!"

All unarmed as they were, they rushed past me, their faces grimly set. I ran after them, my head reeling with the effort. Would they be in time? I moaned with fear as I labored up the stairs, my breath searing my dried-out, cracked throat.

From above me came a roar as of lions. I struggled up the stairs, cursing my failing limbs. At last I reached the battlements. The northern warriors were locked into bloody bare-handed combat with the men-at-arms, and above them, tee-tering upon the sloping parapet, a rope already around his neck, was Taharka.

Then I gasped in horror. The Bearsnake Margrave, was rising from the melee his teeth showing in a grimace of hate and rage, and I realized that he meant to push Taharka off the wall. "No!" I shrieked, and hurled energy I hadn't known I possessed at him. No great bolt it was, only the last dregs of power, a pitiful, slow, lazy ball that rotated as it sailed majestically through the air. The Bearsnake Margrave took step after stately step toward my helpless husband, hands outstretched before him, face contorted with malicious glee.

It was no great searing bolt of energy, but it hit the would-be executioner at just the right moment, convulsing him in a shower of green sparks and deflecting him by just enough that Taharka was able to twist out of his path. Still with a slow and stately grace, he staggered over the parapet and sailed into the blue air where all the height of the wall and of the river bluffs waited to receive him. I didn't stay to watch him fall, but threaded my way through the raging hand-to-hand battles to Taharka. Helping him down from his precarious perch, I tore the rope from his neck and flung it away. Then, sobbing, I gathered his sagging form into my arms, murmuring broken endearments as I cradled him against me.

It was some moments before I gained enough command of myself to realize that he was patiently begging me to untie his hands so that he might join in the fight on the battle-ments. Sniffling, I complied. Scooping up a fallen weapon, bellowing encouragement to his men, he sailed into the fray as ferociously as if he had not already fought a terrible battle against overwhelming odds and come within a hairbreadth of a degrading death—and saved my life as well; it had been his dirk in Ailinis's back. When the choice had come, with no time to think, he had chosen me.

I huddled against a cold stone wall and watched as he waded into the fight. What a hero he was! Even with the light weapon he had found, he cut a circle of destruction around him. Under this new onslaught, bereft of their leader, the men-at-arms wavered and broke. It was only minutes before the fight was over.

Those of the northern warriors who remained standing looked about drunkenly as their battle-rage ebbed. "Round up all the usurpers you can find and throw them out!" bellowed Taharka. "If any resistance they offer, kill them!" There was a low roar of savage agreement, and the northerners trooped off down the stairs.

I was utterly spent. My knees gave way and I slid down the rough stone wall, shaking with weakness and exhaustion. I was alone with the dead and the cold wind.

I was beginning to realize what I had done. In my relief from the horrifying fear that he would be hanged, I had laid my feelings, emotions I had kept carefully hidden even from myself, open for Taharka to see. He would know that I was not angry at him for betraying me with Ailinis. I had never really been as angry with him for that as he seemed to think I ought to be. He had been the victim of magic, and I had been wrong to abandon him, no matter how hurt my feelings had been.

There was a step upon the battlements, and Taharka came into my sight, looking about him. He moved stiffly, and he had found and reclaimed his battle sword, which he carried. He was looking for me, I knew, but I hadn't the strength to call out to him. I only waited numbly for him to see me.

His eye lit upon my huddled form and he came hastily to me. He knelt before me, reaching out to touch my shoulder. "Hurt, are you, Runa?" he asked.

"No," I managed to whisper. "Only spent. Are you hurt?"

"Nothing to mention. A few stitches you will have to take here and there."

I realized that there were no doubt many wounded awaiting my attention in the surgery. I would have to find from somewhere the strength to take care of them. It was part of a mantic's duty. I struggled to rise, and Taharka put his sword into his scabbard to help me. "I must go to the surgery," I said, reeling dizzily.

"No," said Taharka firmly. "Rest you will. No one is so badly injured that you must see to them now."

I raised my head and looked him in the eye. "I am mantic

here. It's part of the mantic's job to take care of the wounded."

His jaw clenched and for a moment I thought we would fall into an argument there on the bloody battlements, both of us reeling with exhaustion. Then suddenly he grinned. "Then help me down the stairs, Runa, my wife, and do what you must. Then come to me, for your husband I am, and I very much want to spend about three hours telling you how wonderful you are and how much I love you."

The warm joy of his words surged through my being. "And another three for me to tell you how magnificent you are and how much I love you. Come on."

And staggering with pain and weariness, laughing like children, we helped one another down the stairs.